The past—mystical and brutal, lecherous and kind—permeates the stories of Isaac Bashevis Singer, whether the scene is Warsaw or New York, shtetl or Miami Beach. But it is not the prettied-up past of the conventional Yiddish writer. Murder, crime, satanism, perversion, lust—all stir up the coals of this past and the pious Hasidim feel the heat. The wisdom of the past is intrinsic in the works of Singer, but it is wisdom purified with the fires of feeling.

Fawcett Crest Books
by Isaac Bashevis Singer:

A CROWN OF FEATHERS   23465 $2.95

THE FAMILY MOSKAT   24066 $2.95

IN MY FATHER'S COURT   24074 $2.50

PASSIONS   24067 $2.95

SATAN IN GORAY   24326 $2.50

THE SÉANCE   24364 $2.75

SHORT FRIDAY   24068 $2.50

SHOSHA   23997 $2.95

THE SLAVE   24188 $2.50

The Séance
and Other Stories

Isaac Bashevis Singer

FAWCETT CREST • NEW YORK

In memory of my beloved sister
MINDA ESTHER

THE SÉANCE

This book contains the complete text of the original hardcover
edition.

Published by Fawcett Crest Books, a unit of CBS Publications,
the Consumer Publishing Division of CBS Inc., by arrange-
ment with Farrar, Straus & Giroux

ISBN: 0-449-24364-8

*"The Dead Fiddler," "The Letter Writer," and "The Slaught-
erer" appeared originally in* The New Yorker; *"Zeitl and
Rickel" appeared originally in* The Hudson Review *and "Henne
Fire" and "The Lecture" in* Playboy. *The other stories in
this volume have appeared in* Harper's Magazine, *Commentary, Encounter, Chicago Review, Hadassah Magazine,
Cosmopolitan, Cavalier, and* American Judaism

Printed in the United States of America

First Fawcett Crest printing: January 1981

10 9 8 7 6 5 4 3 2 1

Contents

AUTHOR'S NOTE

Most of these stories were written in recent years—*The Dead Fiddler,* for example, was written only last year. However, one story, *Two Corpses Go Dancing*, was published in Yiddish in 1943. I am glad that three of the stories— the title story, *The Lecture*, and *The Letter Writer*—deal with events in the United States or Canada. I am grateful to the following translators: Mirra Ginsburg, Cecil Hemley, Ellen Kantarov, Roger Klein, J. M. Lask, Elizabeth Pollet, Alizah Shevrin, Elizabeth Shub, Joseph Singer, Dorothea Straus, Ruth Whitman, Alma Singer. As the reader will see, I was often the co-translator of the stories, all of which were edited by Robert Giroux and some of them by Cecil Hemley, Rachel Mac-Kenzie, and Elizabeth Shub, to all of whom I wish to express my gratitude.

I.B.S

The Séance

It was during the summer of 1946, in the living room of Mrs. Kopitzky on Central Park West. A single red bulb burned behind a shade adorned with one of Mrs. Kopitzky's automatic drawings—circles with eyes, flowers with mouths, goblets with fingers. The walls were all hung with Lotte Kopitzky's paintings, which she did in a state of trance and at the direction of her control—Bhaghavar Krishna, a Hindu sage supposed to have lived in the fourth century. It was he, Bhaghavar Krishna, who had painted the peacock with the golden tail, in the middle of which appeared the image of Buddha; the otherworldly trees hung with elflocks and fantastic fruits; the young women of the planet Venus with their branch-like arms and their ears from which stretched silver nets—organs of telepathy. Over the pictures, the old furniture, the shelves with books, there hovered reddish shadows. The windows were covered with heavy drapes.

At the round table on which lay a Ouija board, a trumpet, and a withered rose, sat Dr. Zorach Kalisher, small, broad-shouldered, bald in front and with sparse tufts of hair in the back, half yellow, half gray. From behind his yellow bushy brows peered a pair of small, piercing eyes. Dr. Kalisher had almost no neck—his head sat directly on his broad shoulders, making him look like a primitive African statue. His nose was crooked, flat at the top, the tip split in two. On his chin

7

sprouted a tiny growth. It was hard to tell whether this
was a remnant of a beard or just a hairy wart. The face
was wrinkled, badly shaven, and grimy. He wore a
black corduroy jacket, a white shirt covered with ash
and coffee stains, and a crooked bow tie.

When conversing with Mrs. Kopitzky, he spoke an
odd mixture of Yiddish and German. "What's keeping
our friend Bhaghavar Krishna? Did he lose his way in
the spheres of heaven?"

"Dr. Kalisher, don't rush me," Mrs. Kopitzky answered. "We cannot give them orders . . . they have
their motives and their moods. Have a little patience."

"Well, if one must, one must."

Dr. Kalisher drummed his fingers on the table. From
each finger sprouted a little red beard. Mrs. Kopitzky
leaned her head on the back of the upholstered chair
and prepared to fall into a trance. Against the dark
glow of the red bulb, one could discern her freshly dyed
hair, black without luster, waved into tiny ringlets;
her rouged face, the broad nose, high cheekbones, and
eyes spread far apart and heavily lined with mascara.
Dr. Kalisher often joked that she looked like a painted
bulldog. Her husband, Leon Kopitzky, a dentist, had
died eighteen years before, leaving no children. The
widow supported herself on an annuity from an
insurance company. In 1929 she had lost her fortune in
the Wall Street crash, but had recently begun to buy
securities again on the advice of her Ouija board,
planchette, and crystal ball. Mrs. Kopitzky even asked
Bhaghavar Krishna for tips on the races. In a few
cases, he had divulged in dreams the names of winning
horses.

Dr. Kalisher bowed his head and covered his eyes
with his hands, muttering to himself as solitary people
often do. "Well, I've played the fool enough. This is the
last night. Even from kreplach one has enough."

"Did you say something, Doctor?"

"What? Nothing."

"When you rush me, I can't fall into the trance."

"Trance-schmance," Dr. Kalisher grumbled to himself. "The ghost is late, that's all. Who does she think she's fooling? Just crazy—meshugga."

Aloud, he said: "I'm not rushing you, I've plenty of time. If what the Americans say about time is right, I'm a second Rockefeller."

As Mrs. Kopitzky opened her mouth to answer, her double chin, with all its warts, trembled, revealing a set of huge false teeth. Suddenly she threw back her head and sighed. She closed her eyes, and snorted once. Dr. Kalisher gaped at her questioningly, sadly. He had not yet heard the sound of the outside door opening, but Mrs. Kopitzky, who probably had the acute hearing of an animal, might have. Dr. Kalisher began to rub his temples and his nose, and then clutched at his tiny beard.

There was a time when he had tried to understand all things through his reason, but that period of rationalism had long passed. Since then, he had constructed an anti-rationalistic philosophy, a kind of extreme hedonism which saw in eroticism the *Ding an sich,* and in reason the very lowest stage of being, the entropy which led to absolute death. His position had been a curious compound of Hartmann's idea of the Unconscious with the Cabala of Rabbi Isaac Luria, according to which all things, from the smallest grain of sand to the very Godhead itself, are Copulation and Union. It was because of this system that Dr. Kalisher had come from Paris to New York in 1939, leaving behind in Poland his father, a rabbi, a wife who refused to divorce him, and a lover, Nella, with whom he had lived for years in Berlin and later in Paris. It so happened that when Dr. Kalisher left for America, Nella went to visit her parents in Warsaw. He had planned to bring her over to the United States as soon as he found a translator, a publisher, and a chair at one of the American universities.

In those days Dr. Kalisher had still been hopeful. He had been offered a cathedra in the Hebrew University in Jerusalem; a publisher in Palestine was about to issue one of his books; his essays had been printed in

Zurich and Paris. But with the outbreak of the Second World War, his life began to deteriorate. His literary agent suddenly died, his translator was inept and, to make matters worse, absconded with a good part of the manuscript, of which there was no copy. In the Yiddish press, for some strange reason, the reviewers turned hostile and hinted that he was a charlatan. The Jewish organizations which arranged lectures for him cancelled his tour. According to his own philosophy, he had believed that all suffering was nothing more than negative expressions of universal eroticism: Hitler, Stalin, the Nazis who sang the Horst Wessel song and made the Jews wear yellow armbands, were actually searching for new forms and variations of sexual salvation. But Dr. Kalisher began to doubt his own system and fell into despair. He had to leave his hotel and move into a cheap furnished room. He wandered about in shabby clothes, sat all day in cafeterias, drank endless cups of coffee, smoked bad cigars, and barely managed to survive on the few dollars that a relief organization gave him each month. The refugees whom he met spread all sorts of rumors about visas for those left behind in Europe, packages of food and medicines that could be sent them through various agencies, ways of bringing over relatives from Poland through Honduras, Cuba, Brazil. But he, Zorach Kalisher, could save no one from the Nazis. He had received only a single letter from Nella.

Only in New York had Dr. Kalisher realized how attached he was to his mistress. Without her, he became impotent.

2.

Everything was exactly as it had been yesterday and the day before. Bhaghavar Krishna began to speak in English with his foreign voice that was half male and half female, duplicating Mrs. Kopitzky's errors in pronunciation and grammar. Lotte Kopitzky came from a village in the Carpathian Mountains. Dr. Kalisher could never discover her nationality—Hungarian, Rumanian, Galician? She knew no Polish or German, and little English; even her Yiddish had been corrupted through her long years in America. Actually she had been left languageless and Bhaghavar Krishna spoke her various jargons. At first Dr. Kalisher had asked Bhaghavar Krishna the details of his earthly existence but had been told by Bhaghavar Krishna that he had forgotten everything in the heavenly mansions in which he dwelt. All he could recall was that he had lived in the suburbs of Madras. Bhaghavar Krishna did not even know that in that part of India Tamil was spoken. When Dr. Kalisher tried to converse with him about Sanskrit, the Mahabharata, the Ramayana, the Sakuntala, Bhaghavar Krishna replied that he was no longer interested in terrestrial literature. Bhaghavar Krishna knew nothing but a few theosophic and spiritualistic brochures and magazines which Mrs. Kopitzky subscribed to.

For Dr. Kalisher it was all one big joke; but if one lived in a bug-ridden room and had a stomach spoiled by cafeteria food, if one was in one's sixties and completely without family, one became tolerant of all kinds of crackpots. He had been introduced to Mrs. Kopitzky in 1942, took part in scores of her séances, read her automatic writings, admired her automatic paintings, listened to her automatic symphonies. A few times he had borrowed money from her which he had been unable to return. He ate at her house—vegetarian suppers, since Mrs. Kopitzky touched neither meat, fish, milk, nor eggs, but only fruit and vegetables which mother earth produces. She specialized in preparing salads with nuts, almonds, pomegranates, avocados.

In the beginning, Lotte Kopitzky had wanted to draw him into a romance. The spirits were all of the opinion that Lotte Kopitzky and Zorach Kalisher derived from the same spiritual origin: *The Great White Lodge*. Even Bhaghavar Krishna had a taste for matchmaking. Lotte Kopitzky constantly conveyed to Dr. Kalisher regards from the Masters, who had con-

nections with Tibet, Atlantis, the Heavenly Hierarchy,
the Shambala, the Fourth Kingdom of Nature and the
Council of Sanat Kumara. In heaven as on the earth,
in the early forties, all kinds of crises were brewing.
The Powers having realigned themselves, the members of the Ashrams were preparing a war on Cosmic
Evil. The Hierarchy sent out projectors to light up the
planet Earth, and to find esoteric men and women to
serve special purposes. Mrs. Kopitzky assured Dr.
Kalisher that he was ordained to play a huge part in
the Universal Rebirth. But he had neglected his mission, disappointed the Masters. He had promised to
telephone, but didn't. He spent months in Philadelphia
without dropping her a postcard. He returned without
informing her. Mrs. Kopitzky ran into him in an auto-
mat on Sixth Avenue and found him in a torn coat, a
dirty shirt, and shoes worn so thin they no longer had
heels. He had not even applied for United States citizenship, though refugees were entitled to citizenship
without going abroad to get a visa.

Now, in 1946, everything that Lotte Kopitzky had
prophesied had come true. All had passed over to the
other side—his father, his brothers, his sisters, Nella.
Bhaghavar Krishna brought messages from them. The
Masters still remembered Dr. Kalisher, and still had
plans for him in connection with the Centennial Con-
ference of the Hierarchy. Even the fact that his family
had perished in Treblinka, Maidanek, Stutthof was
closely connected with the Powers of Light, the Devel-
opment of Karma, the New Cycle after Lemuria, and
with the aim of leading humanity to a new ascent in
Love and a new Aquatic Epoch.

During the last few weeks, Mrs. Kopitzky had become dissatisfied with summoning Nella's spirit in the
usual way. Dr. Kalisher was given the rare opportu-
nity of coming into contact with Nella's materialized
form. It happened in this way: Bhaghavar Krishna
would give a sign to Dr. Kalisher that he should walk
down the dark corridor to Mrs. Kopitzky's bedroom.
There in the darkness, near Mrs. Kopitzky's bureau,

an apparition hovered which was supposed to be Nella. She murmured to Dr. Kalisher in Polish, spoke caressing words into his ear, brought him messages from friends and relatives. Bhaghavar Krishna had admonished Dr. Kalisher time and again not to try to touch the phantom, because contact could cause severe injury to both, to him and Mrs. Kopitzky. The few times that he sought to approach her, she deftly eluded him. But confused though Dr. Kalisher was by these episodes, he was aware that they were contrived. This was not Nella, neither her voice nor her manner. The messages he received proved nothing. He had mentioned all these names to Mrs. Kopitzky and had been questioned by her. But Dr. Kalisher remained curious: Who was the apparition? Why did she act the part? Probably for money. But the fact that Lotte Kopitzky was capable of hiring a ghost proved that she was not only a self-deceiver but a swindler of others as well. Every time Dr. Kalisher walked down the dark corridor, he murmured, "Crazy, meshugga, a ridiculous woman."

Tonight Dr. Kalisher could hardly wait for Bhaghavar Krishna's signal. He was tired of these absurdities. For years he had suffered from a prostate condition and now had to urinate every half hour. A Warsaw doctor who was not allowed to practice in America, but did so clandestinely nonetheless, had warned Dr. Kalisher not to postpone an operation, because complications might arise. But Kalisher had neither the money for the hospital nor the will to go there. He sought to cure himself with baths, hot-water bottles, and with pills he had brought with him from France. He even tried to massage his prostate gland himself. As a rule, he went to the bathroom the moment he arrived at Mrs. Kopitzky's, but this evening he had neglected to do so. He felt a pressure on his bladder. The raw vegetables which Mrs. Kopitzky had given him to eat made his intestines twist. "Well, I'm too old for such pleasures," he murmured. As Bhaghavar Krishna spoke, Dr. Kalisher could scarcely listen. "What is she babbling, the idiot? She's not even a decent ventriloquist."

The instant Bhaghavar Krishna gave his usual sign,
Dr. Kalisher got up. His legs had been troubling him
greatly but had never been as shaky as tonight. "Well,
I'll go to the bathroom first," he decided. To reach the
bathroom in the dark was not easy. Dr. Kalisher walked
hesitantly, his hands outstretched, trying to feel his
way. When he had reached the bathroom and opened
the door, someone inside pulled the knob back. It is
she, the girl, Dr. Kalisher realized. So shaken was he
that he forgot why he was there. "She most probably
came here to undress." He was embarrassed both for
himself and for Mrs. Kopitzky. "What does she need it
for, for whom is she playing this comedy?" His eyes had
become accustomed to the dark. He had seen the girl's
silhouette. The bathroom had a window giving on to
the street, and the shimmer of the street lamp had
fallen on to it. She was small, broadish, with a high
bosom. She appeared to have been in her underwear.
Dr. Kalisher stood there hypnotized. He wanted to cry
out, "Enough, it's all so obvious," but his tongue was
numb. His heart pounded and he could hear his own
breathing.

After a while he began to retrace his steps, but he
was dazed with blindness. He bumped into a clothes
tree and hit a wall, striking his head. He stepped
backwards. Something fell and broke. Perhaps one of
Mrs. Kopitzky's otherworldly sculptures! At that
moment the telephone began to ring, the sound
unusually loud and menacing. Dr. Kalisher shivered.
He suddenly felt a warmth in his underwear. He had
wet himself like a child.

3.

"Well, I've reached the bottom," Dr. Kalisher muttered
to himself. "I'm ready for the junkyard." He walked
toward the bedroom. Not only his underwear, his pants
also had become wet. He expected Mrs. Kopitzky to
answer the telephone; it happened more than once that

she awakened from her trance to discuss stocks, bonds, and dividends. But the telephone kept on ringing. Only now he realized what he had done—he had closed the living-room door, shutting out the red glow which helped him find his way. "I'm going home," he resolved. He turned toward the street door but found he had lost all sense of direction in that labyrinth of an apartment. He touched a knob and turned it. He heard a muffled scream. He had wandered into the bathroom again. There seemed to be no hook or chain inside. Again he saw the woman in a corset, but this time with her face half in the light. In that split second he knew she was middle-aged.

"Forgive, please." And he moved back.

The telephone stopped ringing, then began anew. Suddenly Dr. Kalisher glimpsed a shaft of red light and heard Mrs. Kopitzky walking toward the telephone. He stopped and said, half statement, half question: "Mrs. Kopitzky!"

Mrs. Kopitzky started. "Already finished?"

"I'm not well, I must go home."

"Not well? Where do you want to go? What's the matter? Your heart?"

"Everything."

"Wait a second."

Mrs. Kopitzky, having approached him, took his arm and led him back to the living room. The telephone continued to ring and then finally fell silent. "Did you get a pressure in your heart, huh?" Mrs. Kopitzky asked. "Lie down on the sofa, I'll get a doctor."

"No, no, not necessary."

"I'll massage you."

"My bladder is not in order, my prostate gland."

"What? I'll put on the light."

He wanted to ask her not to do so, but she had already turned on a number of lamps. The light glared in his eyes. She stood looking at him and at his wet pants. Her head shook from side to side. Then she said, "That is what comes from living alone."

"Really, I'm ashamed of myself."

"What's the shame? We all get older. Nobody gets younger. Were you in the bathroom?"

Dr. Kalisher didn't answer.

"Wait a moment, I still have *his* clothes. I had a premonition I would need them someday."

Mrs. Kopitzky left the room. Dr. Kalisher sat down on the edge of a chair, placing his handkerchief beneath him. He sat there stiff, wet, childishly guilty and helpless, and yet with that inner quiet that comes from illness. For years he had been afraid of doctors, hospitals, and especially nurses, who deny their feminine shyness and treat grownup men like babies. Now he was prepared for the last degradations of the body. "Well, I'm finished, *kaput.*" . . . He made a swift summation of his existence. "Philosophy? what philosophy? Eroticism? whose eroticism?" He had played with phrases for years, had come to no conclusions. What had happened to him, in him, all that had taken place in Poland, in Russia, on the planets, on the far-away galaxies, could not be reduced either to Schopenhauer's blind will or to his, Kalisher's, eroticism. It was explained neither by Spinoza's substance, Leibnitz's monads, Hegel's dialectic, or Heckel's monism. "They all just juggle words like Mrs. Kopitzky. It's better that I didn't publish all that scribbling of mine. What's the good of all these preposterous hypotheses? They don't help at all. . . ." He looked up at Mrs. Kopitzky's pictures on the wall, and in the blazing light they resembled the smearings of school children. From the street came the honking of cars, the screams of boys, the thundering echo of the subway as a train passed. The door opened and Mrs. Kopitzky entered with a bundle of clothes: a jacket, pants, and shirt, and underwear. The clothes smelled of mothballs and dust. She said to him, "Have you been in the bedroom?"

"What? No."

"Nella didn't materialize?"

"No, she didn't materialize."

"Well, change your clothes. Don't let me embarrass you."

She put the bundle on the sofa and bent over Dr. Kalisher with the devotion of a relative. She said, "You'll stay here. Tomorrow I'll send for your things."

"No, that's senseless."

"I knew that this would happen the moment we were introduced on Second Avenue."

"How so? Well, it's all the same."

"They tell me things in advance. I look at someone, and I know what will happen to him."

"So? When am I going to go?"

"You still have to live many years. You're needed here. You have to finish your work."

"My work has the same value as your ghosts."

"There *are* ghosts, there are! Don't be so cynical. They watch over us from above, they lead us by the hand, they measure our steps. We are much more important to the Cyclic Revival of the Universe than you imagine."

He wanted to ask her: "Why then, did you have to hire a woman to deceive me?" but he remained silent. Mrs. Kopitzky went out again. Dr. Kalisher took off his pants and his underwear and dried himself with his handkerchief. For a while he stood with his upper part fully dressed and his pants off like some mad jester. Then he stepped into a pair of loose drawers that were as cool as shrouds. He pulled on a pair of striped pants that were too wide and too long for him. He had to draw the pants up until the hem reached his knees. He gasped and snorted, had to stop every few seconds to rest. Suddenly he remembered! This was exactly how as a boy he had dressed himself in his father's clothes when his father napped after the Sabbath pudding: the old man's white trousers, his satin robe, his fringed garment, his fur hat. Now his father had become a pile of ashes somewhere in Poland, and he, Zorach, put on the musty clothes of a dentist. He walked to the mirror and looked at himself, even stuck out his tongue like a child. Then he lay down on the sofa. The telephone rang again, and Mrs. Kopitzky apparently answered it, because this time the ringing stopped immediately. Dr.

Kalisher closed his eyes and lay quietly. He had nothing to hope for. There was not even anything to think about.

He dozed off and found himself in the cafeteria on Forty-second Street, near the Public Library. He was breaking off pieces of an egg cookie. A refugee was telling him how to save relatives in Poland by dressing them up in Nazi uniforms. Later they would be led by ship to the North Pole, the South Pole, and across the Pacific. Agents were prepared to take charge of them in Tierra del Fuego, in Honolulu and Yokohama. . . . How strange, but that smuggling had something to do with his, Zorach Kalisher's, philosophic system, not with his former version but with a new one, which blended eroticism with memory. While he was combining all these images, he asked himself in astonishment: "What kind of relationship can there be between sex, memory, and the redemption of the ego? And how will it work in infinite time? It's nothing but casuistry, casuistry. It's a way of explaining my own impotence. And how can I bring over Nella when she has already perished? Unless death itself is nothing but a sexual amnesia." He awoke and saw Mrs. Kopitzky bending over him with a pillow which she was about to put behind his head.

"How do you feel?"

"Has Nella left?" he asked, amazed at his own words. He must still be half asleep.

Mrs. Kopitzky winced. Her double chin shook and trembled. Her dark eyes were filled with motherly reproach.

"You're laughing, huh? There is no death, there isn't any. We live forever, and we love forever. This is the pure truth."

Translated by Roger H. Klein and Cecil Hemley

The Slaughterer

Yoineh Meir should have become the Kolomir rabbi.
His father and his grandfather had both sat in the
rabbinical chair in Kolomir. However, the followers of
the Kuzmir court had set up a stubborn opposition: this
time they would not allow a Hassid from Trisk to
become the town's rabbi. They bribed the district official and sent a petition to the governor. After long
wrangling, the Kuzmir Hassidim finally had their way
and installed a rabbi of their own. In order not to leave
Yoineh Meir without a source of earnings, they
appointed him the town's ritual slaughterer.

When Yoineh Meir heard of this, he turned even
paler than usual. He protested that slaughtering was
not for him. He was softhearted; he could not bear the
sight of blood. But everybody banded together to persuade him—the leaders of the community; the members of the Trisk synagogue; his father-in-law, Reb
Getz Frampoler; and Reitze Doshe, his wife. The new
rabbi, Reb Sholem Levi Halberstam, also pressed him
to accept. Reb Sholem Levi, a grandson of the Sondz
rabbi, was troubled about the sin of taking away another's livelihood; he did not want the younger man to
be without bread. The Trisk rabbi, Reb Yakov Leibele,
wrote a letter to Yoineh Meir saying that man may not
be more compassionate than the Almighty, the Source
of all compassion. When you slaughter an animal with
a pure knife and with piety, you liberate the soul that

19

resides in it. For it is well known that the souls of
saints often transmigrate into the bodies of cows, fowl,
and fish to do penance for some offense.

After the rabbi's letter, Yoineh Meir gave in. He had
been ordained a long time ago. Now he set himself to
studying the laws of slaughter as expounded in the
Grain of the Ox, the *Shulchan Aruch,* and the Commentaries. The first paragraph of the *Grain of the Ox*
says that the ritual slaughterer must be a Godfearing
man, and Yoineh Meir devoted himself to the Law with
more zeal than ever.

Yoineh Meir—small, thin, with a pale face, a tiny
yellow beard on the tip of his chin, a crooked nose, a
sunken mouth, and yellow frightened eyes set too close
together—was renowned for his piety. When he prayed,
he put on three pairs of phylacteries: those of Rashi,
those of Rabbi Tam, and those of Rabbi Sherira Gaon.
Soon after he had completed his term of board at the
home of his father-in-law, he began to keep all fast
days and to get up for midnight service.

His wife, Reitze Doshe, already lamented that Yoineh
Meir was not of this world. She complained to her
mother that he never spoke a word to her and paid her
no attention, even on her clean days. He came to her
only on the nights after she had visited the ritual bath,
once a month. She said that he did not remember the
names of his own daughters.

After he agreed to become the ritual slaughterer,
Yoineh Meir imposed new rigors upon himself. He ate
less and less. He almost stopped speaking. When a
beggar came to the door, Yoineh Meir ran to welcome
him and gave him his last groschen. The truth is that
becoming a slaughterer plunged Yoineh Meir into melancholy, but he did not dare to oppose the rabbi's will.
It was meant to be, Yoineh Meir said to himself; it was
his destiny to cause torment and to suffer torment. And
only heaven knew how much Yoineh Meir suffered.

Yoineh Meir was afraid that he might faint as he
slaughtered his first fowl, or that his hand might not
be steady. At the same time, somewhere in his heart,

he hoped that he would commit an error. This would release him from the rabbi's command. However, everything went according to rule.

Many times a day, Yoineh Meir repeated to himself the rabbi's words: "A man may not be more compassionate than the Source of all compassion." The Torah says, "Thou shalt kill of thy herd and thy flock as I have commanded thee." Moses was instructed on Mount Sinai in the ways of slaughtering and of opening the animal in search of impurities. It is all a mystery of mysteries—life, death, man, beast. Those that are not slaughtered die anyway of various diseases, often ailing for weeks or months. In the forest, the beasts devour one another. In the seas, fish swallow fish. The Kolomir poorhouse is full of cripples and paralytics who lie there for years, befouling themselves. No man can escape the sorrows of this world.

And yet Yoineh Meir could find no consolation. Every tremor of the slaughtered fowl was answered by a tremor in Yoineh Meir's own bowels. The killing of every beast, great or small, caused him as much pain as though he were cutting his own throat. Of all the punishments that could have been visited upon him, slaughtering was the worst.

Barely three months had passed since Yoineh Meir had become a slaughterer, but the time seemed to stretch endlessly. He felt as though he were immersed in blood and lymph. His ears were beset by the squawking of hens, the crowing of roosters, the gobbling of geese, the lowing of oxen, the mooing and bleating of calves and goats; wings fluttered, claws tapped on the floor. The bodies refused to know any justification or excuse—every body resisted in its own fashion, tried to escape, and seemed to argue with the Creator to its last breath.

And Yoineh Meir's own mind raged with questions. Verily, in order to create the world, the Infinite One had had to shrink His light; there could be no free choice without pain. But since the beasts were not endowed with free choice, why should they have to suffer? Yoineh Meir watched, trembling, as the butchers chopped the cows with their axes and skinned them before they had heaved their last breath. The women plucked the feathers from the chickens while they were still alive.

It is the custom that the slaughterer receives the spleen and tripe of every cow. Yoineh Meir's house overflowed with meat. Reitze Doshe boiled soups in pots as huge as cauldrons. In the large kitchen there was a constant frenzy of cooking, roasting, frying, baking, stirring, and skimming. Reitze Doshe was pregnant again, and her stomach protruded into a point. Big and stout, she had five sisters, all as bulky as herself. Her sisters came with their children. Every day, his mother-in-law, Reitze Doshe's mother, brought new pastries and delicacies of her own baking. A woman must not let her voice be heard, but Reitze Doshe's maidservant, the daughter of a water carrier, sang songs, pattered around barefoot, with her hair down, and laughed so loudly that the noise resounded in every room.

Yoineh Meir wanted to escape from the material world, but the material world pursued him. The smell of the slaughterhouse would not leave his nostrils. He tried to forget himself in the Torah, but he found that the Torah itself was full of earthly matters. He took to the Cabala, though he knew that no man may delve into the mysteries until he reaches the age of forty. Nevertheless, he continued to leaf through the *Treatise of the Hassidim, The Orchard,* the *Book of Creation,* and *The Tree of Life.* There, in the higher spheres, there was no death, no slaughtering, no pain, no stomachs and intestines, no hearts or lungs or livers, no membranes, and no impurities.

This particular night, Yoineh Meir went to the window and looked up into the sky. The moon spread a radiance around it. The stars flashed and twinkled, each with its own heavenly secret. Somewhere above the World of Deeds, above the constellations, Angels were flying, and Seraphim, and Holy Wheels, and Holy

Beasts. In Paradise, the mysteries of the Torah were revealed to souls. Every holy zaddik inherited three hundred and ten worlds and wove crowns for the Divine Presence. The nearer to the Throne of Glory, the brighter the light, the purer the radiance, the fewer the unholy host.

Yoineh Meir knew that man may not ask for death, but deep within himself he longed for the end. He had developed a repugnance for everything that had to do with the body. He could not even bring himself to go to the ritual bath with the other men. Under every skin he saw blood. Every neck reminded Yoineh Meir of the knife. Human beings, like beasts, had loins, veins, guts, buttocks. One slash of the knife and those solid householders would drop like oxen. As the Talmud says, all that is meant to be burned is already as good as burned. If the end of man was corruption, worms, and stench, then he was nothing but a piece of putrid flesh to start with.

Yoineh Meir understood now why the sages of old had likened the body to a cage—a prison where the soul sits captive, longing for the day of its release. It was only now that he truly grasped the meaning of the words of the Talmud: "Very good, this is death." Yet man was forbidden to break out of his prison. He must wait for the jailer to remove the chains, to open the gate.

Yoineh Meir returned to his bed. All his life he had slept on a feather bed, under a feather quilt, resting his head on a pillow; now he was suddenly aware that he was lying on feathers and down plucked from fowl. In the other bed, next to Yoineh Meir's, Reitze Doshe was snoring. From time to time a whistle came from her nostrils and a bubble formed on her lips. Yoineh Meir's daughters kept going to the slop pail, their bare feet pattering on the floor. They slept together, and sometimes they whispered and giggled half the night.

Yoineh Meir had longed for sons who would study the Torah, but Reitze Doshe bore girl after girl. While they were small, Yoineh Meir occasionally gave them a pinch on the cheek. Whenever he attended a circumcision, he would bring them a piece of cake. Sometimes he would even kiss one of the little ones on the head. But now they were grown. They seemed to have taken after their mother. They had spread out in width. Reitze Doshe complained that they ate too much and were getting too fat. They stole tidbits from the pots. The eldest, Bashe, was already sought in marriage. At one moment, the girls quarreled and insulted each other, at the next they combed each other's hair and plaited it into braids. They were forever babbling about dresses, shoes, stockings, jackets, panties. They cried and they laughed. They looked for lice, they fought, they washed, they kissed.

When Yoineh Meir tried to chide them, Reitze Doshe cried, "Don't butt in! Let the children alone!" Or she would scold, "You had better see to it that your daughters shouldn't have to go around barefoot and naked!"

Why did they need so many things? Why was it necessary to clothe and adorn the body so much, Yoineh Meir would wonder to himself.

Before he had become a slaughterer, he was seldom at home and hardly knew what went on there. But now he began to stay at home, and he saw what they were doing. The girls would run off to pick berries and mushrooms; they associated with the daughters of common houses. They brought home baskets of dry twigs. Reitze Doshe made jam. Tailors came for fittings. Shoemakers measured the women's feet. Reitze Doshe and her mother argued about Bashe's dowry. Yoineh Meir heard talk about a silk dress, a velvet dress, all sorts of skirts, cloaks, fur coats.

Now that he lay awake, all those words reechoed in his ears. They were rolling in luxury because he, Yoineh Meir, had begun to earn money. Somewhere in Reitze Doshe's womb a new child was growing, but Yoineh Meir sensed clearly that it would be another girl. "Well, one must welcome whatever heaven sends," he warned himself.

He had covered himself, but now he felt too hot. The

pillow under his head became strangely hard, as though there were a stone among the feathers. He, Yoineh Meir, was himself a body: feet, a belly, a chest, elbows. There was a stabbing in his entrails. His palate felt dry.

Yoineh Meir sat up. "Father in heaven, I cannot breathe!"

2.

Elul is a month of repentance. In former years, Elul would bring with it a sense of exalted serenity. Yoineh Meir loved the cool breezes that came from the woods and the harvested fields. He could gaze for a long time at the pale-blue sky with its scattered clouds that reminded him of the flax in which the citrons for the Feast of Tabernacles were wrapped. Gossamer floated in the air. On the trees the leaves turned saffron yellow. In the twittering of the birds he heard the melancholy of the Solemn Days, when man takes an accounting of his soul.

But to a slaughterer Elul is quite another matter. A great many beasts are slaughtered for the New Year. Before the Day of Atonement, everybody offers a sacrificial fowl. In every courtyard, cocks crowed and hens cackled, and all of them had to be put to death. Then comes the Feast of Booths, the Day of the Willow Twigs, the Feast of Azereth, the Day of Rejoicing in the Law, the Sabbath of Genesis. Each holiday brings its own slaughter. Millions of fowl and cattle now alive were doomed to be killed.

Yoineh Meir no longer slept at night. If he dozed off, he was immediately beset by nightmares. Cows assumed human shape, with beards and side locks, and skullcaps over their horns. Yoineh Meir would be slaughtering a calf, but it would turn into a girl. Her neck throbbed, and she pleaded to be saved. She ran to the study house and spattered the courtyard with her blood. He even dreamed that he had slaughtered Reitze Doshe instead of a sheep.

In one of his nightmares, he heard a human voice come from a slaughtered goat. The goat, with his throat slit, jumped on Yoineh Meir and tried to butt him, cursing in Hebrew and Aramaic, spitting and foaming at him. Yoineh Meir awakened in a sweat. A cock crowed like a bell. Others answered, like a congregation answering the cantor. It seemed to Yoineh Meir that the fowl were crying out questions, protesting, lamenting in chorus the misfortune that loomed over them.

Yoineh Meir could not rest. He sat up, grasped his side locks with both hands, and rocked.

Reitze Doshe woke up. "What's the matter?"

"Nothing, nothing."

"What are you rocking for?"

"Let me be."

"You frighten me!"

After a while Reitze Doshe began to snore again. Yoineh Meir got out of bed, washed his hands, and dressed. He wanted to put ash on his forehead and recite the midnight prayer, but his lips refused to utter the holy words. How could he mourn the destruction of the Temple when a carnage was being readied here in Kolomir, and he, Yoineh Meir, was the Titus, the Nebuchadnezzar!

The air in the house was stifling. It smelled of sweat, fat, dirty underwear, urine. One of his daughters muttered something in her sleep, another one moaned. The beds creaked. A rustling came from the closets. In the coop under the stove were the sacrificial fowls that Reitze Doshe had locked up for the Day of Atonement. Yoineh Meir heard the scratching of a mouse, the chirping of a cricket. It seemed to him that he could hear the worms burrowing through the ceiling and the floor. Innumerable creatures surrounded man, each with its own nature, its own claims on the Creator.

Yoineh Meir went out into the yard. Here everything was cool and fresh. The dew had formed. In the sky, the midnight stars were glittering. Yoineh Meir inhaled deeply. He walked on the wet grass, among the leaves and shrubs. His socks grew damp above his slippers. He came to a tree and stopped. In the branches there seemed to be some nests. He heard the twittering of awakened fledglings. Frogs croaked in the swamp beyond the hill. "Don't they sleep at all, those frogs?" Yoineh Meir asked himself. "They have the voices of men."

Since Yoineh Meir had begun to slaughter, his thoughts were obsessed with living creatures. He grappled with all sorts of questions. Where did flies come from? Were they born out of their mother's womb, or did they hatch from eggs? If all the flies died out in winter, where did the new ones come from in summer? And the owl that nested under the synagogue roof— what did it do when the frosts came? Did it remain there? Did it fly away to warm countries? And how could anything live in the burning frost, when it was scarcely possible to keep warm under the quilt?

An unfamiliar love welled up in Yoineh Meir for all that crawls and flies, breeds and swarms. Even the mice—was it their fault that they were mice? What wrong does a mouse do? All it wants is a crumb of bread or a bit of cheese. Then why is the cat such an enemy to it?

Yoineh Meir rocked back and forth in the dark. The rabbi may be right. Man cannot and must not have more compassion than the Master of the universe. Yet he, Yoineh Meir, was sick with pity. How could one pray for life for the coming year, or for a favorable writ in Heaven, when one was robbing others of the breath of life?

Yoineh Meir thought that the Messiah Himself could not redeem the world as long as injustice was done to beasts. By rights, everything should rise from the dead: every calf, fish, gnat, butterfly. Even in the worm that crawls in the earth there glows a divine spark. When you slaughter a creature, you slaughter God....

"Woe is me, I am losing my mind!" Yoineh Meir muttered.

A week before the New Year, there was a rush of

slaughtering. All day long, Yoineh Meir stood near a
pit, slaughtering hens, roosters, geese, ducks. Women
pushed, argued, tried to get to the slaughterer first.
Others joked, laughed, bantered. Feathers flew, the
yard was full of quacking, gabbling, the screaming of
roosters. Now and then a fowl cried out like a human
being.

Yoineh Meir was filled with a gripping pain. Until
this day he had still hoped that he would get accustomed to slaughtering. But now he knew that if he
continued for a hundred years his suffering would not
cease. His knees shook. His belly felt distended. His
mouth was flooded with bitter fluids. Reitze Doshe and
her sisters were also in the yard, talking with the
women, wishing each a blessed New Year, and voicing
the pious hope that they would meet again next year.

Yoineh Meir feared that he was no longer slaughtering
according to the Law. At one moment, a blackness
swam before his eyes; at the next, everything turned
golden green. He constantly tested the knife blade on
the nail of his forefinger to make sure it was not
nicked. Every fifteen minutes he had to go to urinate.
Mosquitoes bit him. Crows cawed at him from among
the branches.

He stood there until sundown, and the pit became
filled with blood.

After the evening prayers, Reitze Doshe served Yoineh
Meir buckwheat soup with pot roast. But though he
had not tasted any food since morning, he could not
eat. His throat felt constricted, there was a lump in his
gullet, and he could scarcely swallow the first bite. He
recited the Shema of Rabbi Isaac Luria, made his
confession, and beat his breast like a man who was
mortally sick.

Yoineh Meir thought that he would be unable to
sleep that night, but his eyes closed as soon as his head
was on the pillow and he had recited the last benedic-
tion before sleep. It seemed to him that he was examin-
ing a slaughtered cow for impurities, slitting open its
belly, tearing out the lungs and blowing them up.

What did it mean? For this was usually the butcher's task. The lungs grew larger and larger; they covered the whole table and swelled upward toward the ceiling. Yoineh Meir ceased blowing, but the lobes continued to expand by themselves. The smaller lobe, the one that is called "the thief," shook and fluttered, as if trying to break away. Suddenly a whistling, a coughing, a growling lamentation broke from the windpipe. A dybbuk began to speak, shout, sing, pour out a stream of verses, quotations from the Talmud, passages from the Zohar. The lungs rose up and flew, flapping like wings. Yoineh Meir wanted to escape, but the door was barred by a black bull with red eyes and pointed horns. The bull wheezed and opened a maw full of long teeth.

Yoineh Meir shuddered and woke up. His body was bathed in sweat. His skull felt swollen and filled with sand. His feet lay on the straw pallet, inert as logs. He made an effort and sat up. He put on his robe and went out. The night hung heavy and impenetrable, thick with the darkness of the hour before sunrise. From time to time a gust of air came from somewhere, like a sigh of someone unseen.

A tingling ran down Yoineh Meir's spine, as though someone brushed it with a feather. Something in him wept and mocked. "Well, and what if the rabbi said so?" he spoke to himself. "And even if God Almighty had commanded, what of that? I'll do without rewards in the world to come! I want no Paradise, no Leviathan, no Wild Ox! Let them stretch me on a bed of nails. Let them throw me into the Hollow of the Sling. I'll have none of your favors, God! I am no longer afraid of your Judgment! I am a betrayer of Israel, a willful transgressor!" Yoineh Meir cried. "I have more compassion than God Almighty—more, more! He is a cruel God, a Man of War, a God of Vengeance. I will not serve Him. It is an abandoned world!" Yoineh Meir laughed, but tears ran down his cheeks in scalding drops.

Yoineh Meir went to the pantry where he kept his knives, his whetstone, the circumcision knife. He gathered them all and dropped them into the pit of the outhouse. He knew that he was blaspheming, that he was desecrating the holy instruments, that he was mad, but he no longer wished to be sane.

He went outside and began to walk toward the river, the bridge, the wood. His prayer shawl and phylacteries? He needed none! The parchment was taken from the hide of a cow. The cases of the phylacteries were made of calf's leather. The Torah itself was made of animal skin. "Father in Heaven, Thou art a slaughterer!" a voice cried in Yoineh Meir. "Thou art a slaughterer and the Angel of Death! The whole world is a slaughterhouse!"

A slipper fell off Yoineh Meir's foot, but he let it lie, striding on in one slipper and one sock. He began to call, shout, sing. I am driving myself out of my mind, he thought. But this is itself a mark of madness. . . .

He had opened a door to his brain, and madness flowed in, flooding everything. From moment to moment, Yoineh Meir grew more rebellious. He threw away his skullcap, grasped his prayer fringes and ripped them off, tore off pieces of his vest. A strength possessed him, the recklessness of one who had cast away all burdens.

Dogs chased him, barking, but he drove them off. Doors were flung open. Men ran out barefoot, with feathers clinging to their skullcaps. Women came out in their petticoats and nightcaps. All of them shouted, tried to bar his way, but Yoineh Meir evaded them.

The sky turned red as blood, and a round skull pushed up out of the bloody sea as out of the womb of a woman in childbirth.

Someone had gone to tell the butchers that Yoineh Meir had lost his mind. They came running with sticks and rope, but Yoineh Meir was already over the bridge and was hurrying across the harvested fields. He ran and vomited. He fell and rose, bruised by the stubble. Shepherds who take the horses out to graze at night mocked him and threw horse dung at him. The cows at pasture ran after him. Bells tolled as for a fire.

Yoineh Meir heard shouts, screams, the stamping of

running feet. The earth began to slope and Yoineh Meir rolled downhill. He reached the wood, leaped over tufts of moss, rocks, running brooks. Yoineh Meir knew the truth: this was not the river before him; it was a bloody swamp. Blood ran from the sun, staining the tree trunks. From the branches hung intestines, livers, kidneys, The forequarters of beasts rose to their feet and sprayed him with gall and slime. Yoineh Meir could not escape. Myriads of cows and fowls encircled him, ready to take revenge for every cut, every wound, every slit gullet, every plucked feather. With bleeding throats, they all chanted, "Everyone may kill, and every killing is permitted."

Yoineh Meir broke into a wail that echoed through the wood in many voices. He raised his fist to heaven: "Fiend! Murderer! Devouring beast!"

For two days the butchers searched for him, but they did not find him. Then Zeinvel, who owned the watermill, arrived in town with the news that Yoineh Meir's body had turned up in the river by the dam. He had drowned.

The members of the burial society immediately went to bring the corpse. There were many witnesses to testify that Yoineh Meir had behaved like a madman, and the rabbi ruled that the deceased was not a suicide. The body of the dead man was cleansed and given burial near the graves of his father and his grandfather. The rabbi himself delivered the eulogy.

Because it was the holiday season and there was danger that Kolomir might remain without meat, the community hastily dispatched two messengers to bring a new slaughterer.

Translated by Mirra Ginsburg

The Dead Fiddler

In the town of Shidlovtse, which lies between Radom
and Kielce, not far from the Mountains of the Holy
Cross, there lived a man by the name of Reb Sheftel
Vengrover. This Reb Sheftel was supposedly a grain
merchant, but all the buying and selling was done by
his wife, Zise Feige. She bought wheat, corn, barley,
and buckwheat from the landowners and the peasants
and sent it to Warsaw. She also had some of the grain
milled and sold the flour to stores and bakeries. Zise
Feige owned a granary and had an assistant, Zalkind,
who helped her in the business and did all the work
that required a man's hand; he carried sacks, looked
after the horses, and served as coachman whenever Zise
Feige drove out to a fair or went to visit a landowner.

Reb Sheftel held to the belief that the Torah is the
worthiest merchandise of all. He rose at dawn and
went to the study house to pore over the Gemara, the
Annotations and Commentaries, the Midrash, and the
Zohar. In the evenings, he would read a lesson from the
Mishnah with the Mishnah Society. Reb Sheftel also
devoted himself to community affairs and was an ar-
dent Radzymin Hassid.

Reb Sheftel was not much taller than a midget, but
he had the longest beard in Shidlovtse and the sur-
rounding district. His beard reached down to his knees
and seemed to contain every color: red, yellow, even
the color of hay. At Tishah b'Av, when the mischief-

32

makers pelted everyone with burs, Reb Sheftel's beard
would be full of them. At first Zise Feige had tried to
pull them out, but Reb Sheftel would not allow it, for
she pulled out the hairs of the beard too, and a man's
beard is a mark of his Jewishness and a reminder that
he was created in the image of God. The burs remained
in his beard until they dropped out by themselves. Reb
Sheftel did not curl his sidelocks, considering this a
frivolous custom. They hung down to his shoulders. A
tuft of hair grew on his nose. As he studied, he smoked
a long pipe.

When Reb Sheftel stood at the lectern in the synagogue in his prayer shawl and phylacteries, he looked
like one of the ancients. He had a high forehead, and
under shaggy eyebrows, eyes that combined the sharp
glance of a scholar with the humility of a God-fearing
man. Reb Sheftel imposed a variety of penances upon
himself. He drank no milk unless he had been present
at the milking. He ate no meat except on the Sabbath
and on holidays and only if he had examined the
slaughtering knife in advance. It was told of him that
on the eve of Passover he ordered that the cat wear
socklets on its feet, lest it bring into the house the
smallest crumb of unleavened bread. Every night, he
faithfully performed the midnight prayers. People said
that although he had inherited his grain business from
his father and grandfather he still could not distinguish between rye and wheat.

Zise Feige was a head taller than her husband and
in her younger days had been famous for her good
looks. The landlords who sold her grain showered her
with compliments, but a good Jewish woman pays no
attention to idle talk. Zise Feige loved her husband and
considered it an honor to help him serve the Almighty.

She had borne nine children, but only three remained:
a married son, Jedidiah, who took board with his
father-in-law in Wlodowa; a boy Tsadock Meyer, who
was still in heder; and a grown daughter, Liebe Yentl.
Liebe Yentl had been engaged and about to be married,
but her fiancé, Ozer, caught a cold and died. This Ozer

had a reputation as a prodigy and a scholar. His father was the president of the community in Opola. Although Liebe Yentl had seen Ozer only during the signing of the betrothal papers, she wept bitterly when she heard the bad news. Almost at once she was besieged with marriage offers, for she was already a ripe girl of seventeen, but Zise Feige felt that it was best to wait until she got over her misfortune.

Liebe Yentl's betrothed, Ozer, departed this world just after Passover. Now it was already the month of Heshvan. Succoth is usually followed by rains and snow, but this fall was a mild one. The sun shone. The sky was blue, as after Pentecost. The peasants in the villages complained that the winter crops were beginning to sprout in the fields, which could lead to crop failure. People feared that the warm weather might bring epidemics. In the meantime, grain prices rose by three groschen on the pood, and Zise Feige had higher profits. As was the custom between man and wife, she gave Reb Sheftel an accounting of the week's earnings every Sabbath evening, and he immediately deducted a share—for the study house, the prayer house, the mending of sacred books, for the inmates of the poorhouse, and for itinerant beggars. There was no lack of need for charity.

Since Zise Feige had a servant girl, Dunya, and was herself a fine housekeeper, Liebe Yentl paid little attention to household matters. She had her own room, where she would often sit, reading storybooks. She copied letters from the letter book. When she had read through all the storybooks, she secretly took to borrowing from her father's bookcase. She was also good at sewing and embroidery. She was fond of fine clothes. Liebe Yentl inherited her mother's beauty, but her red hair came from her father's side. Like her father's beard, her hair was uncommonly long—down to her loins. Since the mishap with Ozer, her face, always pale, had grown paler still and more delicate. Her eyes were green.

Reb Sheftel paid little attention to his daughter. He

merely prayed to the Lord to send her the right husband. But Zise Feige saw that the girl was growing up as wild as a weed. Her head was full of whims and fancies. She did not allow herring or radishes to be mentioned in her presence. She averted her eyes from slaughtered fowl and from meat on the salting board or in the soaking dish. If she found a fly in her groats, she would eat nothing for the rest of the day. She had no friends in Shidlovtse. She complained that the girls of the town were common and backward; as soon as they were married, they became careless and slovenly. Whenever she had to go among people, she fasted the day before, for fear that she might vomit. Although she was beautiful, clever, and learned, it always seemed to her that people were laughing and pointing at her.

Zise Feige wanted many times to talk to her husband about the troubles she was having with their daughter, but she was reluctant to divert him from his studies. Besides, he might not understand a woman's problems. He had a rule for everything. On the few occasions when Zise Feige had tried to tell him of her fears, his only reply was, "When, God willing, she gets married, she will forget all this foolishness."

After the calamity with Ozer, Liebe Yentl fell ill from grieving. She did not sleep nights. Her mother heard her sobbing in the dark. She was constantly going for a drink of water. She drank whole dippers full, and Zise Feige could not imagine how her stomach could hold so much water. As though, God forbid, a fire was raging inside her, consuming everything.

Sometimes, Liebe Yentl spoke to her mother like one who was altogether unsettled. Zise Feige thought to herself that it was fortunate the girl avoided people. But how long can anything remain a secret? It was already whispered in town that Liebe Yentl was not all there. She played with the cat. She took solitary walks down the Gentile street that led to the cemetery. When anyone addressed her, she turned pale and her answers were quite beside the point. Some people thought that she was deaf. Others hinted that Liebe Yentl might be dabbling in magic. She had been seen on a moonlit night walking in the pasture across the bridge and bending down every now and then to pick flowers or herbs. Women spat to ward off evil when they spoke of her. "Poor thing, unlucky and sick besides."

2.

Liebe Yentl was about to become betrothed again, this time to a young man from Zawiercia. Reb Sheftel had sent an examiner to the prospective bridegroom, and he came back with the report that Shmelke Motl was a scholar. The betrothel contract was drawn up, ready to be signed.

The examiner's wife, Traine, who had visited Zawiercia with her husband (they had a daughter there), told Zise Feige that Shmelke Motl was small and dark. He did not look like much, but he had the head of a genius. Because he was an orphan, the householders provided his meals; he ate at a different home every day of the week. Liebe Yentl listened without a word.

When Traine had gone, Zise Feige brought in her daughter's supper—buckwheat and pot roast with gravy. But Liebe Yentl did not touch the food. She rocked over the plate as though it were a prayer book. Soon afterwards, she retired to her room. Zise Feige sighed and also went to bed. Reb Sheftel had gone to sleep early, for he had to rise for midnight prayers. The house was quiet. Only the cricket sang its night song behind the oven.

Suddenly Zise Feige was wide awake. From Liebe Yentl's room came a muffled gasping, as though someone were choking there. Zise Feige ran into her daughter's room. In the bright moonlight she saw the girl sitting on her bed, her hair disheveled, her face chalk-white, struggling to keep down her sobs. Zise Feige cried out, "My daughter, what is wrong? Woe is me!" She ran to the kitchen, lit a candle, and returned to Liebe Yentl, bringing a cup of water to splash at her if, God forbid, the girl should faint.

But at this moment a man's voice broke from Liebe Yentl's lips. "No need to revive me, Zise Feige," the voice called out. "I'm not in the habit of fainting. You'd better fetch me a drop of vodka."

Zise Feige stood petrified with horror. The water spilled over from the cup.

Reb Sheftel had also wakened. He washed his hands hastily, put on his bathrobe and slippers, and came into his daughter's room.

The man's voice greeted him. "A good awakening to you, Reb Sheftel. Let me have a schnapps—my throat's parched. Or Slivovitz—anything will do, so long as I wet my whistle."

Man and wife knew at once what had happened: a dybbuk had entered Liebe Yentl. Reb Sheftel asked with a shudder: "Who are you? What do you want?"

"Who I am you wouldn't know," the dybbuk answered. "You're a scholar in Shidlovtse, and I'm a fiddler from Pinchev. You squeeze the bench, and I squeezed the wenches. You're still around in the Imaginary World, and I'm past everything. I've kicked the bucket and have already had my taste of what comes after. I've had it cold and hot, and now I'm back on the sinful earth—there's no place for me either in heaven or in hell. Tonight I started out flying to Pinchev, but I lost my way and got to Shidlovtse instead—I'm a musician, not a coachman. One thing I do know, though—my throat's itchy."

Zise Feige was seized by a fit of trembling. The candle in her hand shook so badly it singed Reb Sheftel's beard. She wanted to scream, to call for help, but her voice stuck in her throat. Her knees buckled, and she had to lean against the wall to keep from falling.

Reb Sheftel pulled at his sidelock as he addressed the dybbuk. "What is your name?"

"Getsl."

"Why did you choose to enter my daughter?" he asked in desperation.

"Why not? She's a good-looking girl. I hate the ugly ones—always have, always will." With that, the dybbuk began to shout ribaldries and obscenities, both in ordinary Yiddish and in musician's slang. "Don't make me wait, Feige dear," he called out finally. "Bring me a cup of cheer. I'm dry as a bone. I've got an itching in my gullet, a twitching in my gut."

"Good people, help!" Zise Feige wailed. She dropped the candle and Reb Sheftel picked it up, for it could easily have set the wooden house on fire.

Though it was late, the townsfolk came running. There are people everywhere with something bothering them; they cannot sleep nights. Tevye the night watchman thought a fire had broken out and ran through the street, knocking at the shutters with his stick. It was not long before Reb Sheftel's house was packed.

Liebe Yentl's eyes goggled, her mouth twisted like an epileptic's, and a voice boomed out of her that could not have come from a woman's throat. "Will you bring me a glass of liquor or won't you? What the devil are you waiting for?"

"And what if we don't?" asked Zeinvl the butcher, who was on his way home from the slaughterhouse.

"If you don't, I'll lay you all wide open, you pious hypocrites. And the secrets of your wives—may they burn up with hives."

"Get him liquor! Give him a drink!" voices cried on every side.

Reb Sheftel's son, Tsadock Meyer, a boy of eleven, had also been awakened by the commotion. He knew where his father kept the brandy that he drank on the Sabbath, after the fish. He opened the cupboard, poured out a glass, and brought it to his sister. Reb Sheftel leaned against the chest of drawers, for his legs were giving way. Zise Feige fell into a chair. Neighbors sprinkled her with vinegar against fainting.

Liebe Yentl stretched out her hand, took the glass, and tossed it down. Those who stood nearby could not believe their eyes. The girl didn't even twitch a muscle.

The dybbuk said, "You call that liquor? Water, that's what it is—hey, fellow, bring me the bottle!"

"Don't let her have it! Don't let her have it!"

Zise Feige cried. "She'll poison herself, God help us!"

The dybbuk gave a laugh and a snort. "Don't worry, Zise Feige, nothing can kill me again. So far as I'm concerned, your brandy is weaker than candy."

"You won't get a drink until you tell us who you are and how you got in here," Zeinvl the butcher said. Since no one else dared to address the spirit, Zeinvl took it upon himself to be the spokesman.

"What does the meatman want here?" the dybbuk asked. "Go on back to your gizzards and guts!"

"Tell us who you are!"

"Do I have to repeat it? I am Getsl the fiddler from Pinchev. I was fond of things nobody else hates, and when I cashed in, the imps went to work on me. I couldn't get into paradise, and hell was too hot for my taste. The devils were the death of me. So at night, when the watchman dropped off, I made myself scarce. I meant to go to my wife, may she rot alive, but it was dark on the way and I got to Shidlovtse instead. I looked through the wall and saw this girl. My heart jumped in my chest and I crawled into her breast."

"How long do you intend to stay?"

"Forever and a day."

Reb Sheftel was almost speechless with terror, but he remembered God and recovered. He called out, "Evil spirit, I command you to leave the body of my innocent daughter and go where men do not walk and beasts do not tread. If you don't, you shall be driven out by Holy Names, by excommunication, by the blowing of the Ram's Horn."

"In another minute you'll have me scared!" the dybbuk taunted. "You think you're so strong because your beard's long?"

"Impudent wretch, betrayer of Israel!" Reb Sheftel cried in anger.

"Better an open rake than a sanctimonious fake," the dybbuk answered. "You may have the Shidlovtse schlemiels fooled, but Getsl the fiddler of Pinchev has been around. I'm telling you. Bring me the bottle or I'll make you crawl."

There was an uproar at the door. Someone had wakened the rabbi, and he came with Bendit the beadle. Bendit carried a stick, a Ram's Horn, and the Book of the Angel Raziel.

3.

Once in the bedroom, the rabbi, Reb Yeruchim, ordered the Ram's Horn to be blown. He had the beadle pile hot coals into a brazier, then he poured incense on the coals. As the smoke of the herbs filled the room, he commanded the evil one with Holy Oaths from the Zohar, the Book of Creation, and other books of the Cabala to leave the body of the woman Liebe Yentl, daughter of Zise Feige. But the unholy spirit defied everyone. Instead of leaving, he played out a succession of dances, marches, hops—just with the lips. He boomed like a bass viol, he jingled like a cymbal, he whistled like a flute, and drummed like a drum.

The page is too short for a recital of all that the dybbuk did and said that night and the nights that followed—his brazen tricks, his blasphemies against the Lord, the insults he hurled at the townsfolk, the boasts of all the lecheries he had committed, the mockery, the outbursts of laughing and of crying, the stream of quotations from the Torah and wedding jester's jokes, and all of it in singsong and in rhyme.

The dybbuk made himself heard only after dark. During the day, Liebe Yentl lay exhausted in bed and evidently did not remember what went on at night. She thought that she was sick and occasionally begged her mother to call the doctor or to give her some medicine. Most of the time she dozed, with her eyes and her lips shut tight.

Since the incantations and the amulets of the Shidlovtse rabbi were of no avail, Reb Sheftel went to seek the advice of the Radzymin rabbi. On the very morning he left, the mild weather gave way to wind and snow. The roads were snowed in and it was difficult to reach Radzymin, even in a sleigh. Weeks went by, and no news came from Reb Sheftel. Zise Feige was so hard hit by the calamity that she fell ill, and her assistant Zalkind had to take over the whole business.

Winter nights are long, and idlers look for ways to while away the time. Soon after twilight, they would gather at Zise Feige's house to hear the dybbuk's talk and to marvel at his antics. Zise Feige forbade them to annoy her daughter, but the curiosity of the townspeople was so great that they would break the door open and enter.

The dybbuk knew everyone and had words for each man according to his position and conduct. Most of the time he heaped mud and ashes upon the respected leaders of the community and their wives. He told each one exactly what he was: a miser or a swindler, a sycophant or a beggar, a slattern or a snob, an idler or a grabber. With the horse traders he talked about horses, and with the butchers about oxen. He reminded Chaim the miller that he had hung a weight under the scale on which he weighed the flour milled for the peasants. He questioned Yukele the thief about his latest theft. His jests and his jibes provoked both astonishment and laughter. Even the older folks could not keep from smiling. The dybbuk knew things that no stranger could have known, and it became clear to the visitors that they were dealing with a soul from which nothing could be hidden, for it saw through all their secrets. Although the evil spirit put everyone to shame, each man was willing to suffer his own humiliation for the sake of seeing others humbled.

When the dybbuk tired of exposing the sins of the townsfolk, he would turn to recitals of his own misdeeds. Not an evening passed without revelations of new vices. The dybbuk called everything by its name, denying nothing. When he was asked whether he regretted his abominations, he said with a laugh: "And if I did, could anything be changed? Everything is recorded up above. For eating a single wormy plum, you get six hundred and eighty-nine lashes. For a single moment of lust, you're rolled for a week on a bed of nails."

Between one jest and another, he would sing and bleat and play out tunes so skillfully that no one living could vie with him.

One evening the teacher's wife came running to the rabbi and reported that people were dancing to the dybbuk's music. The rabbi put on his robe and his hat and hurried to the house. Yes, the men and women danced together in Zise Feige's kitchen. The rabbi berated them and warned that they were committing a sacrilege. He sternly forbade Zise Feige to allow the rabble into her house. But Zise Feige lay sick in bed, and her boy, Tsadock Meyer, was staying with relatives. As soon as the rabbi left, the idlers resumed their dancing—a Scissors Dance, a Quarrel Dance, a Cossack, a Water Dance. It went on till midnight, when the dybbuk gave out a snore, and Liebe Yentl fell asleep.

A few days later there was a new rumor in town: a second dybbuk had entered Liebe Yentl, this time a female one. Once more an avid crowd packed the house. And, indeed, a woman's voice now came from Liebe Yentl—not her own gentle voice but the hoarse croaking of a shrew. People asked the new dybbuk who she was, and she told them that her name was Beyle Tslove and that she came from the town of Plock, where she had been a barmaid in a tavern and had later become a whore.

Beyle Tslove spoke differently from Getsl the fiddler, with the flat accents of her region and a mixture of Germanized words unknown in Shidlovtse. Beyle Tslove's language made even the butchers and the combers of pigs' bristles blush. She sang ribald songs and soldiers' ditties. She said she had wandered for eighty years in waste places. She had been reincarnated as a cat, a turkey, a snake, and a locust. For a long time her soul resided in a turtle. When someone mentioned Getsl the fiddler and asked whether she knew him and whether she knew that he was also lodged in the same woman, she answered, "I neither know him nor want to know him."

"Why not? Have you turned virtuous all of a sudden?" Zeinvl the butcher asked her.

"Who wants a dead fiddler?"

The people began to call to Getsl the fiddler, urging him to speak up. They wanted to hear the two dybbuks talk to each other. But Getsl the fiddler was silent.

Beyle Tslove said, "I see no Getsl here."

"Maybe he's hiding?" someone said.

"Where? I can smell a man a mile away."

In the midst of this excitement, Reb Sheftel returned. He looked older and even smaller than before. His beard was streaked with gray. He had brought talismans and amulets from Radzymin, to hang in the corners of the room and around his daughter's neck.

People expected the dybbuk to resist and fight the amulets, as evil spirits do when touched by a sacred object. But Beyle Tslove was silent while the amulets were hung around Liebe Yentl's neck. Then she asked, "What's this? Sacred toilet paper?"

"These are Holy Names from the Radzymin rabbi!" Reb Sheftel cried out. "If you do not leave my daughter at once, not a spur shall be left of you!"

"Tell the Radzymin rabbi that I spit at his amulets," the woman said brazenly.

"Harlot! Fiend! Harridan!" Reb Sheftel screamed.

"What's he bellowing for, that Short Friday? Some man—nothing but bone and beard!"

Reb Sheftel had brought with him blessed six-groschen coins, a piece of charmed amber, and several other magical objects that the Evil Host is known to shun. But Beyle Tslove, it seemed, was afraid of nothing. She mocked Reb Sheftel and told him she would come at night and tie an elflock in his beard.

That night Reb Sheftel recited the Shema of the Holy Isaac Luria. He slept in his fringed garment with the Book of Creation and a knife under his pillow—like a woman in childbirth. But in the middle of the night he woke and felt invisible fingers on his face. An unseen hand was burrowing in his beard. Reb Sheftel wanted to scream, but the hand covered his mouth. In the morning Reb Sheftel got up with his whole beard full of tangled braids, gummy as if stuck together with glue.

Although it was a fearful matter, the Worka Hassidim, who were bitter opponents of the Radzymin rabbi, celebrated that day with honey cake and brandy in their study house. Now they had proof that the Radzymin rabbi did not know the Cabala. The followers of the Worka rabbi had advised Reb Sheftel to make a journey to Worka, but he ignored them, and now they had their revenge.

4.

One evening, as Beyle Tslove was boasting of her former beauty and of all the men who had run after her, the fiddler of Pinchev suddenly raised his voice. "What were they so steamed up about?" he asked her mockingly. "Were you the only female in Plock?"

For a while all was quiet. It looked as though Beyle Tslove had lost her tongue. Then she gave a hoarse laugh. "So he's here—the scraper! Where were you hiding? In the gall?"

"If you're blind, I can be dumb. Go on, Grandma, keep jabbering. Your story had a gray beard when I was still in my diapers. In your place, I'd take such tall tales to the fools of Chelm. In Shidlovtse there are two or three clever men, too."

"A wise guy, eh?" Beyle Tslove said. "Let me tell you something. A live fiddle-scraper's no prize—and when it comes to a dead one! Go back, if you forgive me, to your resting place. They miss you in the Pinchev cemetery. The corpses who pray at night need another skeleton to make up their quorum."

The people who heard the two dybbuks quarrel were so stunned that they forgot to laugh. Now a man's voice came from Liebe Yentl, now a woman's. The Pinchev fiddler's "r"s were soft, the Plock harlot's hard.

Liebe Yentl herself rested against two pillows, her face pale, her hair down, her eyes closed. No one rightly saw her move her lips, though the room was full of people watching. Zise Feige was unable to keep them out, and there was no one to help her. Reb Sheftel no longer came home at night; he slept in the study house. Dunya the servant girl had left her job in the middle of the year. Zalkind, Zise Feige's assistant, went home in the evenings to his wife and children. People wandered in and out of the house as if it did not belong to anyone. Whenever one of the respectable members of the community came to upbraid the merry gang for ridiculing a stricken girl, the two dybbuks hurled curses and insults at him. The dybbuks gave the townspeople new nicknames: Reitse the busybody, Mindl glutton, Yekl tough, Dvoshe the strumpet. On several occasions, Gentiles and members of the local gentry came to see the wonder, and the dybbuks bantered with them in Polish. A landowner said in a tavern afterward that the best theater in Warsaw could not compete with the scenes played out by the two dead rascals in Shidlovtse.

After a while, Reb Sheftel, who had been unbending in his loyalty to the Radzymin rabbi, gave in and went to see the rabbi of Worka; perhaps he might help.

The two dybbuks were meanwhile carrying on their word duel. It is generally thought that women will get the better of men where the tongue is concerned, but the Pinchev fiddler was a match for the Plock whore. The fiddler cried repeatedly that it was beneath his dignity to wrangle with a harlot—a maid with a certificate of rape—but the hoodlums egged him on. "Answer her! Don't let her have the last word!" They whistled, hooted, clapped their hands, stamped their feet.

The battle of wits gradually turned into storytelling. Beyle Tslove related that her mother, a pious and virtuous woman, had borne her husband, a Hassid and a loafer, eight children, all of them girls. When Beyle Tslove made her appearance in the world, her father was so chagrined that he left home. By trickery, he collected the signatures of a hundred rabbis, permitting him to remarry, and her mother became an abandoned wife. To support the family, she went to market every morning to sell hot beans to the yeshiva students. A wicked tutor, with a goat's beard and sidelocks down to his shoulders, came to teach Beyle Tslove to pray, but he raped her. She was not yet eight years old. When Beyle Tslove went on to tell how she had become a barmaid, how the peasants had pinched and cursed her and pulled her hair, and how a bawd, pretending to be a pious woman, had lured her to a distant city and brought her into a brothel, the girls who were listening burst into tears. The young men, too, dabbed their eyes.

Getsl the fiddler questioned her. Who were the guests? How much did they pay? How much did she have to give the procurers and what was left for her to live on? Had she ever gone to bed with a Turk or a blackamoor?

Beyle Tslove answered all the questions. The young rakes had tormented her in their ways, and the old lechers had wearied her with their demands. The bawd took away her last groschen and locked the bread in the cupboard. The pimp whipped her with a wet strap and stuck needles into her buttocks. From fasting and homesickness she contracted consumption and ended by spitting out her lungs at the poorhouse. And because she had been buried behind the fence, without Kaddish, she was immediately seized by multitudes of demons, imps, mockers, and Babuks. The Angel Dumah asked her the verse that went with her name, and when she could not answer he split her grave with a fiery rod. She begged to be allowed into hell, for there the punishment lasts only twelve months, but the Unholy Ones dragged her off to waste places and deserts. She said that in the desert she had come upon a pit that was the door to Gehenna. Day and night, the screams of sinners who were being punished there came from the pit. She was carried to the Congealed Sea, where sailing ships, wrecked by storms, were held immobile, with dead crews and captains turned to stone. Beyle Tslove had also flown to a land inhabited by giants with two heads and single eyes in their foreheads. Few females were born there, and every woman had six husbands.

Getsl the fiddler also began to talk about the events of his life. He told of incidents at the weddings and balls of the gentry where he had played, and of what happened later, in the hereafter. He said that evildoers did not repent, even in the Nether Regions. Although they had already learned the truth of things, their souls still pursued their lusts. Gamblers played with invisible cards, thieves stole, swindlers swindled, and fornicators indulged in their abominations.

The townsfolk who heard the two were amazed, and Zeinvl the butcher asked, "How can anyone sin when he is rotting in the earth?"

Getsl explained that it was, anyway, the soul and not the body that enjoyed sin. This was why the soul was punished. Besides, there were bodies of all kinds—of smoke, of spiderwebs, of shadow—and they could be used for a while, until the Angels of Destruction tore them to pieces. There were castles, inns, and ruins in the deserts and abysses, which provided hiding places from Judgment, and also Avenging Angels who could be bribed with promises or even with the kind of money that has no substance but is used in the taverns and brothels of the Nether World.

When one of the idlers cried out that this was unbelievable, Getsl called on Beyle Tslove to attest to the truth of his words. "Tell us, Beyle Tslove, what did you really do all these years? Did you recite Psalms, or did you wander through swamps and wastes, consorting with demons, Zmoras, and Malachais?"

Instead of replying, Beyle Tslove giggled and coughed. "I can't speak—my mouth's dry."

"Yes, let's have a drop," Getsl chimed in, and when somebody brought over a tumbler of brandy, Liebe Yentl downed it like water. She did not open her eyes or even wince. It was clear to everybody that she was entirely in the sway of the dybbuks within her.

When Zeinvl the butcher realized that the two dybbuks had made peace, he asked, "Why don't you two become man and wife? You'd make a good pair."

"And what are we to do after the wedding?" Beyle Tslove answered. "Pray from the same prayer book?"

"You'll do what all married couples do."

"With what? We're past all doing. Anyway, there's no time—we won't be staying here much longer."

"Why not? Liebe Yentl is still young."

"The Worka rabbi is not the Radzymin schlemiel," Beyle Tslove said. "Asmodeus himself is afraid of his talismans."

"The Worka rabbi can kiss me you know where," Getsl boasted. "But I'm not about to become a bridegroom."

"The match isn't good enough for you?" Beyle Tslove cried. "If you knew who wanted to marry me, you'd croak a second time."

"If she's cursing me now, what can I expect later?" Getsl joked. "Besides, she's old enough to be my great-grandmother—seventy years older than I am, anyway you figure it."

"Numbskull. I was twenty-seven years old when I kicked in, and I can't get any older. And how old are you, bottle-bum? Close to sixty, if you're a day."

"May you get as many carbuncles on your bloated flesh as the years I was short of fifty."

"Just give me the flesh, I won't argue over the carbuncles."

The two kept up their wrangling and the crowd kept up its urging until finally the dybbuks consented. Those who have not heard the dead bride and groom haggle about the dowry, the trousseau, the presents, will never know what unholy spirits are capable of.

Beyle Tslove said that she had long since paid for all her transgressions and was therefore as pure as a virgin. "Is there such a thing as a virgin, anyway?" she argued. "Every soul has lodged countless times both in men and in women. There are no more new souls in heaven. A soul is cleansed in a cauldron, like dishes before Passover. It is purified and sent back to earth. Yesterday's beggar is today's magnate. A rabbi's wife becomes a coachman. A horse thief returns as a Community Elder. A slaughterer comes back as an ox. So what's all the fuss about? Everything is kneaded of the same dough—cat and mouse, bear hunter and bear, old man and infant." Beyle Tslove herself had in previous incarnations been a grain merchant, a dairymaid, a rabbi's wife, a teacher of the Talmud.

"Do you remember any Talmud?" Getsl asked.

"If the Angel of Forgetfulness had not tweaked me on the nose, I would surely remember."

"What do you say to my bride?" Getsl bantered. "A whittled tongue. She could convince a stone. If my wife in Pinchev knew what I was exchanging her for, she'd drown herself in a bucket of slops."

"Your wife filled her bed before you were cold. . . ."

The strange news spread throughout the town: tomorrow there would be a wedding at Reb Sheftel's house; Getsl the fiddler and Beyle Tslove would become man and wife.

5.

When the rabbi heard of the goings on, he issued a proscription forbidding anyone to attend the black wedding. He sent Bendit the beadle to stand guard at the door of Reb Sheftel's house and allow no one to enter. That night, however, there was a heavy snowfall, and by morning it turned bitterly cold. The wind had blown up great drifts and whistled in all the chimneys. Bendit was shrouded in white from head to foot and looked like a snowman made by children. His wife came after him and took him home, half frozen. As soon as dusk began to fall, the rabble gathered at Reb Sheftel's house. Some brought bottles of vodka or brandy; others, dried mutton and honey cake.

As usual, Liebe Yentl had slept all day and did not waken even when the ailing Zise Feige poured a few spoonfuls of broth into her mouth. But once darkness came, the girl sat up. There was such a crush in the house that people could not move.

Zeinvl the butcher took charge. "Bride, did you fast on your wedding day?"

"The way the dead eat, that's how they look," Beyle Tslove replied with a proverb.

"And you, bridegroom, are you ready?"

"Let her first deliver the dowry."

"You can take all I have—a pinch of dust, a moldy crust. . . ."

Getsl proved that evening that he was not only an expert musician but could also serve as rabbi, cantor, and wedding jester. First he played a sad tune and recited "God Is Full of Mercy" for the bride and groom. Then he played a merry tune, accompanying it with appropriate jests. He admonished the bride to be a faithful wife, to dress and adorn herself, and to take good care of her household. He warned the couple to be mindful of the day of death, and sang to them:

> "Weep, bride, weep and moan,
> Dead men fear to be alone.
> In the Sling, beneath the tide,
> A groom is waiting for his bride.
> Corpse and corpse, wraith and wraith,
> Every demon seeks a mate.
> Angel Dumah, devil, Shed,
> A coffin is a bridal bed."

Although it was a mock wedding, many a tear fell from the women's eyes. The men sighed. Everything proceeded according to custom. Getsl preached, sang, played. The guests could actually hear the weeping of a fiddle, the piping of a clarinet, the bleating of a trumpet, the wailing of a bagpipe. Getsl pretended to cover the bride with the veil and played a melody appropriate to the veiling ceremony. After the wedding march he recited the words of "Thou Art Sanctified," which accompany the giving of the ring. He delivered the bridegroom's oration, and announced the wedding presents: a shrouded mirror, a little sack of earth from the Holy Land, a burial cleansing spoon, a stopped clock.

When the spirits of the guests seemed to droop, Getsl struck up a kozotsky. They tried to dance, but there was scarcely room to take a step. They swayed and gesticulated.

Beyle Tslove suddenly began to wail. "Oi, Getsl!"

"What, my dove!"

"Why couldn't this be real? We weren't born dead!"

"Pooh! Reality itself hangs by a thread."

"It's not a game to me, you fool."

"Whatever it is, let's drink and keep cool. May we rejoice and do well until all the fires are extinguished in hell."

A glass of wine was brought, and Liebe Yentl emptied it to the last drop. Then she dashed it against the wall, and Getsl began to recite in the singsong of the cheder boys:

> "Such is Noah's way,
> Wash your tears away.
> Take a drink instead,
> The living and the dead.
> Wine will make you strong,
> Eternity is long."

Zise Feige could not endure any more. She rose from her sickbed, wrapped herself in a shawl, and shuffled into her daughter's room in her slippers. She tried to push through the crowd. "Beasts," she cried. "You are torturing my child!"

Beyle Tslove screamed at her, "Don't you worry, old sourpuss! Better a rotten fiddler than a creep from Zawiercia!"

6.

In the middle of the night there were sounds of steps and shouts outside the door. Reb Sheftel had come home from Worka, bringing a bagful of new amulets, charms, and talismans. The Hassidim of the Worka rabbi entered with him, ready to drive out the rabble.

They swung their sashes, crying, "Get out, you scum!"

Several young fellows tried to fight off the Worka Hassidim, but the Shidlovtse crowd was tired from standing so long, and they soon began to file out the door. Getsl called after them, "Brothers, don't let the holy schlemiels get you! Give them a taste of your fists! Hey, you, big shot!"

"Cowards! Bastards! Mice!" Beyel Tslove screeched.

A few of the Worka Hassidim got a punch or two, but after a while the riffraff slunk off. The Hassidim burst into the room, panting and threatening the dybbuks with excommunication.

The warden of the Worka synagogue, Reb Avigdor Yavrover, ran up to Liebe Yentl's bed and tried to hang a charm around her neck, but the girl pulled off his hat and skullcap with her right hand, and with her left she seized him by the beard. The other Hassidim tried to pull him away, but Liebe Yentl thrashed out in all directions. She kicked, bit, and scratched. One man got a slap on the cheek, another had his sidelock pulled, a third got a mouthful of spittle on his face, a fourth a punch in the ribs. In order to frighten off the pious, she cried that she was in her unclean days. Then she tore off her shift and exhibited her shame. Those who did not avert their eyes remarked that her belly was distended like a drum. On the right and the left were two bumps as big as heads, and it was clear that the spirits were there. Getsl roared like a lion, howled like a wolf, hissed like a snake. He called the Worka rabbi a eunuch, a clown, a baboon, insulted all the holy sages, and blasphemed against God.

Reb Sheftel sank to the floor and sat there like a mourner. He covered his eyes with both hands and rocked himself as over a corpse. Zise Feige snatched a broom and tried to drive away the men who swarmed around her daughter, but she was dragged aside and fell to the ground. Two neighboring women helped her to get up. Her bonnet fell off, exposing her shaven head with its gray stubble. She raised two fists and screamed, sobbing, "Torturers, you're killing my child! Lord in heaven, send Pharaoh's curses upon them!"

Finally, several of the younger Hassidim caught Liebe Yentl's hands and feet and tied her to the bed with their sashes. Then they slipped the Worka rabbi's amulets around her neck.

Getsl, who had fallen silent during the struggle, spoke up. "Tell your miracle worker his charms are tripe."

"Wretch, you're in Hell, and you still deny?" Reb Avigdor Yavrover thundered.

"Hell's full of your kind."

"Dog, rascal, degenerate!"

"Why are you cursing, you louses?" Beyle Tslove yelled. "Is it our fault that your holy idiot hands out phony talismans? You'd better leave the girl alone. We aren't doing her any harm. Her good is our good. We're also Jews, remember—not Tatars. Our souls have stood on Mount Sinai, too. If we erred in life, we've paid our debt, with interest."

"Strumpet, hussy, slut, out with you!" one of the Hassidim cried.

"I'll go when I feel like it."

"Todres, blow the Ram's Horn—a long blast!"

The Ram's Horn filled the night with its eerie wail. Beyle Tslove laughed and jeered. "Blow hot, blow cold, who cares!"

"A broken trill now!"

"Don't you have enough breaks under your rupture bands?" Getsl jeered.

"Satan, Amalekite, apostate!"

Hours went by, but the dybbuks remained obdurate. Some of the Worka Hassidim went home. Others leaned against the wall, ready to do battle until the end of their strength. The hoodlums who had run away returned with sticks and knives. The Hassidim of the Radzymin rabbi had heard the news that the Worka talismans had failed, and they came to gloat.

Reb Sheftel rose from the floor and in his anguish began to plead with the dybbuks. "If you are Jews, you should have Jewish hearts. Look what has become of my innocent daughter, lying bound like a sheep prepared for slaughter. My wife is sick. I myself am ready to drop. My business is falling apart. How long will you torture us? Even a murderer has a spark of pity."

"Nobody pities us."

"I'll see to it that you get forgiveness. It says in the Bible, 'His banished be not expelled from Him.' No Jewish soul is rejected forever."

"What will you do for us?" asked Getsl. "Help us moan?"

"I will recite Psalms and read the Mishnah for you. I will give alms. I will say Kaddish for you for a full twelve months."

"I'm not one of your peasants. You can't fool me."

"I have never fooled anyone."

"Swear that you will keep your word!" Getsl commanded.

"What's the matter, Getsl? You anxious to leave me already?" Beyle Tslove asked with a laugh.

Getsl yawned. "I'm sorry for the old folks."

"You want to leave me a deserted wife the very first night?"

"Come along if you can."

"Where to? Behind the Mountains of Darkness?"

"Wherever our eyes take us."

"You mean sockets, comedian!"

"Swear, Reb Sheftel, that you will keep all your promises," Getsl the fiddler repeated. "Make a holy vow. If you break your word, I'll be back with the whole Evil Host and scatter your bones to the four winds."

"Don't swear, Reb Sheftel, don't swear!" the Hassidim cried. "Such a vow is a desecration of the Name!"

"Swear, my husband, swear. If you don't, we shall all perish."

Reb Sheftel put his hand on his beard. "Dead souls, I swear that I will faithfully fulfill all that I take upon myself. I will study the Mishnah for you. I will say Kaddish for twelve months. Tell me when you died, and I will burn memorial candles for you. If there are no headstones on your graves, I will journey to the cemeteries and have them erected."

"Our graves have been leveled long since. Come, Beyle Tslove, let's go. Dawn is rising over Pinchev."

"Imp, you made a fool of a Jewish daughter all for nothing!" Beyle Tslove reproached him.

"Hey, men, move aside!" Getsl cried. "Or I shall enter one of you!"

There was such a crush that, though the door stood open, no one could get out. Hats and skullcaps fell off. Caftans caught on nails and ripped. A muffled cry rose from the crowd. Several Hassidim fell, and others trampled them. Liebe Yentl's mouth opened wide and there was a shot as from a pistol. Her eyes rolled and she fell back on the pillow, white as death. A stench swept across the room—a foul breath of the grave. Zise Feige stumbled on weak legs toward her daughter and untied her. The girl's belly was now flat and shrunken like the belly of a woman after childbirth.

Reb Sheftel attested afterward that two balls of fire came out of Liebe Yentl's nostrils and flew to the window. A pane split open, and the two sinful souls returned through the crack to the World of Delusion.

7.

For weeks after the dybbuks had left her, Liebe Yentl lay sick. The doctor applied cups and leeches; he bled her, but Liebe Yentl never opened her eyes. The woman from the Society of Tenders of the Sick who sat with the girl at night related that she heard sad melodies outside the window, and Getsl's voice begging her to remove the amulets from the girl's neck and let him in. The woman also heard Beyle Tslove's giggling.

Gradually Liebe Yentl began to recover, but she had almost stopped speaking. She sat in bed and stared at the window. Winter was over. Swallows returned from the warm countries and were building a nest under the eaves. From her bed Liebe Yentl could see the roof of the synagogue, where a pair of storks were repairing last year's nest.

Reb Sheftel and Zise Feige feared that Liebe Yentl would no longer be accepted in marriage, but Shmelke Motl wrote from Zawiercia that he would keep to his agreement if the dowry were raised by one third. Reb Sheftel and Zise Feige consented at once. After Pentecost, Shmelke Motl made his appearance at the Shidlovtse prayer house—no taller than a cheder boy but with a large head on a thin neck and tightly twisted sidelocks that stood up like a pair of horns. He had thick eyebrows and dark eyes that looked down at the tip of his nose. As soon as he entered the study house, he took out a Gemara and sat down to study. He sat there, swaying and mumbling, until he was taken to the ceremony of betrothal.

Reb Sheftel invited only a selected few to the engagement meal, for during the time that his daughter had been possessed by the dybbuks he had made many enemies both among the Radzymin Hassidim and among those of Worka. According to custom, the men sat at one table, the women at another. The bridegroom delivered an impromptu sermon on the subject of the Stoned Ox. Such sermons usually last half an hour, but two hours went by and the groom still talked on in his high, grating voice, accompanying his words with wild gestures. He grimaced as though gripped with pain, pulled at a sidelock, scratched his chin, which was just beginning to sprout a beard, grasped the lobe of his ear. From time to time his lips stretched in a smile, revealing blackened teeth, pointed as nails.

Liebe Yentl never once took her eyes from him. The women tried to talk to her; they urged her to taste the cookies, the jam, the mead. But Liebe Yentl bit her lips and stared.

The guests began to cough and fidget, hinting in various ways that it was time to bring the oration to an end, and finally the bridegroom broke off his sermon. The betrothal contract was brought to him, but he did not sign it at once. First he read the page from beginning to end. He was evidently nearsighted, for he brought the paper right up to his nose. Then he began to bargain. "The prayer shawl should have silver braid."

"It will have any braid you wish," Reb Sheftel agreed.

"Write it in."

It was written in on the margin. The groom read on, and demanded, "I want a Talmud printed in Slovita."

"Very well, it will be from Slovita."

"Write it in."

After much haggling and writing in, the groom signed the contract: Shmelke Motl son of the late Catriel Godl. The letters of the signature were as tiny as flyspecks.

When Reb Sheftel brought the contract over to Liebe Yentl and handed her the pen, she said in a clear voice, "I will not sign."

"Daughter, you shame me!"

"I will not live with him."

Zise Feige began to pinch her wrinkled cheeks. "People, go home!" she called out. She snuffed the candles in the candlesticks. Some of the women wept with the disgraced mother; others berated the bride. But the girl answered no one. Before long, the house was dark and empty. The servant went out to close the shutters.

Reb Sheftel usually prayed at the synagogue with the first quorum, but that morning he did not show himself at the holy place. Zise Feige did not go out to do her shopping. The door of Reb Sheftel's house stood locked; the windows were shuttered. Shmelke Motl returned at once to Zawiercia.

After a time Reb Sheftel went back to praying at the synagogue, and Zise Feige went again to market with her basket. But Liebe Yentl no longer came out into the street. People thought that her parents had sent her away somewhere, but Liebe Yentl was at home. She kept to her room and refused to speak to anyone. When her mother brought her a plate of soup, she first knocked at the door as though they were gentry. Liebe Yentl scarcely touched the food, and Zise Feige sent it to the poorhouse.

For some months the matchmakers still came with

offers, but since a dybbuk had spoken from her and she
had shamed a bridegroom Liebe Yentl could no longer
make a proper match. Reb Sheftel tried to obtain a
pardon from the young man in Zawiercia, but he had
gone away to some yeshiva in Lithuania. There was a
rumor that he had hanged himself with his sash. Then
it became clear that Liebe Yentl would remain an old
maid. Her younger brother, Tsadock Meyer, had in the
meantime grown up and got married to a girl from
Bendin.

Reb Sheftel was the first to die. This happened on a
Thursday night in winter. Reb Sheftel had risen for
midnight prayers. He stood at the reading desk, with
ash on his head, reciting a lament on the Destruction of
the Temple. A beggar was spending that night at the
prayer house. About three o'clock in the morning, the
man awakened and put some potatoes into the stove to
bake. Suddenly he heard a thud. He stood up and saw
Reb Sheftel on the floor. He sprinkled him with water
from the pitcher, but the soul had already departed.

The townspeople mourned Reb Sheftel. The body was
not taken home but lay in the prayer house with
candles at its head until the time of burial. The rabbi
and some of the town's scholars delivered eulogies. On
Friday, Liebe Yentl escorted the coffin with her mother. Liebe Yentl was wrapped in a black shawl from
head to toe; only a part of her face showed, white as the
snow in the cemetery. The two sons lived far from
Shidlovtse, and the funeral could not be postponed till
after the Sabbath; it is a dishonor for a corpse to wait
too long for burial. Reb Sheftel was put to rest near the
grave of the old rabbi. It is known that those who are
buried on Friday after noon do not suffer the pressure
of the grave, for the Angel Dumah puts away his fiery
rod on the eve of the Sabbath.

Zise Feige lingered a few years more, but she was
fading day by day. Her body bent like a candle. In her
last year she no longer attended to the business, rely-
ing entirely on her assistant, Zalkind. She began to
rise at dawn to pray at the women's synagogue, and

she often went to the cemetery and prostrated herself on Reb Sheftel's grave. She died as suddenly as her husband. It happened during evening prayer on Yom Kippur. Zise Feige had stood all day, weeping, at the railing that divided the women's section from the men's in the prayer house. Her neighbors, seeing her waxen-yellow face, urged her to break her fast, for human life takes precedence over all laws, but Zise Feige refused. When the cantor intoned, "The gates of Heaven open," Zise Feige took from her bosom a vial of aromatic drops, which are a remedy against faintness. But the vial slipped from her hand and she fell forward onto the reading desk. There was an outcry and women ran for the doctor, but Zise Feige had already passed into the True World. Her last words were: "My daughter. . . ."

This time the funeral was delayed until the arrival of the two sons. They sat in mourning with their sister. But Liebe Yentl avoided all strangers. Those who came to pray with the mourners and to comfort them found only Jedidiah and Tsadock Meyer. Liebe Yentl would lock herself away in her room.

Nothing was left of Reb Sheftel's wealth. People muttered that the assistant had pocketed the money, but it could not be proved. Reb Sheftel and Zise Feige had kept no books. All the accounting had been done with a piece of chalk on the wall of a wardrobe. After the seven days of mourning, the sons called Zalkind to the rabbi's court, but he offered to swear before the Holy Scrolls and black candles that he had not touched a groschen of his employers' money. The rabbi forbade such an oath. He said that a man who could break the commandment "Thou Shalt Not Steal" could also violate the commandment "Thou Shalt Not Take the Name of Thy God the Lord in Vain."

After the judgment, the two sons went home. Liebe Yentl remained with the servant. Zalkind took over the business and merely sent Liebe Yentl two gulden a week for food. Soon he refused to give even that and sent only a few groschen. The servant woman left and went to work elsewhere.

Now that Liebe Yentl no longer had a servant, she was compelled to show herself in the street, but she never came out during the day. She would leave the house only after dark, waiting until the streets were empty and the stores without other customers. She would appear suddenly, as though from nowhere. The storekeepers were afraid of her. Dogs barked at her from Christian yards.

Summer and winter she was wrapped from head to toe in a long shawl. She would enter the store and forget what she wanted to buy. She often gave more money than was asked, as though she no longer remembered how to count. A few times she was seen entering the Gentile tavern to buy vodka. Tevye the night watchman had heard Liebe Yentl pacing the house at night, talking to herself.

Zise Feige's good friends tried repeatedly to see the girl, but the door was always bolted. Liebe Yentl never came to the synagogue on holidays to pray for the souls of the deceased. During the months of Nissan and Elul, she never went to visit the graves of her parents. She did not bake Sabbath bread on Fridays, did not set roasts overnight in the oven, and probably did not bless the candles. She did not come to the women's synagogue even on the High Holy Days.

People began to forget Liebe Yentl—as if she were dead—but she lived on. At times, smoke rose from her chimney. Late at night, she was sometimes seen going to the well for a pail of water. Those who caught sight of her swore that she did not look a day older. Her face was becoming even more pale, her hair redder and longer. It was said that Liebe Yentl played with cats. Some whispered that she had dealings with a demon. Others thought that the dybbuk had returned to her. Zalkind still delivered a measure of flour to the house every Thursday, leaving it in the larder in the entrance hall. He also provided Liebe Yentl with firewood.

There had formerly been several other Jewish households on the street, but gradually the owners had sold to Gentiles. A hog butcher had moved into one house and built a high fence around it. Another house was occupied by a deaf old widow who spent her days spinning flax, guarded by a blind dog at her feet.

Years went by. One early morning in Elul, when the rabbi was sitting in his study writing commentary and drinking tea from a samovar, Tevye the night watchman knocked at his door. He told the rabbi that he had seen Liebe Yentl on the road leading to Radom. The girl wore a long white dress; she had no kerchief on her head and walked barefoot. She was accompanied by a man with long hair, carrying a violin case. The full moon shone brightly. Tevye wanted to call out, but since the figures cast no shadow he was seized with fear. When he looked again, the pair had vanished.

The rabbi ordered Tevye to wait until the worshippers assembled for morning prayer in the synagogue. Then Tevye told the people of the apparition, and two men—a driver and a butcher—went to Reb Sheftel's house. They knocked, but no one answered. They broke open the door and found Liebe Yentl dead. She lay in the middle of the room among piles of garbage, in a long shift, barefoot, her red hair loose. It was obvious that she had not been among the living for many days—perhaps a week or even more. The women of the burial society hastily carried off the corpse to the hut for the cleansing of the dead. When the shroud-makers opened the wardrobe, a cloud of moths flew out, filling the house like a swarm of locusts. All the clothes were eaten, all the linens moldy and decayed.

Since Liebe Yentl had not taken her own life and since she had exhibited all the signs of madness, the rabbi permitted her to be buried next to her parents. Half the town followed the body to the cemetery. The brothers were notified and came later to sell the house and order a stone for their sister's grave.

It was clear to everyone that the man who had appeared with Liebe Yentl on the road to Radom was the dead fiddler of Pinchev. Dunya, Zise Feige's former servant, told the women that Liebe Yentl had not been able to forget her dead bridegroom Ozer and that Ozer had become a dybbuk in order to prevent the marriage to Shmelke Motl. But where would Ozer, a scholar and the son of a rich man, have learned to play music and to perform like a wedding jester? And why would he appear on the Radom road in the guise of a fiddler? And where was he going with the dead Liebe Yentl that night? And what had become of Beyle Tslove? Heaven and earth have sworn that the truth shall remain forever hidden.

More years went by, but the dead fiddler was not forgotten. He was heard playing at night in the cold synagogue. His fiddle sang faintly in the bathhouse, the poorhouse, the cemetery. It was said in town that he came to weddings. Sometimes, at the end of a wedding after the Shidlovtse band had stopped playing, people still heard a few lingering notes, and they knew that it was the dead fiddler.

In autumn, when leaves fell and winds blew from the Mountains of the Holy Cross, a low melody was often heard in the chimneys, thin as a hair and mournful as the world. Even children would hear it, and they would ask, "Mamma, who is playing?" And the mother would answer, "Sleep, child. It's the dead fiddler."

Translated by Mirra Ginsburg

The Lecture

I was on my way to Montreal to deliver a lecture. It was midwinter and I had been warned that the temperature there was ten degrees lower than in New York. Newspapers reported that trains had been stalled by the snow and fishing villages cut off, so that food and medical supplies had to be dropped to them by plane.

I prepared for the journey as though it were an expedition to the North Pole. I put on a heavy coat over two sweaters and packed warm underwear and a bottle of cognac in case the train should be halted somewhere in the fields. In my breast pocket I had the manuscript that I intended to read—an optimistic report on the future of the Yiddish language.

In the beginning, everything went smoothly. As usual, I arrived at the station an hour before train departure and therefore could find no porter. The station teemed with travelers and I watched them, trying to guess who they were, where they were going, and why.

None of the men was dressed as heavily as I. Some even wore spring coats. The ladies looked bright and elegant in their minks and beavers, nylon stockings and stylish hats. They carried colorful bags and illustrated magazines, smoked cigarettes and chattered and laughed with a carefree air that has never ceased to amaze me. It was as though they knew nothing of the existence of world problems or eternal questions, as though they had never heard of death, sickness, war, poverty, betrayal, or even of such troubles as missing a train, losing a ticket, or being robbed. They flirted like young girls, exhibiting their blood-red nails. The station was chilly that morning, but no one except myself seemed to feel it. I wondered whether these people knew there had been a Hitler. Had they heard of Stalin's murder machine? They probably had, but what does one body care when another is tortured?

I was itchy from the woolen underwear. Now I began to feel hot. But from time to time a shiver ran through my body. The lecture, in which I predicted a brilliant future for Yiddish, troubled me. What had made me so optimistic all of a sudden? Wasn't Yiddish going under before my very eyes?

The prompt arrival of American trains and the ease in boarding them have always seemed like miracles to me. I remember journeys in Poland when Jewish passengers were not allowed into the cars and I had to hang on to the handrails. I remember railway strikes when trains were halted midway for many hours and it was impossible in the dense crowd to push through to the washroom.

But here I was, sitting on a soft seat, right by the window. The car was heated. There were no bundles, no high fur hats, no sheepskin coats, no boxes, and no gendarmes. Nobody was eating bread and lard. Nobody drank vodka from a bottle. Nobody was berating Jews for state treason. In fact, nobody discussed politics at all. As soon as the train started, a huge Negro in a white apron came in and announced lunch. The train was not rattling, it glided smoothly on its rails along the frozen Hudson. Outside, the landscape gleamed with snow and light. Birds that remained here for the winter flew busily over the icy river.

The farther we went, the wintrier the landscape. The weather seemed to change every few miles. Now we went through dense fog, and now the air cleared and the sun was shining again over silvery distances.

A heavy snowfall began. It suddenly turned dark.

The day was flickering out. The express no longer ran but crept slowly and cautiously, as though feeling its way. The heating system in the train seemed to have broken down. It became chilly and I had to put on my coat. The other passengers pretended for a while that they did not notice anything, as though reluctant to admit too quickly that they were cold. But soon they began to tap their feet, grumble, grin sheepishly, and rummage in their valises for sweaters, scarves, boots, or whatever else they had brought along. Collars were turned up, hands stuffed into sleeves. The makeup on women's faces dried up and began to peel like plaster.

The American dream gradually dissolves and harsh Polish reality returns. Someone is drinking whiskey from a bottle. Someone is eating bread and sausage to warm his stomach. There is also a rush to the toilets. It is difficult to understand how it happened, but the floor of the car becomes wet and muddy. The windowpanes become crusted with ice and bloom with frost patterns.

Suddenly the train stops. I look out and see a sparse wood. The trees are thin and bent, and though they are covered with snow, they look bare and charred, as after a fire. The sun has already set, but purple stains still glow in the west. The snow on the ground is no longer white, but violet. Crows walk on it, flap their wings, and I can hear their cawing. The snow falls in gray, heavy lumps, as though the guardians of the Treasury of Snow up above had been too lazy to flake it more finely. Passengers walk from car to car, leaving the doors open. Conductors and other train employees run past; when they are asked questions, they do not stop, but mumble something rudely.

We are not far from the Canadian border, and Uncle Sam's domain is virtually at an end. Some passengers begin to take down their luggage; they may have to show it soon to the customs officials. A naturalized American citizen gets out his citizenship papers and studies his own photograph, as if trying to convince himself that the document is not a false one.

One or two passengers venture to step out of the train, but they sink up to their knees into the snow. It is not long before they clamber back into the car. The twilight lingers for a while, then night falls.

I see people using the weather as a pretext for striking up acquaintance. Women begin to talk among themselves and there is sudden intimacy. The men have also formed a group. Everyone picks up bits of information. People offer each other advice. But nobody pays any attention to me. I sit alone, a victim of my own isolation, shyness, and alienation from the world. I begin to read a book, and this provokes hostility, for reading a book at such a time seems like a challenge and an insult to the other passengers. I exclude myself from society, and all the faces say to me silently: You don't need us and we don't need you. Never mind, you will still have to turn to us, but we won't have to turn to you. . . .

I open my large, heavy valise, take out the bottle of cognac, and take a stealthy sip now and then. After that, I lean my face against the cold windowpane and try to look out. But all I see is the reflection of the interior of the car. The world outside seems to have disappeared. The solipsistic philosophy of Bishop Berkeley has won over all the other systems. Nothing remains but to wait patiently until God's idea of a train halted in its tracks by snowdrifts will give way to God's ideas of movement and arrival.

Alas for my lecture! If I arrive in the middle of the night, there will not even be anyone waiting for me. I shall have to look for a hotel. If only I had a return ticket. However, was Captain Scott, lost in the polar ice fields, in a better position after Amundsen had discovered the South Pole? How much would Captain Scott have given to be able to sit in a brightly lit railway car? No, one must not sin by complaining.

The cognac had made me warm. Drunken fumes rise from an empty stomach to the brain. I am awake and dozing at the same time. Whole minutes drift away, leaving only a blur. I hear talk, but I don't quite know what it means. I sink into blissful indifference. For my part, the train can stand here for three days and three nights. I have a box of crackers in my valise. I will not die of hunger. Various themes float through my mind. Something within me mutters dreamlike words and phrases.

The diesel engine must be straining forward. I am aware of dragging, knocking, growling sounds, as of a monstrous ox, a legendary steel bull. Most of the passengers have gone to the bar or the restaurant car, but I am too lazy to get up. I seem to have grown into the seat. A childish obstinacy takes possession of me: I'll show them all that I am not affected by any of this commotion; I am above the trivial happenings of the day.

Everyone who passes by—from the rear cars to the front, or the other way—glances at me; and it seems to me that each one forms some judgment of his own about the sort of person I am. But does anyone guess that I am a Yiddish writer late for his lecture? This, I am sure, occurs to no one. This is known only to the higher powers.

I take another sip, and another. I have never understood the passion for drinking, but now I see what power there is in alcohol. This liquid holds within itself the secrets of nirvana. I no longer look at my wristwatch. I no longer worry about a place to sleep. I mock in my mind the lecture I had prepared. What if it is not delivered? People will hear fewer lies! If I could open the window, I would throw the manuscript out into the woods. Let the paper and ink return to the cosmos, where there can be no errors and no lies. Atoms and molecules are guiltless; they are a part of the divine truth. . . .

2.

The train arrived exactly at half past two. No one was waiting for me. I left the station and was caught in a blast of icy night wind that no coat or sweaters could keep out. All taxis were immediately taken. I returned to the station, prepared to spend the night sitting on a bench.

Suddenly I noticed a lame woman and a young girl looking at me and pointing with their fingers. I stopped and looked back. The lame woman leaned on two thick, short canes. She was wrinkled, disheveled, like an old woman in Poland, but her black eyes suggested that she was more sick and broken than old. Her clothes also reminded me of Poland. She wore a sort of sleeveless fur jacket. Her shoes had toes and heels I had not seen in years. On her shoulders she wore a fringed woolen shawl, like one of my mother's. The young woman, on the other hand, was stylishly dressed, but also rather slovenly.

After a moment's hesitation, I approched them.

The girl said: "Are you Mr. N.?"

I answered, "Yes, I am."

The lame woman made a sudden movement, as though to drop her canes and clap her hands. She immediately broke into a wailing cry so familiar to me.

"Dear Father in heaven!" she sang out. "I was telling my daughter it's he, and she said no. I recognized you! Where were you going with the valise? It's a wonder you came back. I'd never have forgiven myself! Well, Binele, what do you say now? Your mother still has some sense. I am only a woman, but I am a rabbi's daughter, and a scholar has an eye for people. I took one look and I thought to myself—it's he! But nowadays the eggs are cleverer than the chickens. She says to me: 'No, it can't be.' And in the meantime you disappear. I was already beginning to think, myself: Who knows, one's no more than human, anybody can make a mistake. But when I saw you come back, I knew it was you. My dear man, we've been waiting here since half past seven in the evening. We weren't alone; there was a whole group of teachers, educators, a few writers too. But then it grew later and later and people went home. They have wives, children. Some have to get up in the morning to go to work. But I said to my daughter, 'I won't go. I won't allow my favorite writer, whose every word I treasure as a pearl, to come here and find no one waiting for him. If you want, my child,' I said to her, 'you can go home and go to bed.' What's a night's sleep? When I was young, I used to think that if you missed a night's sleep the world would go under. But Hitler taught us a lesson. He taught us a lesson I won't forget until I lie with shards over my eyes. You look at me and you see an old, sick woman, a cripple, but I did hard labor in Hitler's camps. I dug ditches and loaded railway cars. Was there anything I didn't do? It was there that I caught my rheumatism. At night we slept on plank shelves not fit for dogs, and we were so hungry that—"

"You'll have enough time to talk later, Momma. It's the middle of the night," her daughter interrupted.

It was only then that I took a closer look at the daughter. Her figure and general appearance were those of a young girl, but she was obviously in her late twenties, or even early thirties. She was small, narrow, with yellowish hair combed back and tied into a bun. Her face was of a sickly pallor, covered with freckles. She had yellow eyes, a round forehead, a crooked nose, thin lips, and a long chin. Around her neck she wore a mannish scarf. She reminded me of a Hassidic boy.

The few words she spoke were marked by a provincial Polish accent I had forgotten during my years in America. She made me think of rye bread, caraway seeds, cottage cheese, and the water brought by water carriers from the well in pails slung on a wooden yoke over their shoulders.

"Thank you, but I have patience to listen," I said.

"When my mother begins to talk about those years, she can talk for a week and a day—"

"Hush, hush, your mother isn't as crazy as you think. It's true, our nerves were shattered out there. It is a wonder we are not running around stark mad in the streets. But what about her? As you see her, she too was in Auschwitz waiting for the ovens. I did not even know she was alive. I was sure she was lost, and you can imagine a mother's feelings! I thought she had gone the way of her three brothers; but after the liberation we found each other. What did they want from us, the beasts? My husband was a holy man, a scribe. My sons worked hard to earn a piece of bread, because inscribing mezuzahs doesn't bring much of an income. My husband, himself, fasted more often than he ate. The glory of God rested on his face. My sons were killed by the murderers—"

"Momma, will you please stop?"

"I'll stop, I'll stop. How much longer will I last, anyway? But she is right. First of all, my dear man, we must take care of you. The president gave me the name of a hotel—they made all the reservations for you—but my daughter didn't hear what he said, and I forgot it. This forgetting is my misfortune. I put something down and I don't know where. I keep looking for things, and that's how my whole days go by. So maybe, my dear writer, you'll spend the night with us? We don't have such a fine apartment. It's cold, it's shabby. Still, it's better than no place at all. I'd telephone the president, but I'm afraid to wake him up at night. He has such a temper, may he forgive me; he keeps shouting that we aren't civilized. So I say to him: 'The Germans are civilized, go to them. . . .' "

"Come with us, the night is three quarters gone, anyway," the daughter said to me. "He should have written it down instead of just saying it; and if he said it, he should have said it to me, not to my mother. She forgets everything. She puts on her glasses and cries, 'Where are my glasses?' Sometimes I have to laugh. Let me have your valise."

"What are you saying? I can carry it myself, it isn't heavy."

"You are not used to carrying things, but I have learned out there to carry heavy loads. If you would see the rocks I used to lift, you wouldn't believe your eyes. I don't even believe it myself anymore. Sometimes it seems to me it was all an evil dream. . . ."

"Heaven forbid, you will not carry my valise. That's all I need. . . ."

"He is a gentleman, he is a fine and gentle man. I knew it at once as soon as I read him for the first time," the mother said. "You wouldn't believe me, but we read your stories even in the camps. After the war, they began to send us books, and I came across one of your stories. I don't remember what it was called, but I read it and a darkness lifted off my heart. 'Binele,' I said—she was already with me then—'I've found a treasure.' Those were my words. . . ."

"Thank you, thank you very much."

"Don't thank me, don't thank me. It's we who have to thank you. All the troubles come from people being deaf and blind. They don't see the next man and so they torture him. We are wandering among blind evildoers. . . . Binele, don't let this dear man carry the valise. . . ."

"Yes, please give it to me!"

I had to plead with Binele to let me carry it. She almost tried to pull it out of my hands.

We went outside and a taxi drove up. It was not easy to get the mother into it. I still cannot understand how she had managed to come to the station. I had to lift her up and put her in. In the process, she dropped one of her canes, and Binele and I had to look for it in the snow. The driver had already begun to grumble and scold in his Canadian French. Afterward, the car began to pitch and roll over dimly lit streets covered with snow and overgrown with mountains of ice. The tires had chains on them, but the taxi skidded backward several times.

We finally drove into a street that was reminiscent of a small town in Poland: murky, narrow, with wooden houses. The sick woman hastily opened her purse, but I paid before she had time to take out her money. Both women chided me, and the driver demanded that we get out as quickly as possible. I virtually had to carry the crippled woman out of the taxi. Again, we had to look for her cane in the deep snow. Afterward, her daughter and I half led, half dragged her up a flight of steps. They opened the door and I was suddenly enveloped in odors I had long forgotten: moldy potatoes, rotting onions, chicory, and something else I could not even name. In some mysterious way the mother and daughter had managed to bring with them the whole atmosphere of wretched poverty from their old home in Poland.

They lit a kerosene lamp and I saw an apartment with tattered wallpaper, a rough wooden floor, and spider webs in every corner. The kerosene stove was out and the rooms were drafty. On a bench stood cracked pots, chipped plates, cups without handles. I even caught sight of a besom on a pile of sweepings. No stage director, I thought, could have done a better job of reproducing such a scene of old-country misery.

Binele began to apologize. "What a mess, no? We were in such a hurry to get to the station, we didn't even have time to wash the dishes. And what's the good of washing or cleaning here, anyway? It's an old, run-down shanty. The landlady knows only one thing: to come for the rent every month. If you're late one day, she's ready to cut your throat. Still, after everything we went through over there, this is a palace. . . ."

And Binele laughed, exposing a mouthful of widely spaced teeth with gold fillings that must have been made when she was still across the ocean.

3.

They made my bed on a folding cot in a tiny room with barred windows. Binele covered me with two blankets and spread my coat on top of them. But it was still as cold as outside. I lay under all the coverings and could not warm up.

Suddenly I remembered my manuscript. Where was the manuscript of my lecture? I had had it in the breast pocket of my coat. Afraid to sit up, lest the cot should collapse, I tried to find it. But the manuscript was not there. I looked in my jacket, which hung on a chair

nearby, but it was not there either. I was certain that I
            the valise, for I had opened the
        cognac. I had intended to open it
       ers, but they had only waved me
    s not necessary.

      that I had lost the manuscript. But
     d daughter had told me that the
     ed to the next day, but what would
    ly one hope: perhaps it had dropped
    Binele was covering me with the
    rying not to make a sound, but the
    ightest movement. It even seemed
    to creak in advance, when I only
    Inanimate things are not really

    aughter were evidently not asleep.
    g, a mumbling from the next room.
    about something quietly, but about

The loss of the manuscript, I thought, was a Freud-
ian accident. I was not pleased with the essay from the
very first. The tone I took in it was too grandiloquent.
Still, what was I to talk about that evening? I might
get confused from the very first sentences, like that
speaker who had started his lecture with, "Peretz was
a peculiar man," and could not utter another word.

If only I could sleep! I had not slept the previous night
either. When I have to make a public appearance, I
don't sleep for nights. The loss of the manuscript was a
real catastrophe! I tried to close my eyes, but they kept
opening by themselves. Something bit me; but as soon
as I wanted to scratch, the cot shook and screamed like
a sick man in pain.

I lay there, silent, stiff, wide-awake. A mouse
scratched somewhere in a hole, and then I heard a
sound, as of some beast with saw and fangs trying to
saw through the floorboards. A mouse could not have
raised such noise. It was some monster trying to cut
down the foundations of the building. . . .

"Well, this adventure will be the end of me!" I said to myself. "I won't come out of here alive."

I lay benumbed, without stirring a limb. My nose was stuffed and I was breathing the icy air of the room through my mouth. My throat felt constricted. I had to cough, but I did not want to disturb the mother and daughter. A cough might also bring down the ramshackle cot. . . . Well, let me imagine that I had remained under Hitler in wartime. Let me get some taste of that, too. . . .

I imagined myself somewhere in Treblinka or Maidanek. I had done hard labor all day long. Now I was lying on a plank shelf. Tomorrow there would probably be a "selection," and since I was no longer well, I would be sent to the ovens. . . . I mentally began to say goodbye to the few people close to me. I must have dozed off, for I was awakened by loud cries. Binele was shouting: "Momma! Momma! Momma! . . ." The door flew open and Binele called me: "Help me! Mother is dead!"

I wanted to jump off the cot but it collapsed under me, and instead of jumping, I had to raise myself. I cried: "What happened?"

Binele screamed: "She is cold! Where are the matches? Call a doctor! Call a doctor! Put on the light! Oh, Momma! . . . Momma! Momma!"

I never carry matches with me, since I do not smoke. I went in my pajamas to the bedroom. In the dark I collided with Binele. I asked her: "How can I call a doctor?"

She did not answer, but opened the door into the hallway and shouted, "Help, people, help! My mother is dead!" She cried with all her strength, as women cry in the Jewish small towns in Poland, but nobody responded. I tried to look for matches, knowing in advance that I would not find them in this strange house. Binele returned and we collided again in the dark. She clung to me with unexpected force and wailed: "Help! Help! I have nobody else in the world! She was all I had!"

And she broke into a wild lament, leaving me stunned and speechless.

"Find a match! Light the lamp!" I finally cried out, although I knew that my words were wasted.

"Call a doctor! Call a doctor!" she screamed, undoubtedly realizing herself the senselessness of her demand.

She half led, half pulled me to the bed where her mother lay. I put out my hand and touched her body. I began to look for her hand, found it, and tried to feel her pulse, but there was no pulse. The hand hung heavy and limp. It was cold as only a dead thing is cold. Binele seemed to understand what I was doing and kept silent for a while.

"Well, well? She's dead? . . . She's dead! . . . She had a sick heart! . . . Help me! Help me!"

"What can I do? I can't see anything!" I said to her, and my words seemed to have double meaning.

"Help me! . . . Help me! . . . Momma!"

"Are there no neighbors in the house?" I asked.

"There is a drunkard over us. . . ."

"Perhaps we can get matches from him?"

Binele did not answer. I suddenly became aware of how cold I felt. I had to put something on or I would catch pneumonia. I shivered and my teeth chattered. I started out for the room where I had slept but found myself in the kitchen. I returned and nearly threw Binele over. She was, herself, half naked. Unwittingly I touched her breast.

"Put something on!" I told her. "You'll catch a cold!"

"I do not want to live! I do not want to live! . . . She had no right to go to the station! . . . I begged her, but she is so stubborn. . . . She had nothing to eat. She would not even take a glass of tea. . . . What shall I do now? Where shall I go? Oh, Momma, Momma!"

Then, suddenly, it was quiet. Binele must have gone upstairs to knock on the drunkard's door. I remained alone with a corpse in the dark. A long-forgotten terror possessed me. I had the eerie feeling that the dead woman was trying to approach me, to seize me with her cold hands, to clutch at me and drag me off to where she was now. After all, I was responsible for her death.

The strain of coming out to meet me had killed her. I
started toward the outside door, as though ready to run
out into the street. I stumbled on a chair and struck my
knee. Bony fingers stretched after me. Strange beings
screamed at me silently. There was a ringing in my
ears and saliva filled my mouth as though I were about
to faint.

Strangely, instead of coming to the outside door, I
found myself back in my room. My feet stumbled on the
flattened cot. I bent down to pick up my overcoat and
put it on. It was only then that I realized how cold I was
and how cold it was in that house. The coat was like an
ice bag against my body. I trembled as with ague. My
teeth clicked, my legs shook. I was ready to fight off
the dead woman, to wrestle with her in mortal combat.
I felt my heart hammering frighteningly loud and fast.
No heart could long endure such violent knocking. I
thought that Binele would find two corpses when she
returned, instead of one.

I heard talk and steps and saw a light. Binele had
brought down the upstairs neighbor. She had a man's
coat over her shoulders. The neighbor carried a burning
candle. He was a huge man, dark, with thick black hair
and a long nose. He was barefoot and wore a bathrobe
over his pajamas. What struck me most in my panic
was the enormous size of his feet. He went to the bed
with his candle and shadows danced after him and
wavered across the dim ceiling.

One glance at the woman told me that she was dead.
Her face had altered completely. Her mouth had become strangely thin and sunken; it was no longer a
mouth, but a hole. The face was yellow, rigid, and
claylike. Only the gray hair looked alive. The neighbor
muttered something in French. He bent over the woman
and felt her forehead. He uttered a single word and
Binele began to scream and wail again. He tried to
speak to her, to tell her something else, but she evidently did not understand his language. He shrugged
his shoulders, gave me the candle, and started back.
My hand trembled so uncontrollably that the small

flame tossed in all directions and almost went out. I let some tallow drip on the wardrobe and set the candle in it.

Binele began to tear her hair and let out such a wild lament that I cried angrily at her: "Stop screaming!"

She gave me a sidelong glance, full of hate and astonishment, and answered quietly and sensibly: "She was all I had in the world. . . ."

"I know, I understand. . . . But screaming won't help."

My words appeared to have restored her to her senses. She stood silently by the bed, looking down at her mother. I stood on the opposite side. I clearly remembered that the woman had had a short nose; now it had grown long and hooked, as though death had made manifest a hereditary trait that had been hidden during her lifetime. Her forehead and eyebrows had acquired a new and masculine quality. Binele's sorrow seemed for a while to have given way to stupor. She stared, wide-eyed, as if she did not recognize her own mother.

I glanced at the window. How long could a night last, even a winter night? Would the sun never rise? Could this be the moment of that cosmic catastrophe that David Hume had envisaged as a theoretical possibility? But the panes were just beginning to turn gray.

I went to the window and wiped the misty pane. The night outside was already intermingled with blurs of daylight. The contours of the street were becoming faintly visible; piles of snow, small houses, roofs. A street lamp glimmered in the distance, but it cast no light. I raised my eyes to the sky. One half was still full of stars; the other was already flushed with morning. For a few seconds I seemed to have forgotten all that had happened and gave myself up entirely to the birth of the new day. I saw the stars go out one by one. Streaks of red and rose and yellow stretched across the sky, as in a child's painting.

"What shall I do now? What shall I do now?" Binele began to cry again. "Whom shall I call? Where shall I

go? Call a doctor! Call a doctor!" And she broke into
sobs.

I turned to her. "What can a doctor do now?"

"But someone should be called."

"You have no relatives?"

"None. I've no one in the world."

"What about the members of your lecture club?"

"They don't live in this neighborhood. . . ."

I went to my room and began to dress. My clothes
were icy. My suit, which had been pressed before my
journey, was crumpled. My shoes looked like misshapen
clodhoppers. I caught sight of my face in a mirror, and
it shocked me. It was hollow, dirty, paper-gray, covered
with stubble. Outside, the snow began to fall again.

"What can I do for you?" I asked Binele. "I'm a
stranger here. I don't know where to go."

"Woe is me! What am I doing to you? You are the
victim of our misfortune. I shall go out and telephone
the police, but I cannot leave my mother alone."

"I'll stay here."

"You will? She loved you. She never stopped talking
about you. . . . All day yesterday. . . ."

I sat down on a chair and kept my eyes away from
the dead woman. Binele dressed herself. Ordinarily I
would be afraid to remain alone with a corpse. But I
was half frozen, half asleep. I was exhausted after the
miserable night. A deep despair came over me. It was a
long, long time since I had seen such wretchedness and
so much tragedy. My years in America seemed to have
been swept away by that one night and I was taken
back, as though by magic, to my worst days in Poland,
to the bitterest crisis of my life. I heard the outside door
close. Binele was gone. I could no longer remain sitting
in the room with the dead woman. I ran out to the
kitchen. I opened the door leading to the stairs. I stood
by the open door as though ready to escape as soon as
the corpse began to do those tricks that I had dreaded
since childhood. . . . I said to myself that it was foolish
to be afraid of this gentle woman, this cripple who had
loved me while alive and who surely did not hate me

now, if the dead felt anything. But all the boyhood
fears were back upon me. My ribs felt chilled, as if
some icy fingers moved over them. My heart thumped
and fluttered like the spring in a broken clock. . . .
Everything within me was strained. The slightest rus-
tle and I would have dashed down the stairs in terror.
The door to the street downstairs had glass panes, but
they were half frosted over, half misty. A pale glow
filtered through them as at dusk. An icy cold came
from below. Suddenly I heard steps. The corpse? I
wanted to run, but I realized that the steps came from
the upper floor. I saw someone coming down. It was the
upstairs neighbor on his way to work, a huge man in
rubber boots and a coat with a kind of cowl, a metal
lunch box in his hands. He glanced at me curiously and
began to speak to me in Canadian French. It was good
to be with another human being for a moment. I
nodded, gestured with my hands, and answered him in
English. He tried again and again to say something in
his unfamiliar language, as though he believed that if I
listened more carefully I would finally understand
him. In the end he mumbled something and threw up
his arms. He went out and slammed the door. Now I
was all alone in the whole house.

What if Binele should not return? I began to toy with
the fantasy that she might run away. Perhaps I'd be
suspected of murder? Everything was possible in this
world. I stood with my eyes fixed on the outside door. I
wanted only one thing now—to return as quickly as
possible to New York. My home, my job seemed totally
remote and insubstantial, like memories of a previous
incarnation. Who knows? Perhaps my whole life in
New York had been no more than a hallucination? I
began to search in my breast pocket. . . . Did I lose my
citizenship papers, together with the text of my lecture?
I felt a stiff paper. Thank God, the citizenship papers
are here. I could have lost them, too. This document
was now testimony that my years in America had not
been an invention.

Here is my photograph. And my signature. Here is

the government stamp. True, these were also inanimate, without life, but they symbolized order, a sense
of belonging, law. I stood in the doorway and for the
first time really read the paper that made me a citizen
of the United States. I became so absorbed that I had
almost forgotten the dead woman. Then the outside
door opened and I saw Binele, covered with snow. She
wore the same shawl that her mother had worn yesterday.

"I cannot find a telephone!"

She broke out crying. I went down to meet her,
slipping the citizenship papers back into my pocket.
Life had returned. The long nightmare was over. I put
my arms around Binele and she did not try to break
away. I became wet from the melting snow. We stood
there midway up the stairs and rocked back and forth—a
lost Yiddish writer, and a victim of Hitler and of my
ill-starred lecture. I saw a number tattooed above her
wrist and heard myself saying: "Binele, I won't aban-
don you. I swear by the soul of your mother. . . ."

Binele's body became limp in my arms. She raised
her eyes and whispered: "Why did she do it? She just
waited for your coming. . . ."

Cockadoodledoo

Cockadoodledoo! In your language this means good morning, time to get up, day is breaking in Pinchev. What a lot of words you people use! For us chickens, cockadoodledoo says everything. And how much it can mean! It all depends on the melody, the accent, the tone.

I am a great-grandson of the rooster who perched on King Solomon's chair and I know languages. Therefore I tell you that one cockadoodledoo is worth more than a hundred words. It's not so much a matter of voice as it is of the flap of the wings, the way the comb quivers, the eye tilts, the neck feathers ruffle.

We even have what you call dialects. A Litvak rooster crows cookerikoo, a Polish rooster crows cookerikee, and there are some who can even manage a cockerikko. Each has a style inherited from generations of roosters. Even the same chicken will never crow the same way twice. But for such distinctions you need a good ear.

On my mother's side I have blood of the Ancient Prophetic Woodcock. If you put me in a dark cage, I can tell by the pitch of the roosters' crowing and the hens' clucking whether it is daybreak or twilight, clear or cloudy, whether it is mild or a frost is coming, if it's raining, snowing, or hailing. My ear tells me that the moon is full, half full, or new. I even can tell an eclipse

81

of the sun. I know a thousand things that don't even occur to you. You talk too much, you drown in your own words. All truth lies hidden in one word: cockadoodledoo.

I wasn't born yesterday. A world of hens and roosters has passed before my eyes. I have seen a rooster castrated and force-fed. I know the end all too well: death. Whether they'll make a sacrifice of me for Yom Kippur, whether they'll put me aside until Passover, Succoth or for the Sabbath of Moses' Song of the Red Sea, the slaughterer waits, the knife is sharp, everything is prepared: the tub for soaking, the salting board, the gravy bowl, the stew pot, or maybe the roasting oven.

The garbage dump is crammed with our heads and entrails. Every good-for-nothing housewife carries around one of our wings for a whisk broom. Even if by some chance I should miss the slaughterer's knife, I still can't last indefinitely. I might get a nail in my gizzard. I might catch the pip. I might have—may it not happen to you—pox in my bowels. I might gulp down a wire, a pebble, a needle, a little snake. Every fowl ends up in the bowl.

So then what? Cockadoodledoo resolves all questions, solves all riddles. The rooster may die but not the cockadoodledoo. We were crowing long before Adam and, God willing, we'll go on crowing long after all slaughterers and chicken-gluttons have been laid low. What is rooster, then, and what is hen? Nothing more than a nesting place for the cockadoodledoo. No butcher in the world can destroy that.

There exists a heavenly rooster—his image is our own; and there is a heavenly Cockadoodledoo. The Rooster on High crows through our windpipes, he performs the midnight services through us, gets up with us for prayers when the morning stars sing together. You people pore over the Cabala and rack your brains. But for us the Cabala is in the marrow of our bones. What is cockadoodledoo? A magical name.

Maybe I'm betraying secrets. But to whom am I

talking? To deaf ears. Your ancestors were never able to find out the secret of the cockadoodledoo; it is certain that you won't either. It is said that in distant countries there are machines where they hatch out hens by the millions and pull them out by the shelfful. The slaughterhouse is as big as our marketplace. One butcher boy ties, one cuts, one plucks. Tubs fill up with blood. Feathers fly. Every moment a thousand fowl give up their souls. And yet, can they really finish us this way?

Right now, while I'm talking, the under side of my wing begins to itch. I want to hold myself back, but I can't. My throat tickles, my tongue trembles, my beak itches, my comb burns. The quill of every feather tingles. It must come out! Cockadoodledoo!

2.

Apropos of what you say about hens: you mustn't take them too lightly. When I was a young rooster, a hen was less than nothing to me. What is a hen? No comb, no spurs, no color in her tail, no strength in her claws. She cackles her few years away, lays eggs, hatches them, rubs her what-do-you-call-it in the dirt, puts on pious airs.

At an early age I began to see the hypocrisy of hens. They bow down to every big shot. Among themselves, in their own yard, whoever is stronger picks on the others. I have a hatred of gossip and a hen just can't hold her tongue. Cluck-cluck and cluck-cluck. My rule is: don't talk too much with a chicken. It is true that you can't get along without them. Everybody has a mother. But what of it? You can't stay stuck in the eggshell forever.

But that's the conceit of young roosters. With age I found that it must be this way. In all lands and in all the heavens there is male and female. Everything is paired, from the fly to the elephant, from the Rooster on High to the ordinary cock. It is true that cluck-cluck is just not the same as cockadoodledoo, but a hen, too, is not to be sneezed at.

Your so-called philosophers love to ask: which came first, the chicken or the egg? Garrulous chickens argue endlessly: which came first, the cockadoodledoo or the cluck-cluck? But all this is empty chatter. My opinion is that there was no first egg and there's not going to be any last egg. First is last and last is first. You don't understand? The answer is: cockadoodledoo.

I have five wives and each one is a tale in herself. Kara is a princess. Where she got her pedigree, I couldn't say. She is fat, easygoing, has golden eyes and a tranquil heart. She does not hobnob with the other hens. When the mistress scatters a handful of millet, the rabble runs to grab it, but Kara has both patience and faith. The kernel destined for her will reach her. She keeps herself clean, doesn't look at other cocks, avoids bickering. She has the right to peck at all her competitors but considers it beneath her dignity to start up with every silly hen. She clucks less than the others and the eggs that she lays are big and white.

I have no great passion for her nor she for me, but I have more chicks by her than by any of the others. Every year she hatches two dozen eggs and without complaint she does everything that a hen should. When she's through with her laying, they'll put her away and she'll make a rich soup. I suspect that she doesn't even know that there's such a thing as death, because she likes to play around with the guts of her sisters. That's Kara.

Tsip is the exact opposite: red, thin, bony, a screecher, a glutton, and jealous—fire and flame. She picks on all the hens, but loves me terribly. Just let her see me coming and down she plops and spreads her wings. In your language you would say she is oversexed, but I forgive her everything. She twitches, every limb quivers. Her eggs are tiny, with bloody specks. In all the time I've known her she's never stopped screaming. She runs around the yard as though she were possessed. She complains and complains. This one pecked her, that one bit her, the third one pulled some down from her breast, the fourth grabbed a crumb from under her beak. Lays eggs and doesn't remember where. Tries to fly and almost breaks a leg. Suddenly she's in a tree and then on a roof. At night in the coop she doesn't close an eye. Fidgets, cackles, can't find any place for herself. A witch with an itch. They would have slaughtered her long ago if she were not so skinny, eating herself up alive—and for what? That's Tsip.

Chip is completely white, a hen without any meanness in her, as good as a sunny day, quiet as a dove. She runs from quarrels as from fire. At the least hubbub she stops laying. She loves me with a chaste love, considers me a hen-chaser, but keeps everything to herself. She clucks with a soft-tongued cluck and gets fatter every day.

If she feels like sitting on eggs and there are none to sit on, she might sit on a little white stone; she isn't very bright. The other day she hatched out three duck eggs. As long as the ducklings didn't crawl into the water, Chip thought they were chicks; but as soon as they began to swim in the pond, she almost dropped dead. Chip stood by the bank, her mother's heart close to bursting. I tried to explain to her what a bastard is, but try to talk to a frightened mother.

For some strange reason, Chip loves Tsip and does everything to please her. But Tsip is her blood enemy. Anyone else in Chip's place would have scratched her eyes out long ago; but Chip is good and asks for no reward. She's full of the mercy which comes from the Heavenly Chicken. That's Chip.

Pre-pre is the lowest hen I've ever met. Has all the vices a hen can have: black as coal, thin as a stick, a thief, a tattletale, a scrapper, and blind in one eye from a fight with her first husband, may the dunghill rest lightly on him. She carries on with strange roosters, slips into other people's yards, rummages in all kinds of garbage. She has the comb of a rooster and the voice of a rooster. When the moon is full, she starts to crow as though possessed by a dybbuk.

She lays an egg and devours it herself or cracks it open from sheer meanness. I hate her, that Black Daughter of a Black Mother. How many times I've sworn to have no dealings with the slut, but when she wants what's coming to her, she begins to fawn, flatter, gaze into my eyes like a beggar.

I'm no fighter by nature, but Pre-pre has a bad effect on me. I grab her by the head feathers and chase her all over the yard. My other wives avoid her like the plague. Many times our mistress wanted to catch her and send her to the slaughterer, but just when she's wanted she's not at home, that gadabout, that dog of a hen. That's Pre-pre.

Cluckele is my own little daughter, Kara is her mother, and a father doesn't gossip about his daughter even when she's his wife. I look at her and I don't believe my own eyes: when did she grow up? Only yesterday, it seems, this was a tiny little chick, just out of the eggshell, hardly covered with down. But she's already coquettish, already knows hennish wiles and lays eggs, although they're small. Very soon I'll be the father of my own grandchildren.

I love her, but I suspect that her little heart belongs to another rooster, that cross-eyed idiot on the other side of the fence. What she sees in that sloppy tramp, I have no idea. But how can a rooster know what a hen sees in another rooster? Her head could be turned by a feather in the tail, a tooth in the comb, a side spur, or even the way he shuffles his feet in the sand and stirs up the dust.

I'm good to her, but she doesn't appreciate it. I give her advice, but she doesn't listen. I guard her like the apple of my eye, but she's always looking for excitement. . . . The new generation is completely spoiled, but what can I do? One thing I want: as long as I live, may she live too. What happens afterward is not up to me.

3.

Your experts in the Cabala know that cockadoodledoo is based on sheer faith. What else, logic? But faith itself has different degrees. A rooster's little faith may give out and he will become crestfallen. His wings droop, his comb turns white, his eyes glaze over and his crow sticks in his gullet. Why crow? For whom and for how long? Roosters have been crowing since ancient times and for what? When one begins to think about time, it's no good. Occasionally a rooster will even weep. Yes, roosters are capable of weeping. Listen sometime to the roosters crowing the night before Yom Kippur when you people are reciting the midnight prayers. If your human ears could hear our weeping, you would throw away all your slaughtering knives.

But let me tell you something that happened.

The night was dark. The chickens dozed or pretended to doze. It was during the Ten Days of Repentance before the Yom Kippur sacrifice of fowls. All day long it was oppressively hot. At night the sky clouded over, hiding a sliver of moon. The air was warm and humid like the mud in the duck pond. There was lightning, but no thunder, no rain. People closed their shutters and snored under their feather comforters. The grass stood motionless; the leaves on the apple trees were still; even the grasshoppers fell asleep. The frogs in the swamp were voiceless. The moles rested in their mole-hills.

Everything was silent, everything held its breath. It seemed as if the world had asked the ultimate question and was waiting for an answer: yes or no, one way or another. Things cannot go on like this. If a clear answer does not come, creation will return to primeval chaos. I did not move. My heart didn't beat, my blood didn't flow, nothing stirred. It was midnight, but I had no urge to crow. Had the end come?

Suddenly a flap of wings and from somewhere close at hand: cockadoodledoo! I trembled. I became all ears.

It was the old cockadoodledoo, but with a new meaning. No, not the old one, but a brand-new one: a new style, another approach, a different melody. I didn't know what it was saying, but suddenly everything was light, I felt rejuvenated. Is it possible? I asked myself. Millions of generations of roosters had crowed, but no one before had ever crowed like that. It opened doors in my brain, it cheered my heart. It spilled over with hope and happiness. Could it really be? I asked. And I, fool that I was, had doubted! I felt both shame and joy. I, too, wanted to crow, but I was shy. What could I say after him? Tsip woke up and asked, "What's that?"

"A new voice, a new word," I said. "Chickens, let us join in a blessing. We have not lived in vain."

"Who is he, where is he?" asked Chip.

"What difference does it make who he is? The power lies in the crowing, not in the rooster."

"Still—"

I didn't answer her. I closed my eyes. The crowing had stopped, but its sound still echoed in the silence from trees, roofs, chimneys, birdhouses. It sang like a fiddle, rang like a bell, resounded like a ram's horn. It sang and didn't stop singing.

The dog in the kennel awoke and barked once. The pig in his sty uttered a grunt; the horse in the stable thumped the ground with his hoof. The clouds parted in the sky and a moon appeared, white as chalk. For a while I thought: who knows, perhaps I only imagined it. True, the hens heard it too, but perhaps it was a dream, perhaps it was only the wind. Perhaps it was a wolf howling, the sound of a trumpet, a hunter's call, a drunkard's shout.

Even though fowl wait all their lives for a miracle, still, when it happens, they can't believe it. I expected the other roosters to answer him as usual, but I didn't hear a sound. Had all the roosters been slaughtered, with only this one left? Perhaps I myself was already slaughtered and the voice I heard was only the dream of a chopped-off head? The stillness was not of this world. I stuck my beak in my feathers and pinched my own skin to see if it hurt. Suddenly: cockadoodledoo! It was the same rooster and the same crow. No, not the same, already different: a song which rent the soul and then revived it; a melody lifting a rooster's heart into heights where no eagle ever flew, above all towers, all clouds, into a brightness that made the stars seem dark.

Everything I know I learned that night. I can't reveal secrets—my tongue is tied—but there is a cockadoodledoo which rights every wrong, forgives every sin, straightens all crookedness. Everything is cockadoodledoo: butcher and fowl; knife and throat; feathers and plucker; the blood in the veins and the blood in the ditch. Crow, rooster, and ask no questions! We must accept all: the crow of the rooster, the cluck of the hen, the egg which is hatched, the egg which is eaten, the egg which is stepped upon, and the egg with the splotch of blood in it.

Sing, rooster, praise God, love your hens, don't fight with other roosters unless they attack you. Eat your grain, drink your water, stand on the rooftop and crow as if the whole world—all four corners of it—were waiting for your crowing. It is really waiting. Without your crowing, something would be missing. You don't understand? God willing, you will understand. You have eternity behind you and eternity before you. You will go through many lives. If you knew what awaits you, you would die of joy. But that wouldn't do. As long as you live, you must live. . . .

All night long that rooster crowed and not a single rooster dared answer him. He was a cantor without a choir. Just at daybreak, when it began to redden in the East, he let out his last crow—the loudest, the loveliest, the most divine.

The next day there was a furor among the neighboring roosters. Some swore by their comb and spurs that they had heard nothing. Others admitted they had heard something, but it wasn't a rooster. As for the hens, every one of them had forgotten. What will chickens not do to avoid the truth? They fear the truth more than the knife, and this is in itself a mystery.

But since that rooster crowed—exalted be his name— and I had the privilege to hear and to remember, I have wanted to spread the word, especially since tomorrow is the day before Yom Kippur. Happy is he who believes. A time will come when all will see and hear, and the cockadoodledoo of the Rooster on High will ring throughout heaven and earth.

Cockadoodledoo!

Translated by Ruth Whitman

The Plagiarist

The rabbi of Machlev, Reb Kasriel Dan Kinsker, paced back and forth in his study. From time to time he would stop, grasp his white beard with his left hand, and let go, spreading all five fingers, a typical gesture when he was faced with a problem. He was talking to himself: "How could he ever do such a thing? He's actually copied word for word!"

The rabbi was alluding to one of his disciples, Shabsai Getsel. During the several years that Shabsai Getsel had studied with the rabbi, he had often made use of the latter's manuscripts. As a matter of fact, the rabbi had even asked him to copy out several of his responsa.

Reb Kasriel Dan had for the last forty years been writing homilies and commentaries on Talmudic texts, but he had never yet been able to bring himself to permit the publication of even one of his works. He had heeded the verse in Ecclesiastes: "And further, by these, my son, be admonished: of making many books there is no end."

Authors streamed to Machlev to sell prepublication subscriptions or to raise money to pay for getting their works printed. Some asked Reb Kasriel Dan for approbatory prefaces. There were those whose disquisitions totally missed the point of the Talmud text. Instead, they piled sophistry on sophistry and read into the words of the ancients meanings that had never been intended.

The rabbi hesitated before refusing to write such a preface lest his unwillingness be interpreted as an offense against the author. On the other hand, to praise work he could not approve was equally wrong. It also took a lot of time and good eyesight to read these manuscripts. Some of the handwriting was difficult to decipher, with afterthoughts frequently scribbled in the margins. Whenever the matter of why Reb Kasriel Dan did not bring out a book of his own came up, he would say: "There are quite enough books, thank the Lord, without mine. Let Jews abide by what has been written until now."

One of his grandfather's pithy Bible interpretations occurred to the rabbi. "It is written in Psalms that when the Messiah comes, 'Then shall all the trees of the wood rejoice.' The question that arises is: Why should the trees rejoice? What concern is it of theirs? The answer is that by the time the Messiah arrives, authors will have written so many volumes that books will supply the necessary fuel for stoves. Thus there will no longer be any need to burn wood, and the trees will rejoice at having been spared."

That was all very well, but what Shabsai Getsel had done was so heinous that the rabbi for weeks on end was like a man obsessed. The young fellow had copied whole sections of the rabbi's manuscripts and had them printed under his own name. That was theft plain and simple. The rabbi could not believe that Shabsai Getsel was capable of such behavior, and he was still trying to think up some excuse on Getsel's behalf.

Yet the more the rabbi compared his own manuscripts with Shabsai Getsel's printed book, the more astounded he became. The rabbi realized that Shabsai Getsel knew himself to be safe against exposure. He could be sure that the rabbi would not stoop to shaming another man even though that man had sinned. Besides, Shabsai Getsel was also the son-in-law of Reb Tevia, the warden of the congregation, who had many relatives in Machlev. To bring the matter into the open would cause a scandal and profanation of the Holy Name.

But what had Shabsai Getsel been thinking as he sat copying out dozens of pages of Reb Kasriel Dan's manuscripts? Had he imagined some kind of heavenly dispensation for himself? Or was he, God forbid, a heretic who did not believe either in the Creator or in his judgment?

The more Reb Kasriel Dan pondered the matter, the more confounded he became. He grasped at his beard over and over again. It was not his habit to talk to himself, but the words forced themselves from his lips. He wrinkled his lofty forehead under his skullcap, knitted his brows, grimaced as if he were in physical pain. He paused in front of his bookcase, as though seeking an answer in the spines of the ancient volumes.

There was, of course, the fact that no man sinned unless a touch of madness entered his soul. On the other hand, that was true only of sins committed on impulse in a fit of rage, even if one went so far as to steal, or, God forbid, to commit adultery. But to sit day in, day out, week in, week out, plagiarizing another's works was sheer wantonness. Moreover, how did Shabsai Getsel still dare to look Reb Kasriel Dan in the face?

The whole thing was a riddle. Reb Kasriel Dan called out to himself and to the world at large: "The End of the Days is at hand!" Was not this event similar to those described in the Sotah tractate when it speaks of the omens preceding the coming of the Messiah: "In the Messiah's footsteps brazenness will grow, prices will soar, the vine will bear fruit, but wine will be dear. Idolatry will become heresy practiced with impunity . . . And the wisdom of the scribes will be dulled, while those who fear sin will be held in contempt; the truth will be absent. Boys will mock their elders, and the aged will rise before youth. . . ."

"Have things really gone so far?" the rabbi asked himself.

The rabbi knew he ought not to be wasting so much

time on this matter. His duty was to pray, study, and serve the Lord. This brooding over Shabsai Getsel led only to vexation. It robbed the rabbi of his sleep, so that he had difficulty in concentrating on his predawn studies. He had even vented his bitterness on his wife. He must keep the whole business hushed up. Certainly now he would have to give up any idea of publishing his own writings, for that would set tongues wagging and result in gossip and accusations.

"Who knows?" thought the rabbi. "Perhaps this is heaven's way of preventing the publication of my works. But was this reconcilable with the free will which is granted to all men?"

The door opened and in came Shabsai Getsel.

Outwardly there was nothing unusual in this. Shabsai Getsel had been coming to see the rabbi for years and still acted the part of pupil. Indeed, it was Reb Kasriel Dan who had ordained him the year before. But now the sight of Shabsai Getsel alarmed the rabbi.

"I'll not utter a cross word, heaven forbid, nor make any insinuations," Reb Kasriel resolved. He forced himself to say, "Welcome, Shabsai Getsel!"

Shabsai Getsel, short, swarthy, with pitch-black eyes, black eyebrows, and a little black beard, was wearing a fox coat, with foxtails dangling from the hem; a sable hat was perched on his head. He trod softly in his fur-lined top-boots. He applied two fingers to the mezuzah on the doorpost and kissed it. Carefully he removed his fur coat and woolen scarf, remaining in his caftan.

The rabbi indicated a chair at the table for Shabsai Getsel and seat d himself in his armchair.

Reb Kasriel Dan was taller than Shabsai Getsel. From under his white bristly eyebrows, a pair of gray eyes peered forth. He was wearing a satin robe, breeches, half-shoes, and white knee-length stockings. The rabbi was barely sixty years old but looked closer to eighty. Only his gait was still firm and his gaze piercing. Wheras Shabsai Getsel did everything with deliberation, the rabbi moved with haste. He opened a

book and promptly closed it again. He shifted pen and ink forward and drew them back.

"Well, Shabsai Getsel, what's the news?" he inquired.

"I've received several letters."

"Aha!"

"Would you like to see them?"

"Yes, let's have them."

Reb Kasriel Dan knew in advance what letters these were. Shabsai Getsel had sent copies of his book out to various rabbis, who had written back praising his work. He was already being addressed as "The Great Luminary," "The Living Library," "The Uprooter of Mountains."

The rabbis were eloquent in expressing their pleasure in his exegeses, describing them as "deep as the sea," "sweet as honey," "precious as pearls and jewels."

As the rabbi read the ornate scripts, he prayed to God to preserve him from evil thoughts. "Well, that's fine. 'A good name is better than precious ointment,'" he declared.

Suddenly the rabbi saw it all. He was being tempted. Heaven was testing him to see how much he could stand. One false move and he would fall into the trap laid for him by Satan. He would sink into hatred, sorrow, fury, and who knows what other transgressions. There was only one thing to do: keep his lips sealed and his brain pure. Most assuredly, Shabsai Getsel had erred; but he, Reb Kasriel Dan, was not the Lord of the Universe. It was not for him to pass judgment on a fellow man. Who could tell what went on in another's heart? Who could measure the forces which drove flesh and blood to vanity, covetousness, folly? Reb Kasriel Dan had long since come to understand that many people were made half mad by their passions.

The rabbi took out his pocket handkerchief and wiped his forehead. "What good errand brings you here?"

"I'd like to take a look at the responsum you wrote to the Rabbi of Sochatchov."

Reb Kasriel Dan was about to ask whether Shabsai Getsel was preparing another book. But he stopped himself and said: "It's in the drawer of the commode. Wait, I'll fetch it."

And the rabbi went into the next room, where he kept his manuscripts. He soon returned and handed Shabsai Getsel a copy of the responsum.

2.

Shabsai Getsel remained with the rabbi for several hours. No sooner had he left than the rabbi's wife came in.

Reb Kasriel Dan saw at once that she was angry. She swept into the room, the hem of her dress swishing over the floor. The tassel on her bonnet shook. Her narrow, deeply wrinkled face was paler than usual. Even before she reached the table at which her husband sat, she began shrieking: "What does he want here, that worm? Why does he spent entire days here? He is your enemy, not a friend! Your worst enemy . . . !"

Reb Kasriel Dan pushed his book away. "Why are you screaming? I can't show people the door."

"He comes here to spy, the hypocrite! He wants to sit in your chair! May he never live that long, dear Father in heaven! He's inciting everybody against you. He's in league with all your enemies . . .!"

Reb Kasriel Dan pounded his fist on the table. "How do you know?"

The old woman's narrow chin, sprouting a few white hairs, began to tremble. Her bloodshot eyes, embedded in pouches, flashed angrily. "Everybody knows, except simpletons like you! Apart from that Talmud of yours, you're blind, you don't know your hands from your feet. He's determined to be rabbi here. He's produced a book and sent it out to everyone. You scribble a whole lifetime and nothing comes of it. But he, a young man, is already famous. Wait until they throw you out and appoint him in your place."

"Let them! I must get on with my studies."

"I'll not let you study! What comes of your learning? You get paid eighteen guldens a week. Other rabbis live in comfort, while we starve. I have to knead the dough with my own crippled hands. Your daughter does the washing, because we cannot afford a washer-woman. Your robe is worn through. If I didn't patch and mend every night, you'd go about in rags. And what's to become of your son? They promised to make him your assistant. It's two years since they promised, and not a penny has he seen."

"Is it my fault if they don't keep their word?"

"A proper father would do something for his child. He wouldn't allow the matter to drag on and on. You know the communal busybodies, you know they can't be counted on. Let me tell you something." The rabbi's wife changed her tone. "They're going to appoint Shabsai Getsel as your assistant. And when your time comes—a hundred years from now—it will be he who steps into your shoes. As for Pessachia, he'll be left without bread."

She uttered the last words in a hoarse shriek and clenched her hands into tiny fists. Everything about her was aquiver: her bonnet, her earrings, her sunken mouth, in which not a single tooth remained, her empty double chin.

Reb Kasriel Dan watched her with grief. He pitied his son, who for these past twenty years had not been able to find himself a living and had to be supported by his father. Reb Kasriel Dan was afraid that his wife was about to suffer an attack of gallstones—inevitably they came when she got overly excited. Indeed, the moans that presaged the first spasms had already begun.

Reb Kasriel Dan knew full well that the town worthies had no use for Pessachia. Pessachia did not know how to flatter the elders. He held himself aloof. His appointment as assistant rabbi was constantly being deferred on all manner of pretexts. But, after all, could a man be foisted on a community against their will?

This was, however, the first time Reb Kasriel Dan

had heard any mention of appointing Shabsai Getsel in
Pessachia's place. "Still waters run deep," he thought.
"Shabsai Getsel, my pupil, has become my deadly
enemy. He wants to take everything from me."

Involuntarily something within Reb Kasriel Dan
cried out, "He'll not live to see the day!" But he immediately remembered that it is forbidden to curse anyone, even in thought. Aloud he said to his wife, "Stop
fuming! We don't know whether it's true or not. People
concoct all kinds of lies."

"It's true. The whole town knows it. One hears about
it wherever one goes. Beginning next Sabbath, Shabsai
Getsel is to preach in the House of Study. He's to
receive twenty guldens a week, two more than you do,
just to show who's the real master here."

Reb Kasriel Dan felt a void around his heart. "Like
Absalom rising against David," flitted through his
mind. "May he share Absalom's fate."

Reb Kasriel Dan could no longer contain his ire. He
lowered his head, his eyelids dropped. After a while he
roused himself. "Heaven's will be done!"

"Ay, while you sit with folded hands doing nothing,
others are busy. In heaven, too, you're of no impor-
tance."

"I have not deserved better."

"Old fool!"

Never had Reb Kasriel Dan heard such language
from his wife. He was sure that she would soon be
sorry for what she had said. Suddenly he heard her
gulp and suppress a wail. She began to sway as though
she were about to fall. Reb Kasriel Dan jumped up and
caught her by the arms. She trembled and moaned. He
half walked, half carried her to a bench. In his alarm
he called for help.

The door opened, and in ran Teltsa Mindel, the
rabbi's divorced daughter. Teltsa Mindel's husband
had turned Hassid and gone to live at the court of
the Wonder Rebbe of Belz, from where he had sent her
a bill of divorcement. When Shabsai Getsel, as a yeshiva student and orphan, first came to board and

study with Reb Kasriel Dan, the townsfolk assumed he would marry Teltsa Mindel, despite the fact that she was several years his elder. Reb Kasriel Dan himself had favored the match.

But Shabsai Getsel had instead become betrothed to the daughter of Reb Tevia, a rich man and leader in the community. Reb Kasriel Dan had borne his pupil no grudge. He had officiated at the wedding. When the rabbi's wife had railed against Shabsai Getsel, calling him a hypocrite and a wolf in sheep's clothing, the rabbi had scolded her and reminded her that matches were made in heaven.

The incident of the book and now Shabsai Getsel's attempt to take Pessachia's place as assistant rabbi could not be forgiven so easily. Reb Kasriel Dan shot a quick glance at his daughter and ordered: "Put your mother to bed. Heat up a warming pan. Call Feitel the leech."

"Don't drag me! I'm not dead yet!" cried his wife. "Woe is me! Alas and woe for all that has come upon me!"

Reb Kasriel Dan again looked toward his daughter. It seemed such a short time since she had been a little girl, since Reb Kasriel Dan played with her, seated her on his knees and rocked her up and down on an imaginary "coach ride." Now there stood before him a woman with a grubby kerchief on her head, misshapen slippers on her feet, and a soiled apron. She was short like her mother, had yellow eyebrows and freckles. There was a silent dejection in her pale blue eyes, the misery of an abandoned woman. She was getting fat. She looked older than her age.

Reb Kasriel Dan had had little joy in his children. Several had died in infancy. He had lost a grown son and a daughter. Pessachia had been a boy prodigy, but after his marriage he had grown taciturn. It was impossible to get a word out of him. He slept by day and stayed awake at night. Pessachia had immersed himself in the Cabala.

Was it any wonder that the community rejected him?

Nowadays a rabbi needed to be businesslike, to know how to keep accounts and even speak a little Russian. Reports had reached Reb Kasriel Dan that rabbis in the big towns themselves dealt with the authorities and went to Lublin to see the governor. They enjoyed the hospitality of the wealthy. One rabbi had actually published an appeal to Jews calling on them to settle in colonies in the Land of Israel, where they would speak Hebrew every day, not just on the Sabbath. Conferences were being called, newspapers were being read. Machlev was a blind alley, cut off from the world.

Just the same, why should Shabsai Getsel, who had a rich father-in-law, take away a poor man's living?

Mother and daughter, taking tiny steps, made their way out of the room. Reb Kasriel Dan began to pace back and forth. "The wicked haven't taken over yet," he murmured to himself. "There is a Creator. There is Providence. The Torah is still the Torah. . . ."

Reb Kasriel Dan's thoughts reverted to Shabsai Getsel's book. As a result of his plagiarism, the only thing for the rabbi to do with his own works was put them out of reach once and for all. Otherwise they would be found after his death and Shabsai Getsel would be discovered and shamed, or it could even happen that Reb Kasriel Dan would be suspected of plagiarizing from the younger man. But where could he hide the manuscripts so that they would not be found? The only thing to do was to burn them.

Reb Kasriel Dan glanced at the stove. After all, what difference did it make who the author was? The main thing was that the commentaries were published and would be studied. In heaven the truth was known.

3.

The rabbi lay in bed all night without closing an eye. He recited "Hear, O Israel" and then pronounced the blessing "Causing sleep to descend," after which one is not supposed to utter a word. But sleep would not come.

Reb Kasriel Dan knew what his duty was. The

Biblical injunction stated, "Thou shalt rebuke thy neighbor and not suffer sin upon him." He should summon Shabsai Getsel and bring his grievances out into the open. What would be the use? Reb Kasriel Dan could already hear the other's slippery excuses. He would play the innocent, shrug his shoulders, insist he was being pressed by the congregation to accept the office. As for the manuscripts, the rabbi no longer possessed them. They had all gone up in smoke. Reb Kasriel Dan tossed from side to side. He either froze under the eiderdown or became flushed with heat. When he was not thirsty, he felt the need to urinate. He had put on fresh underwear, yet he itched. His pillow and mattress, although made of down, were as hard to his head and back as though someone had placed stones in the bedding.

Frenzied thoughts came to him of the sort that jeopardized his chances in the hereafter. Who knows? Perhaps the heretics were right, perhaps neither Judge nor Judgment existed . . . Maybe heaven, too, sided with the strong. Was it not written in the Talmud that "he who is stronger, to him shall victory go . . ." Maybe that was why the Jews suffered exile, because they were the feeblest among the nations. Maybe the slaughter of beasts was permitted simply because man was clever enough to wield a knife. It might even be that the strong sat in paradise while the weak fried in hell . . ."

"I'm headed for perdition," Reb Kasriel warned himself. He placed his hand on his forehead. "Father in heaven, save me . . . I'm sinking, God forbid, into the infernal depths . . ." The rabbi sat up so abruptly that the boards under his mattress creaked. "Why do I lie here allowing the evil spirits to tear me to pieces? There's only one remedy—the Torah!"

The rabbi dressed hastily. He lit a lamp and entered his study. Shadows wavered on the wall, on the crossbeams. Though the stove was stoked up Reb Kasriel Dan's teeth chattered with cold. Normally, on rising before dawn, he would light the samovar and brew tea;

but now he did not have the energy to fill it with coals
and pour water into it. He opened a book, but the
letters danced giddily before his eyes. They darted
about, played leapfrog with one another, changed color.

"Am I going blind, heaven forbid?" Reb Kasriel Dan
asked himself. "Or perhaps the end has come. Well, so
much the better. It seems that I have lost the power to
control my will . . ."

Reb Kasriel Dan's head slowly dropped down on his
book and he drowsed off. He apparently slept several
hours, for when he awoke, the gray of daylight lined
the cracks in the shutters. Snow was falling outside.

"What have I been dreaming?" the rabbi asked himself. "Shouting and yelling and the ringing of bells. A
fire, a funeral, slaughter, all at one and the same
time. . . ." The cold ran along his spine. His legs had
grown stiff. He wanted to wash his hands and say the
morning prayers, but he was unable to rise to his feet.

The door opened slowly and Pessachia came in, a
little fellow with a gray face, wide-set eyes almost
devoid of eyebrows, a roundish little beard that was
usually yellow but on this wintry morning looked like
gray cotton wool. Pessachia did not walk but shuffled
in his slippers. His caftan was unbuttoned, revealing
the long, ritual fringes and shabby trousers tied with
tape. His shirt was wide open at the neck, and his
skullcap was covered with bits of feather down.

"What do you want?" the rabbi asked.

Pessachia did not reply immediately. His yellow eyes
blinked and his lips twitched like those of a stutterer.
"Father!"

"What's the matter?"

"Shabsai Getsel is ill . . . very ill . . . Collapsed . . . He
needs mercy . . ."

Reb Kasriel Dan felt a pang all the way from his
throat to his intestines. "What's wrong with him?"

"They called the doctor . . . They don't know . . . His
wife has come to ask you to pray for him . . ."

"What value have my prayers? Well, leave me!"

"Father, his mother's name was Fruma Zlata . . ."

"Very well . . ."

Pessachia went out. The rabbi noticed that his son was limping. "What's happened to him," Reb Kasriel Dan wondered. "He doesn't look well, either."

Reb Kasriel Dan closed his eyes. The reason for Shabsai Getsel's sickness was clear enough. The rabbi's involuntary curse was to blame. A verse from the Book of Proverbs came to his mind: "Also to punish the just is not good." According to the commentaries the real meaning of it is: "Nor is it proper for the righteous to mete out punishment." Even calling himself righteous in his thoughts made the rabbi feel ashamed. "I, a righteous man? A man with evil power like Balaam the Wicked!"

The rabbi began praying for Shabsai Getsel: "Lord of the Universe, send him perfect healing . . . I have done much harm, but I do not wish to be a murderer . . . I forgive him everything, absolutely and forever."

The rabbi rose and took a Psalter from the bookcase. He located the Psalm of intercession for the sick: "Happy is he who comprehends the feeble . . ." It was time for the morning prayers but the rabbi continued his argument with Providence: "I have no strength left for all these upsets. If I cannot have peace in my old age, then better take me . . ."

For several days Shabsai Getsel contended with the Angel of Death. At times it looked as though he were improving but then he would have another relapse. A doctor came from Zamosc. The sick man was treated with cups and leeches. He was rubbed with alcohol and turpentine. His mother-in-law and his wife visited the graveyard to invoke the aid of dead ancestors. Candles were lit in the House of Study. The doors of the Holy Ark were flung wide open. Schoolchildren were made to recite the Psalms.

Reb Kasriel Dan went to visit his sick disciple. He passed through a corridor and a drawing room, entered a carpeted bedroom with curtained windows. On a chair stood bottles of medicine. The rabbi saw an orange, cookies, and sweets. Shabsai Getsel's face was livid. He murmured something, and his little beard moved up and down as though he were chewing. A pointed Adam's apple protruded from his throat. His brow was knotted as though he were considering a difficult problem.

Reb Kasriel Dan bowed his head low. This is what happens to flesh and blood. Aloud he said: "Shabsai Getsel, get well! You are needed here, you are needed . . ."

Shabsai Getsel opened one eye. "Rabbi!"

"Yes, Shabsai Getsel. I pray for you day and night."

It seemed as though Shabsai Getsel wished to say something, but nothing came out except a gurgling sound. After a while he closed his eyes again. The rabbi murmured: "Be healed! In the name of the Torah . . ." Yet all the time he knew, with a certainty that was beyond his understanding, that Shabsai Getsel would never rise from his sickbed.

He died that same night and the funeral was held in the morning. In the House of Study the rabbi spoke the eulogy. Reb Kasriel Dan had never wept when delivering a funeral oration, but this time he covered his face with his handkerchief. He choked over his words. Shabsai Getsel's father-in-law demanded that a copy of his son-in-law's book be placed on the bier; and thus they bore him away to the cemetery. Shabsai Getsel had left no children; the rabbi recited the first Kaddish for him.

A few days later the congregation appointed Pessachia assistant rabbi. They drank brandy, ate honey cake. Pessachia wore a new caftan, new shoes, a skullcap without feather down on it. He promised to fulfill all his rabbinical duties and to help his father lead the congregation. The elders wished him luck.

A few weeks went by. The rabbi remained secluded during the day, delegating the handling of all ritual questions and law cases to his son. He even stopped going to the House of Study to pray. As a rule, he ate one meal a day, gruel, bread, meat. Now he left his food almost untouched. On the Sabbath he sang no hymns. He no longer prepared the samovar at night. The household would hear the rabbi striding about in the dark, sighing and talking to himself. His face grew yellow and his beard shriveled.

All at once Reb Kasriel Dan announced that he was giving up his position as rabbi. He requested the community to appoint Reb Pessachia in his place. He stated that he had sinned and must go into exile to do penance.

The weeping of his wife was of no avail. Reb Kasriel Dan took off his satin robe and round rabbinical fur hat. He put on a shaggy long coat and peaked cap of cloth. He said farewell to his wife, to Teltsa Mindel, to Reb Pessachia, to the townfolk. A wagoner gave him a lift to Lublin.

As the rabbi sat in the wagon, a young man noted for his insolence dared to ask him what sin he had committed. And the rabbi answered: "The Commandment 'Thou shalt not kill' includes all sins."

Translated by J. M. Lask and Elizabeth Shub

Zeitl and Rickel

I often hear people say, "This cannot happen, that cannot be, nobody has ever heard of such a thing, impossible." Nonsense! If something is destined to happen, it does. My grandmother used to say: "If the devil wants to, he can make two walls come together. If it is written that a rabbi will fall off a roof, he will become a chimney sweep." The Gentiles have a proverb: "He who must hang will not drown."

Take this thing that happened in our own town. If anybody told me about it, I'd say he was a liar. But I knew them both, may they intercede for us in heaven. They've surely served their punishment by now. The older one was called Zeitl; the younger one, Rickel.

Zeitl's father, Reb Yisroel Bendiner, was already an old man of eighty when I knew him. He had buried three wives, and Zeitl was the daughter of the third. I don't know whether he had any children with the others. He was in his late fifties when he came to live in our town. He married a young girl, who died, may God preserve us, in childbirth. Zeitl was taken out of her with pincers. Reb Yisroel's father-in-law had left his daughter a large brick building in the marketplace, with thirteen stores, and Reb Yisroel inherited it.

Strange stories were told in town about Reb Yisroel. There had once lived in Poland a false Messiah, Jacob Frank; he had converted many Jews. After he died, a sect remained. He had a daughter somewhere, and barrels full of gold were sent to her. These people pretended to live like other Jews, but at night they would gather in secret and read forbidden parchments.

Reb Yisroel dressed like a rabbi, in a velvet caftan, a round rabbinical hat, slippers, and white socks. He was forever writing something, standing before a high desk, and people said that Zeitl copied all his manuscripts. He had a wide beard, white as snow, and a high forehead. When he looked at anyone, it seemed as though he saw right through him. Zeitl taught the daughters of rich families to read and write. I was one of her pupils.

It was said of the members of the sect that they liked loose women and secretly practiced all sorts of abominations. But with whom could Reb Yisroel have sinned in our town?

Zeitl got married, but six months later she was divorced. Her husband had come from Galicia, and people whispered that he was one of "the clan"; that was how our townsmen called the sect. Nobody knew why the marriage had come to such a quick end. Everything in Reb Yisroel's house was veiled in secrecy. He had trunks hung with double locks. He had large cases full of books. He came to prayer only on the Sabbath, at the cold synagogue. He seldom exchanged a word with anyone. When the storekeepers came to pay their rent, he would put the money into his pocket without counting it.

In those years it was unheard of that groceries should be delivered to anyone at home. The richest women went to market with baskets to do their own shopping. But Zeitl had everything sent to her from the stores: bread, rolls, butter, eggs, cheese, meat. Once a month she received a bill, as though she were living in Warsaw. She had aristocratic ways.

I remember her as if it were yesterday: tall, dark, with a narrow face and black hair braided like a round Sabbath bread. Imagine, in those years—and she did not shave her hair. When she went out, she wore a kerchief. But when was she seen in the street? Reb

Yisroel had a balcony upstairs, looking out upon the
church garden, and Zeitl would sit there on summer
evenings, getting fresh air.

She would give us girls dictation twice a week, not
from a letter book but from her head: "My most esteemed
betrothed! To start with, I wish to let you know that I
am in good health, pray God that I may hear the same
from you. Secondly. . . ." Zeitl also knew Polish and
German. Her eyes were wild, huge as a calf's, and filled
with melancholy. But suddenly she would burst into
such loud laughter that all the rooms would echo with
it. In the middle of the year she might take a fancy to
bake matzo pancakes. She was fond of asking us riddles and of telling tales that made our hair stand on
end.

And now about Rickel. Rickel's father was the town's
ritual slaughterer, Reb Todie. All slaughterers are
pious men, but Reb Todie had the reputation of a saint.
Yet he had bad luck. His son had gone one day to the
ritual bath and was found drowned. He must have
gotten a cramp. One of his daughters died in an epi-
demic. A few years later strange noises began to be
heard in his house. Something knocked, and no one
knew what or where. Something would give a bang so
that the walls would shake. The whole town came
running, even the Gentiles. They searched the attic,
the cellar, every corner.

A regiment of soldiers was stationed in our town.
The colonel's name was Semiatitsky. He was supposed
to have descended from converted Jews. He had a red
beard and cracked jokes till your sides would split with
laughter. When Semiatitsky heard that a demon was
banging in Todie's house, he brought a platoon of
soldiers and commanded them to look into every crack
and every hole. He did not believe in devils; he called
them nothing but old wives' tales. He ordered everybody out and Cossacks stood guard with whips, allowing
nobody to come near. But suddenly there was a crash
that nearly brought the roof down.

I was not there, but people said that Semiatitsky

called to the unholy one to tell his name and what he wanted and that the spirit gave one knock for yes, and two knocks for no.

Every man has enemies, especially if he has a job with the community, and people began to say that Todie should be dismissed as a slaughterer. It was whispered that he had slaughtered an ox with a blemished knife. Reb Todie's wife took it so hard that she died.

Rickel was small, thin, with red hair and freckles. When her father slaughtered fowl, she would pluck the feathers and do other small chores. When the knocking began, suspicion fell on Rickel. Some people said that she was doing it. But how could she? And why? It was said that when she went away for the night the knocking stopped. There's no limit to what evil tongues can invent. One night there was such a loud bang that three windows were shattered. Before that, the devil had not touched the windows. This was the last time. From then on, it was quiet again.

But Reb Todie was already without his job, and he became a teacher of beginners. The family had gone through Rickel's dowry and she was now affianced to a yeshiva student from Krashnik, a lame young man. He was a Hassid, and soon after the wedding he went on a pilgrimage to his rabbi. At first he would come home for Passover and the High Holy Days. Afterwards he disappeared altogether. Rickel became an abandoned wife. Her father had died in the meantime and all she had left was the old house—little more than a ruin.

What could a husbandless wife do? She went around, teaching girls how to pray. She took in sewing and mending. On Purim she carried presents of holiday delicacies for wealthy families. On Passover she would become a sort of women's beadle and deliver gifts of herbs. When a woman was sick and someone was needed to watch at the bedside, Rickel was called. She learned how to cup and bleed the sick. She did not shave her head but wore a kerchief. She read many storybooks and loved to invent wild and improbable tales.

Old maids, you know, also end up half crazy. But when a woman who has had a man is left alone, it goes to her head. Rickel might have found her husband if she had had the money to send a messenger to look for him, but Todie left her without a groschen. Why did her husband forsake her? Who can tell? There are such men. They get married and then they tire of it. They wander away and nobody knows where their bones have come to rest.

2.

I do not know exactly how Zeitl and Rickel got together. It seems that Reb Yisroel fell ill and Rickel came to rub him down with turpentine. People said he had cast an eye on her, but I don't believe it. He was already more dead than alive. He died soon afterwards, and both girls, Zeitl and Rickel, were left alone in the world. At first people thought that Rickel had stayed on with Zeitl as a servant. But if Zeitl had never had a servant before, why would she need one now?

When Reb Yisroel was alive, few matchmakers came to Zeitl with offers. They knew that Reb Yisroel wanted his daughter for himself. There are such fathers, even among Jews. She waited on him hand and foot. If his pipe went out, she would bring him an ember to relight it. I don't know why, but he never went to the bath, and it was whispered that Zeitl bathed him in a wooden bathtub. I've never seen it, but those false believers are capable of anything. To them, a sin is a virtue.

Anyway, Reb Yisroel gave the matchmakers such a reception that they forswore repeating their visits to the tenth generation. But as soon as Zeitl was alone, they were back at her doorstep. She sent them off with all sorts of excuses: later, tomorrow, it's not yet time. She had a habit, whenever she spoke to anyone, of looking over his head. Rickel had moved in with her, and now whenever anyone knocked, she would answer from behind the door chain: Zeitl is out, she is asleep, she is reading.

How long could the matchmakers keep coming? Nobody is dragged to the wedding canopy by force. But in a small town people have time, and they talk. No matter how you may try to keep away from strangers' eyes, you can't hide everything.

It was said that Zeitl and Rickel ate together, drank together, slept together. Rickel wore Zeitl's dresses, shortened and made smaller to fit her. Rickel became the cashier, and she paid the bills sent by the storekeepers. She also collected the rents. In the daytime the two girls seldom went out together, but on summer evenings they went strolling down Church Street, along the avenues leading to the woods. Zeitl's arm would be around Rickel's shoulders, and Rickel's around Zeitl's waist. They were absorbed in their talk. When people said good evening, they did not hear. Where did two women find so much to talk about? Some people tried to follow them and listen in, but they were whispering, as though they had secrets between them. They would walk all the way to the mill or the woods.

Rumors were brought to Reb Eisele, our rabbi, but he said: "There is no law to keep two women from walking to the mill."

Reb Eisele was a Misnagid, a Lithuanian, and they have a law for everything: either it is permitted or it's a sin.

But the talk would not die down. Naftali, the night watchman, had seen Zeitl and Rickel kissing each other on the mouth. They had stopped by the sawmill, near the log pile, and embraced like a loving couple. Zeitl called Rickel dove, and Rickel called her kitten. At first nobody believed Naftali; he was fond of a drop and could bring you tales of a fair up in heaven. Still, where there's smoke, there must be fire. My dear folks, the two girls seemed so much in love that all the tongues in town started wagging. The Tempter can make anybody crazy in his own way. Something flips in your head, and everything turns upside down. I heard talk of a lady in Krasnostaw who made love with a stallion. At the time of the Flood, even beasts paired themselves with other kinds. I read about it in the Women's Bible.

People went to Reb Eisele, but he insisted: "There is nothing in the Torah to forbid it. The ban applies only to men. Besides, since there are no witnesses, it is forbidden to spread rumors." Nevertheless, he sent the beadle for them. Rickel came alone and denied everything. She had a whittled tongue, that girl. Reb Eisele said to her: "Go home and don't worry about it. It is the slanderers who will be punished, not you. It is better to burn in a lime pit than to put another to shame."

I forgot to mention that Zeitl had stopped teaching the girls how to write.

I was still very young at that time, but something of all that talk had reached me too. You can't keep everything from a child's ears. Zeitl and Rickel, it was said, were studying Reb Yisroel's books together. Their lamp burned until late at night. Those who passed their bedroom window saw shadows moving this way and that behind the drapes, and coming together as in a dance. Who knows what went on there?

Now listen to a story.

One summer it turned terribly hot. I've lived through many a summer, but I don't remember such heat. Right in the morning the sun began to burn like fire. Not only men but even girls and older women would go down to the river to bathe. When the sun blazes, the water gets warm. My mother, may she plead for us, took me along.

This was the first time I bathed in the river. Men went into the water naked, but the girls wore their shifts. The roughnecks came running to peep at them, and it was impossible to drive them off. Each time there'd be a squealing and a panic. One woman started drowning. Another screamed that a frog had bitten her. I bathed and even tried to swim until I was so tired that I lay down among the bushes near the bank to rest. I thought I'd cool off in the shade and go home, but a strange sleep came over me. Not just sleep; may heaven preserve us, it was more like death. I put my head down and remained there like a rock. A darkness seemed to fall over me and I sank into it. I must have slept for many hours.

When I awakened, it was night. There was no moon. The sky was cloudy. I lay there and did not know where I was or who I was. I felt the grass around me, moist with dew, but I did not remember that I was on the outskirts of town. I touched myself; I had nothing on but my shift. I wanted to cry, to call for help, when suddenly I heard voices. I thought of demons and was terror-stricken, yet I tried to hear what they were saying. Two women were speaking, and their voices seemed familiar.

I heard one ask: "Must we go through hell?"

The other answered: "Yes, my soul, but even going through hell together with you will be a delight. God is merciful. The punishment never lasts more than twelve months. We shall be purified and enter paradise. Since we have no husbands, we shall be no one's footstools. We shall bathe in balsam and eat of the leviathan. We shall have wings and fly like birds. . . ."

I cannot recall all their talk. I gasped. I knew who they were now: the questioner was Rickel, and Zeitl gave the answers. I heard Zeitl say: "We shall meet our fathers and mothers there, and our grandparents, and all the generations: Abraham and Isaac, Jacob and Rachel, Leah, Bilhah, Zilpah, Abigail, Bathsheba. . . ." She spoke as though she had just come from there, and every word was like a pearl. I forgot that I was half naked and alone out late at night.

Zeitl went on: "Father is waiting for us. He comes to me in dreams. He is together with your mother." Rickel asked: "Did they get married there?" And Zeitl answered: "Yes. We shall get married up there too. In heaven there is no difference between men and women. . . ."

It must have been past midnight. There was a flash of lightning, and I saw my clothing, shoes, and stockings on the grass nearby. I caught a glimpse of them too. They sat by the river in nothing but their shifts, their hair down, pale as death. If I did not die of fright that night, I'll never die.

"And then?"

Wait a minute. I came home in the middle of the night, but my mother had left earlier in the evening for the fair; she was a storekeeper. My father was spending the night at the study house. I slipped into bed, and when I woke next morning, the whole thing seemed like a dream. I was ashamed to tell anyone about it. However, as the saying goes, heaven and earth conspired that there should be no secrets.

People began to say that Zeitl and Rickel were fasting. They would eat nothing all day and merely take a bite at night. We had pious women in town who would climb up the stairs into the women's section of the synagogue at dawn to pray. Every Monday and Thursday they went to visit graves in the cemetery. Suddenly we heard that Zeitl and Rickel had joined the pious company in lamentations and penitential prayers. They had shaved their heads and put on bonnets, as though they had just gotten married. They omitted no line or word, and wept as on the Day of the Destruction of the Temple. They also visited the cemetery, prostrating themselves on Reb Yisroel's grave and wailing.

People ran to Reb Eisele again, but the rabbi sent them off with a scolding. If Jewish daughters wanted to do penance, he said, was that wrong too? He was fond of poring over his books, but the affairs of the town meant little to him. He was later dismissed, but that's another story.

There are busybodies everywhere, and they took the matter to the colonel. But he said, "Leave me out of your Jewish squabbles. I have trouble enough with my soldiers." Cossacks are good soldiers, but sometimes they got letters from home that their wives were carrying on with other men and they went wild. More than one Cossack would go galloping off on his horse, slashing away with his sword right and left. After they had served their five-year terms, they would come into the stores to buy presents for their mothers and fathers, sisters and brothers, the whole family. The shopkeeper would ask, "And what will you get for your wife, Nikita?" "A horsewhip," he would say. They'd go back to their steppes on the Don and find bastards at home. They'd chop off the wife's head and be sent to Siberia for hard labor. . . .

Where was I? Oh, yes, penance. Zeitl and Rickel clung to each other and spoke only of the next world. They bought up all the books from every peddler passing through town. Whenever a preacher came, they questioned him: How long was the punishment inflicted on transgressors after death? How many hells were there? Who meted out the penalties? Who did the whipping? With what kind of rods? Iron? Copper? The wags had plenty to joke about.

We had many visiting preachers, but one, Reb Yuzel, was famous. Whenever he went up to the lectern, it was like the Day of Atonement all over again. When he painted a picture of hell, everybody shuddered. People said that it was dangerous for pregnant women to hear him; several had had miscarriages after his sermons. But that's how it is: when you must not do a thing, you're sure to do it. When Reb Yuzel preached, the synagogue was full. The railing closing off the women's section was almost bursting with the crush. He had a voice that reached into every corner. Every word cut like a knife.

The last time he came, I also ran to hear him. There was not one hell, he said, but seven, and the flames in each were sixty times hotter than in the last. There was a man in our town, Alterl Kozlover. He had a screw loose, and he figured out that the seventh hell was myriads of time hotter than the first. Men cried like babies. Women screamed and wailed.

Zeitl and Rickel were also there. They had entered among the men and stood on a bench, wrapped in their shawls. Ordinarily, women are admitted in the men's section only on the Festival of Rejoicing in the Law.

But when the women's section was too crowded, some women were allowed into the antechamber, and from there they'd move inside.

Reb Yuzel handed out punishment to everybody, but the worst of his wrath was reserved for the women. He described how they were hung by the breasts and by the hair; how the imps laid them out on boards of nails and tore pieces from them. From fiery coals they were thrown into snow, and from the snow back onto heaps of coals. Before they were admitted to hell, they were first tortured in the Sling, by devils, imps and evil spirits. It made your hair stand on end to hear him. I was still a young girl, but I began to sob and choke. I glanced at Zeitl and Rickel: they did not cry, but their eyes were twice as big as usual, and their faces were like chalk. A madness seemed to stare out of them, and I had a feeling that they would come to a terrible end.

On the next day Reb Yuzel preached again, but I had had enough. Someone said later that Zeitl had come up to him after the sermon and invited him to be her guest. Many people asked him to their homes, but he went with Zeitl. Nobody knows what they spoke about. I don't remember whether he had stayed there for the night. Probably not; how could a man remain with two women? Although it's true the Lithuanians have an argument for everything. They interpret the Law as they like. That's why they are nicknamed "heathens." My grandfather, may he intercede for us, used to tell of a Lithuanian Jew from Belaya Tserkov who had married a Gentile woman and had gone on studying the Talmud.

After Reb Yuzel left, the town was quiet again. By then the summer was over.

One winter night, long after all the shutters had been closed, we heard a wild outcry. People ran out in panic. They thought the peasants had attacked. The moon was bright, and we saw a strange sight—Fivel the butcher carrying Rickel in his arms. She screamed and struggled and tried to scratch his eyes out. He was a giant of a man and he brought her straight into the rabbi's judgment chamber. Reb Eisele sat up late, studying and drinking tea from a samovar. Everybody shouted, and Rickel kept fighting to break away and run out. It took two men to hold her. The rabbi began to question her.

· I was there myself. Ordinarily I went to bed early, but that night we had been chopping cabbage and all the girls had gathered at our house. This was the custom in our town. We chopped cabbage for pickling in barrels, and everybody ate bread with cracklings and told stories. One day the girls would gather in one house, the next in another. Sometimes they'd break into a dance in pairs. I had a sister-in-law who could play all the dances on a comb: a Scissor Dance, a Quarrel Dance, a Good Day.

When we heard the uproar, we all ran out.

At first Rickel would not say anything. She merely screamed to be allowed to go. But Fivel testified that she had wanted to throw herself into the well. He had caught her when she had already flung her leg over the edge.

"How did it come into your head to do such a thing?" the rabbi asked, and Rickel answered: "I am sick of this world. I want to know what goes on in the next." The rabbi argued: "Those who lay their hands upon themselves do not share the rewards of the next world." But Rickel said: "Hell is also for people, not for goats." She screamed: "I want to go to my mother and my father, my grandmother and grandfather. I don't want to keep wandering in this vale of tears." Those were her words. It was clear at once that she had learned all this from Zeitl, because the other knew the texts printed in small letters too. Somebody asked: "Where is Zeitl?" And Rickel answered: "She is all right, she is already up there. . . ." My dear folks, Zeitl had thrown herself into the well a moment earlier. She had gone first.

Half the town came running. Torches were lit, and we went to the well. Zeitl lay with her head in the water, her feet up. A ladder was lowered, and she was dragged up, dead.

Rickel had to be watched, and the men of the burial society took her to the poorhouse. She was turned over to the caretaker, who was told to keep an eye on her. Zeitl was later buried outside the fence. Rickel pretended that she had come to her senses and regretted her deed. But the next day at dawn, when everybody was asleep, she rose from the bundle of straw and went to the river. It was frozen, but she must have broken the ice with a stone. It was only in the afternoon that people realized she was gone. They found her footprints in the snow and ran down to the river. Rickel had followed Zeitl. She was buried near the other one, without a mound, without as much as a board to mark the place.

The burgomaster locked and sealed Zeitl's house, but later on, a letter she had written was discovered. She explained why she was leaving the world: she wanted to know what went on in the hereafter.

Who can tell what goes on in another's head? A person gets hold of some melancholy notion and it grows like a mushroom. Zeitl was the leader, and Rickel drank in every word she said. Forty years have gone by since their deaths, and they have probably suffered their allotted share.

As long as I was in the town, Reb Yisroel's house was boarded up and nobody moved into it. People saw lights flickering in the windows. A man said that he was passing by at night and heard Zeitl speak and Rickel answer. They kissed, laughed, cried. Lost souls remain on earth and do not even know they don't belong. . . .

I was told that an officer had later moved into the house. One morning he was found hanged.

A house is not simply a pile of logs and boards. Whoever lives there leaves something behind. A few years later the whole marketplace burned down. Thank God for fires. If it were not for them, the stench that would accumulate would reach high heaven. . . .

Translated by Mirra Ginsburg

The Warehouse

In a warehouse in heaven, a number of naked souls stood around waiting for the issuance of their new bodies. Bagdial, the angel in charge of such goods, was a trifle late that morning. To be precise, Bagdial handed out a card entitling the spirit to receive a body but did not hand out the body itself. In heaven there is as much red tape as on earth, the dignitaries finding it necessary to make work to keep unemployed angels busy. But angels who have got used to an easy life resent having to do anything too strenuous.

It was now ten o'clock in the morning. The angelic choirs had long since finished chanting their lauds. The righteous in paradise had already had their second helping of leviathan. The wicked, lying on their fiery beds in hell, had just been turned onto their other side. But in the commissariat not a single card had been issued. Finally Bagdial, a corpulent angel whose wings were not sufficiently large to conceal either his massive legs or his navel, entered and, without even bothering to say good morning, shouted, "Cut out that shoving. There are enough bodies for all. The day's still young. When your number is called, step forward. In the meantime, shut up." Bagdial headed for his private office. "I'll be back in a minute."

"The morning's almost over, but he must see to his private business," an impatient soul muttered. "According to regulations, work is supposed to begin promptly with the cock's crow."

"Stop that grumbling. If you don't like what goes on here, report me to the Lord Malbushial. You keep your right of appeal until your departure."

"No, Bagdial, we're more than satisfied," a number of humble souls called out.

"I will return soon."

As Bagdial shut the door of his office, one of the souls remarked, "An absolutely worthless caterpillar. In the old days that sort of angel was kicked out of heaven and exiled to earth to consort with the daughters of Adam. Some were changed into devils and imps. Now, since they have organized, they do as they please. It almost seems that God Himself is afraid of them."

"How can God be afraid of His own creations?"

The soul of one who had once been a philosopher tugged at its spiritual beard. "That's one of the ancient problems. My opinion is that though God is very powerful, He is not omnipotent. He can destroy a world or two if He has a tantrum, but not the entire cosmos. Omnipotence would mean He could destroy Himself and leave the universe godless, an obvious contradiction. Although I've roasted in Gehenna for a full year, it's made me no wiser. I still concur with Aristotle that the world had no beginning. The notion that the world was created from nothing is repugnant to reason."

"I am no scholar, just an ordinary woman," another soul said, "but it's obvious to me that there's no order here. Thirty-one years ago I was exiled to earth from the Throne of Glory, where I used to polish one of the legs, and imprisoned in a beautiful body. Why they sent me to earth I did not understand until today. People say it's men who are the lecherous ones; my lust was more powerful than that of any ten men. My mother baked delicious pretzels with caraway seeds which the yeshiva boys loved, but they liked me even better. She warned me against men, but already when I was nine I could think of nothing else. I saw two dogs coupling once and after that. . . ."

"All right, we catch on. You became a whore."

"Not right away."

"How long did you fry in Gehenna?"

"An entire year."

"Well, you got off easy. There are lots of whores that they sling into the desert. When they get to Gehenna, they think it's paradise. What did they do to you?"

"The usual. I was hung by my breasts, hurled from fire into ice, and from ice into fire, and so on, except, of course, Sabbaths and holidays."

"You were lucky not to have to remain in the vale of tears longer," another soul remarked. "I lived there for eighty-nine years three months five days two hours and eight minutes."

"Were you also a whore?"

"No, a man."

"That's what I'd like to be. If I have to be dressed in blood and flesh, let it be male."

"What's so wonderful about being a man?"

"You are not a female."

"So I became a miser. A woman of pleasure has at least some pleasure. My sack of bones could do nothing but gather money. I got married but never gave my wife enough for the household and accused her of being a spendthrift. You don't need me to tell you that women hate a tightwad. All females are wasteful. My wife was always cooking twice the porridge we could eat. There was always a pot of spoiling food in our larder. We had so much schmaltz it turned rancid. Our flour became mouldy. The Angel of Good pleaded with me: 'Let her have her will. She enjoys it. Why quarrel?' But my bag of money obsessed me."

"Was she any good in bed?"

"Even there I was stingy. Those who hoard money hoard everything. The upshot of it was that she ran off with a shoemaker."

"I would have done it, too."

"After that happened, I was afraid to take another wife. For all I knew, the woman I got would be crazy about marzipan. It got so bad I broke my teeth on stale bread because it cost a half cent a loaf less than the fresh. The moment I entered my house, I took off my

gaberdine and, forgive my expression, even my underwear to keep them from wearing. I even saved snuff."

"How did you do that?"

"I would stretch out my hand when I saw someone
taking a pinch and ask him for some. Instead of using
it, I hid it in a bag."

"Did you save much?"

"Two sacks full."

"How long did it take you to do that?"

"More than forty years."

"If I become a man, I won't stint my wife. I'll give her
anything she wants. If you ever become a woman,
you'll find out what pleases women."

"If you become a man, you'll forget all this feminine
nonsense."

"What do you want to be?" the whore asked.

"I don't want to be anyone," the miser answered.

"Perhaps they will make you a woman."

"For all I care, they can make me a flea."

"It could be that you'll be stillborn."

"The stiller the better."

"I don't care what you say, I would like the taste of
being a man."

"You won't be consulted. You'll be handed a body
whether it fits or not. I know. I've been here now for
more than thirty years. For ten years I worked sorting
bodies. The whole thing's just one enormous mess. A
woman's torso is given a man's head. Just a short time
ago, a man's body turned up with a pair of breasts of a
wet nurse. They even get mixed up on who gets what
genitals. You know about hermaphrodites, don't you?
That Bagdial is both lazy and incompetent. If he weren't
Malbushial's second cousin, he would have been scrapped
long ago."

"What about God?"

"Does anyone believe in God here? Here in the lowest
heaven we have only atheists. He is supposed to dwell
in the seventh heaven, which is an infinity away. One
thing we can be sure of, He's not here."

"Be quiet. Here comes Bagdial."

2.

Bagdial scratched his left buttock with his right wing. "''m not deaf, miser. If Malbushial knew of your barkings, he'd give you the body of a dog. No, we're not atheists here. But when you've hung around here some 689,000 years and been continually told about a boss who never shows up, you begin to have your doubts. Why does He sit there forever in His seventh heaven? Oughtn't He to come down here occasionally and see what's going on? Souls are shipped in this direction and that, wearing this or that body.

"You think that we warehouse people are negligent, but can we do anything if the manufacturers and the cutters send us poor products? We almost never receive a well-lathed nose. The noses we get are almost all either long as a ram's horn or short as a bean. Our suppliers have been in the nose business since the time of Methuselah, but they don't know their trade. The lips we're sent are either too thin or too thick. Almost none of the ears has decent proportions. The angel in charge of procreation is supposed to adjust the genitals of the sexes to fit correctly, and he's the worst bungler of all. He is capable of mating an elephant to a mouse.

"All of you clamor for beautiful bodies, but if you get one, what use do you make of it? It's destroyed, either by drinking or by lechery or by sloth. A short time ago we did a splendid job; soul and body fitted perfectly. Once a millennium we do such a good job. But that pampered little body started eating as if it had been given a bottomless stomach. It ate for forty years and returned round as a barrel, a mere heap of repulsive flesh. Miser, if you continue your blasphemies, I will. . . ."

"I didn't blaspheme. Honest, I didn't. What style body am I to get?"

"A eunuch."

"Why a eunuch? I was just saying that for all I cared I could be turned into a flea."

"I heard you. We have one eunuch-style body on

hand which will fit you perfectly. You'll never be in a position to support a wife. And you certainly don't deserve to have someone else support you."

"What sort of temptations does a eunuch have?"

"Money."

"Will I be rich?"

"The wealthiest inmate in the poorhouse of Pinchev."

"What do I have to correct?"

"You'll return all the tobacco you stole to its rightful owners. The snuff was given to you to use, not to hoard."

"Where will I get so much snuff?"

"That's your problem. Hey there, whore."

"What style have I been given?"

"A woman."

"Again?"

"Exactly."

"Why not a man this time?"

"Don't bargain with me. I distribute the cards, not the bodies. We don't have our full quota of males in this batch. Eighty male bodies were ruined in the factory yesterday. This year we've overproduced women. But we'll get rid of them all because Rabbi Gershom's edict against polygamy is about to be repealed. Every schlemiel dreams of having a harem. Even tailor's assistants want to become King Solomons. If you ask me, it's better to be a mortar than a pestle."

"I would like to be a man just once."

"We all have unfulfilled desires. I would have preferred to have been a seraph and sit in paradise between Bathsheba and Abigail. Instead, I have to come here six days a week and hand out cards for defective bodies. Everyone haggles with me as though I had the power of Metatron. I don't know what it's like in the other heavens; here in the warehouse it's chaos. At times I even envy the miserable creatures who are sent down to earth. At least there are temptations in the lower world. If you try hard you can achieve sainthood and receive your reward in paradise. What do I have? Nothing. No one tempts me and I'm fed with sour moon milk. I'm slandered disgracefully. I'm begrudged even a little stardust. Evil tongues make me feel that if I weren't Malbushial's second cousin I'd be nowhere."

"Maybe you could do me a small favor?"

"What sort of a favor, whore? Take your card and leave. You were a wanton for eighteen years; you'll be chaste now for exactly the same amount of time. If not, you'll return again, a double hunchback, one in the front and one in the rear."

"Have you already had a look at my body?"

"I caught a glimpse of it."

"What does it look like?"

"What's the use of telling you? Once you get to earth, you'll forget that the body is only a garment. Down there they think the body is everything. All around you, people will be saying that there isn't a soul."

"What will I look like?"

"Since you must correct the errors you made in your former existence, you will not be exactly a beauty. The body you receive will make your task easier."

"Ugly, eh?"

"Men will not care for you, nor will you care for men. You have been given nine measures of shyness, which is exactly what is required to create a spinster."

"You dirty scoundrel."

Another soul flew over.

"Who are you?" Bagdial asked. "I don't recognize you."

"Leibke the thief."

"Well, no more stealing for you. You'll be robbed by others. Everything will be taken from you—your money, your wife, even the pillow you rest your head on. You'll hide your money in your boot tops, go to the steam bath, and leave your boots behind you. You'll swear never to hide anything in your boots again and yet not be able to resist the urge to do so. Every body is made with its own particular obsession.

"Once we had a gambler here. Do you know what he'd done? He was playing draw poker and threw his wife into the pot. Can you imagine what he had? A pair of jacks. He was a big bluffer, only you can't bluff a man who has four aces. When his wife came back to him three months later, she was pregnant. He swallowed a ladle in an attempt to kill himself!"

"Did he get it down?"

"It stuck in his throat. Was there any sense to it? But you know how people are. The angels are no wiser. Who are you?"

"Hayim the coachman."

"Since you had a beautiful wife and in addition fornicated with a Gentile, what did you need the mare for?"

"I don't know."

"Hadn't you ever heard that horses kick?"

"It just slipped my mind."

"Those down below are always forgetting. Is it their fault? The most defective of all the organs is the portion of the brain containing the memory. They put on two pairs of underwear in the winter and only take off one when they go to the outhouse. The only things they never forget are the injuries done them. Two sisters in Frampol quarreled over the tail of a herring for sixty years. When the older died, the younger urinated on her grave. You, Hayim, will be the horse this time. You'll pull freight from Izbitza to Krasnistaw."

"Has that road been fixed?"

"It's as muddy as it was, but a little bumpier."

"If that's so, there is no God."

"And suppose there isn't. Will that make pulling the wagon any easier? Anyway, you'll only last three years. Zelig the Red will whip you to death."

"Is that murderer still around?"

"He has a score to settle. He hasn't forgotten that you sold him a lame stallion."

"That happened thirty years ago. I was swindled myself. I got the horse from a gypsy."

"We know that. It's all on record here. The gypsy is now a stallion, and the stallion a gypsy. But the whip remains what it was and still has seven knots. Hey, who are you?"

"Shiffra the cook."

"You're not supposed to spit into your employer's porridge, even though he did spit in your face."

"What will I become?"

"Your employer's spittoon."

"Will I feel his spit?"

"Everything knows and feels. Your employer suffers from consumption and will spit out his last piece of lung into you. Both of you will be back in three quarters of a year."

"Together?"

"You will be married. You will be his footstool in the antechamber of paradise."

"I'd rather be a pisspot in Gehenna."

"Little fool, that amorous ass loved you. That's how men are. What they can't have, they spit at."

Bagdial scratched the nape of his neck with one of his lower wings and brooded in silence. "Is it much better in heaven?" he finally asked. "I stay here all day surrounded by rabble and listen to their needling. Other angels sing hymns three times a day and that's the end of it. Some can't even sing, only bellow. The higher your position, the less work you do. He created the world in six short winter days and has been resting ever since. There are those who are of the opinion that He didn't even work that hard."

"Do you mean by that that He wasn't the First Cause?" the philosopher demanded.

"Who else is the First Cause? He is a jealous God. He would never delegate such power. But being the cause and keeping order are different things altogether."

Henne Fire

Yes, there are people who are demons. God preserve us! Mothers see things when they give birth, but they never tell what they see!

Henne Fire, as she was called, was not a human being but a fire from Gehenna. I know one should not speak evil of the dead and she suffered greatly for her sins. Was it her fault that there was always a blaze within her? One could see it in her eyes: two coals. It was frightening to look at them. She was black as a gypsy, with a narrow face, sunken cheeks, emaciated—skin and bone. Once I saw her bathing in the river. Her ribs protruded like hoops. How could someone like Henne put on fat? Whatever one said to her, no matter how innocently, she immediately took offense. She would begin to scream, shake her fists, and spin around like a crazy person. Her face would turn white with anger. If you tried to defend yourself, she was ready to swallow you alive and she'd start smashing dishes. Every few weeks her husband, Berl Chazkeles, had to buy a new set.

She suspected everybody. The whole town was out to get her. When she flew into a rage, she said things that would not even occur to an insane person. Swear words poured from her mouth like worm-eaten peas. She knew every curse in the holy book by heart. She was not beyond throwing rocks. Once, in the middle of winter, she broke a neighbor's windowpane and the neighbor never learned why.

Henne had children, four girls, but as soon as they grew up they ran away from home. One became a servant in Lublin; one left for America; the most beautiful, Malkeleh, died of scarlet fever; and the fourth married an old man. Anything was better than living with Henne.

Her husband, Berl, must have been a saint. Only a saint could have stood such a shrew for twenty years. He was a sieve-maker. In those days, in the wintertime, work started when it was still dark. The sievemaker had to supply his own candle. He earned only a pittance. Of course, they were poor, but they were not the only ones. A wagonload of chalk would not suffice to write down the complaints she hurled at him. I lived next door to her and once, when he left for work at dawn, I heard her call after him: "Come back feet first!" I can't imagine what she blamed him for. He gave her his last penny, and he loved her too. How could one love such a fiend? Only God knows. In any case, who can understand what goes on in the heart of a man?

My dear people, even he finally ran away from her. One summer morning, a Friday, he left to go to the ritual bath and disappeared like a stone in the water. When Henne heard he was seen leaving the village, she fell down in an epileptic fit right in the gutter. She knocked her head on the stones, hissed like a snake, and foamed at the mouth. Someone pushed a key into her left hand, but it didn't help. Her kerchief fell off and revealed the fact that she did not shave her head. She was carried home. I've never seen such a face, as green as grass, her eyes rolled up. The moment she came to, she began to curse and I think from then on never stopped. It was said that she even swore in her sleep. At Yom Kippur she stood in the women's section of the synagogue and, as the rabbi's wife recited the prayers for those who could not read, Henne berated the rabbi, the cantor, the elders. On her husband she called forth a black judgment, wished him smallpox and gangrene. She also blasphemed against God.

After Berl forsook her, she went completely wild. As
a rule, an abandoned woman made a living by kneading
dough in other people's houses or by becoming a servant. But who would let a malicious creature like
Henne into the house? She tried to sell fish on Thurs-
days, but when a woman asked the price, Henne would
reply, "You are not going to buy anyhow, so why do
you come here just to tease me? You'll poke around and
buy elsewhere."

One housewife picked up a fish and lifted its gills to
see if it was fresh. Henne tore it from her hands,
screaming, "Why do you smell it? Is it beneath your
dignity to eat rotten fish?" And she sang out a list of
sins allegedly committed by the woman's parents,
gradparents, and great-grandparents back to the tenth
generation. The other fishmongers sold their wares
and Henne remained with a tubful. Every few weeks
Henne washed her clothes. Don't ask me how she
carried on. She quarreled about everything: the wash-
tubs, the clotheslines, the water pump. If she found a
speck of dust on a shirt hanging up to dry, she blamed
it on her neighbors. She herself tore down the lines of
others. One heard her yelling over half the town.
People were afraid of her and gave in, but that was no
good either. If you answered her she raised a rumpus,
and if you kept silent she would scream, "Is it a
disgrace to talk to me?" There was no dealing with her
without being insulted.

At first her daughters would come home from the big
towns for the holidays. They were good girls, and they
all took after their father. One moment mother and
daughter would kiss and embrace and before you knew
it there would be a cat fight in Butcher Alley, where we
lived. Plates crashed, windows were broken. The girl
would run out of the house as though poisoned and
Henne would be after her with a stick, screaming,
"Bitch, slut, whore, you should have dissolved in your
mother's belly!" After Berl deserted her, Henne suspected
that her daughters knew his whereabouts. Although
they swore holy oaths that they didn't, Henne would

rave, "Your mouths will grow out the back of your heads for swearing falsely!"

What could the poor girls do? They avoided her like the plague. And Henne went to the village teacher and made him write letters for her saying that she disowned them. She was no longer their mother and they were no longer her daughters.

Still, in a small town one is not allowed to starve. Good people took pity on Henne. They brought her soup, garlic borscht, a loaf of bread, potatoes, or whatever they had to offer, and left it on the threshold. Entering her house was like walking into a lion's den. Henne seldom tasted these gifts. She threw them into the garbage ditch. Such people thrive on fighting.

Since the grownups ignored her, Henne began to quarrel with the children. A boy passed by and Henne snatched his cap because she imagined he had stolen pears from her tree. The pears were as hard as wood and tasted the same; a pig wouldn't eat them. She just needed an excuse. She was always lying and she called everybody else a liar. She went to the chief of police and denounced half the town, accusing this one of being a forger and that one of smuggling contraband from Galicia. She reported that the Hassidim were disrespectful of the Tsar. In the fall, when the recruits were being drafted, Henne announced in the marketplace that the rich boys were being deferred and the poor ones taken. It was true, too. But if they had all been taken, would it have been better? Somebody had to serve. But Henne, good sort that she was, could not suffer injustice. The Russian officials were afraid that she would cause trouble and had her sent to the insane asylum.

I was there when a soldier and a policeman came to get her. She turned on them with a hatchet. She made such a commotion that the whole town came running. But how strong is a female? As she was bound and loaded into a cart, she cursed in Russian, Polish, and Yiddish. She sounded like a pig being slaughtered. She was taken to Lublin and put in a strait jacket.

I don't know how it happened, but she must have been on her good behavior, because in less than half a year she was back in town. A family had moved into her hut, but she drove the whole lot out in the middle of a cold night. The next day Henne announced that she had been robbed. She went to all the neighbors to look for her belongings and humiliated everybody. She was no longer allowed into the women's synagogue and was even refused when she wanted to buy a seat for the Days of Awe. Things came to such a pass that when she went to the well to get water everybody ran away. It was simply dangerous to come near her.

She did not even respect the dead. A hearse passed by and Henne spat at it, screaming that she hoped the dead man's soul would wander in the wastelands forever. The better type of people turned a deaf ear to her, but when the mourners were of the common kind she got beaten up. She liked to be beaten; that is the truth. She would run around showing off a bump given her by this one, a black eye by that one. She ran to the druggist for leeches and salves. She kept summoning everybody to the rabbi, but the beadle would no longer listen to her and the rabbi had issued an order forbidding her to enter his study. She also tried her luck with the Gentiles, but they only laughed at her. Nothing remained to her but God. And according to Henne she and the Almighty were on the best of terms.

Now listen to what happened. There was a coachman called Kopel Klotz who lived near Henne. Once in the middle of the night he was awakened by screams for help. He looked out the window and saw that the house of the shoemaker across the street was on fire. He grabbed a pail of water and went to help put it out. But the fire was not at the shoemaker's; it was at Henne's. It was only the reflection that he had seen in the shoemaker's window. Kopel ran to her house and found everything burning: the table, the bench, the cupboard. It wasn't a usual fire. Little flames flew around like birds. Henne's nightshirt was burning. Kopel tore it off her and she stood there as naked as the day she was born.

A fire in Butcher Alley is no small thing. The wood of the houses is dry even in winter. From one spark the whole alley could turn into ashes. People came to the rescue, but the flames danced and turned somersaults. Every moment something else became ignited. Henne covered her naked body with a shawl and the fringes began to burn like so many candles. The men fought the fire until dawn. Some of them were overcome by the smoke. These were not flames, but goblins from hell.

In the morning there was another outburst. Henne's bed linen began to burn of itself. That day I visited Henne's hut. Her sheet was full of holes; the quilt and feather bed, too. The dough in the trough had been baked into a flat loaf of bread. A fiery broom had swept the floor, igniting the garbage. Tongues of flame licked everything. God save us, these were tricks of the Evil Host. Henne sent everybody to the devil; and now the devil had turned on her.

Somehow the fire was put out. The people of Butcher Alley warned the rabbi that if Henne could not be induced to leave they would take matters into their own hands. Everyone was afraid for his kin and possessions. No one wanted to pay for the sins of another. Henne went to the rabbi's house and wailed, "Where am I to go? Murderers, robbers, beasts!"

She became as hoarse as a crow. As she ranted, her kerchief took fire. Those who weren't there will never know what the demons can do.

As Henne stood in the rabbi's study, pleading with him to let her stay, her house went up in flames. A flame burst from the roof and it had the shape of a man with long hair. It danced and whistled. The church bells rang an alarm. The firemen tried their best, but in a few minutes nothing was left but a chimney and a heap of burning embers.

Later, Henne spread the rumor that her neighbors had set her house on fire. But it was not so. Who would

try a thing like that, especially with the wind blowing?
There were scores of witnesses to the contrary. The
fiery image had waved its arms and laughed madly.
Then it had risen into the air and disappeared among
the clouds.

It was then that people began to call her Henne Fire.
Up to then she had been known as Black Henne.

2.

When Henne found herself without a roof over her
head, she tried to move into the poorhouse but the poor
and sick would not let her in. Nobody wants to be
burned alive. For the first time she became silent. A
Gentile woodchopper took her into his house. The moment she crossed the threshold the handle of his ax
caught fire and out she went. She would have frozen to
death in the cold if the rabbi hadn't taken her in.

The rabbi had a booth not far from his house which
was used during the Succoth holidays. It had a roof
which could be opened and closed by a series of pulleys.
The rabbi's son installed a tin stove so that Henne
would not freeze. The rabbi's wife supplied a bed with a
straw mattress and linen. What else could they do?
Jews don't let a person perish. They hoped the demons
would respect a Succoth booth and that it would not
catch fire. True, it had no mezuzah, but the rabbi hung
a talisman on the wall instead. Some of the townspeople offered to bring food to Henne, but the rabbi's wife
said, "The little she eats I can provide."

The winter cold began immediately after the Succoth
holiday and it lasted until Purim. Houses were snowed
under. In the morning one had to dig oneself out with a
shovel. Henne lay in bed all day. She was not the same
Henne: she was docile as a sheep. Yet evil looked out of
her eyes. The rabbi's son fed her stove every morning.
He reported in the study house that Henne lay all day
tucked into her feather bed and never uttered a word.
The rabbi's wife suggested that she come into the
kitchen and perhaps help a little with the housework.

Henne refused. "I don't want anything to happen to the rabbi's books," she said. It was whispered in the town that perhaps the Evil One had left her.

Around Purim it suddenly became warm. The ice thawed and the river overflowed. Bridge Street was flooded. The poor are miserable anyway, but when there is a flood at night and the household goods begin to swim around, life becomes unbearable. A raft was used to cross Bridge Street. The bakery had begun preparing matzos for Passover, but water seeped into the sacks and made the flour unusable.

Suddenly a scream was heard from the rabbi's house. The Succoth booth had burst into flames like a paper lantern. It happened in the middle of the night. Later Henne related how a fiery hand had reached down from the roof and in a second everything was consumed. She had grabbed a blanket to cover herself and had run into the muddy courtyard without clothes on. Did the rabbi have a choice? He had to take her in. His wife stopped sleeping at night. Henne said to the rabbi, "I shouldn't be allowed to do this to you." Even before the booth had burned down, the rabbi's married daughter, Taube, had packed her trousseau into a sheet so she could save it at a moment's notice in case of fire.

Next day the community elders called a meeting. There was much talk and haggling, but they couldn't come to a decision. Someone proposed that Henne be sent to another town. Henne burst into the rabbi's study, her dress in tatters, a living scarecrow. "Rabbi, I've lived here all my life, and here I want to die. Let them dig me a grave and bury me. The cemetery will not catch fire." She had found her tongue again and everybody was surprised.

Present at the meeting was Reb Zelig, the plumber, a decent man, and he finally made a suggestion. "Rabbi, I will build her a little house of brick. Bricks don't burn."

He asked no pay for his work, just his costs. Then a roofer promised to make the roof. Henne owned the lot in Butcher Alley, and the chimney had remained standing.

To put up a house takes months, but this little building was erected between Purim and Passover, everyone lending a hand. Boys from the study house dumped the ashes. Schoolchildren carried bricks. Yeshiva students mixed mortar. Yudel, the glazier, contributed windowpanes. As the proverb goes: a community is never poor. A rich man, Reb Falik, donated tin for the roof. One day there was a ruin and the next day there was the house. Actually it was a shack without a floor, but how much does a single person need? Henne was provided with an iron bed, a pillow, a straw mattress, a feather bed. She didn't even watch the builders. She sat in the rabbi's kitchen on the lookout for fires.

The house was finished just a day before Passover. From the poor fund, Henne was stocked with matzos, potatoes, eggs, horseradish, all that was necessary. She was even presented with a new set of dishes. There was only one thing everybody refused to do, and that was to have her at the Seder. In the evening they looked in at her window: no holiday, no Seder, no candles. She was sitting on a bench, munching a carrot.

One never knows how things will turn out. In the beginning nothing was heard from Henne's daughter, Mindel, who had gone to America. How does the saying go? Across the sea is another world. They go to America and forget father, mother, Jewishness, God. Years passed and there was not a single word from her. But Mindel proved herself a devoted child after all. She got married and her husband became immensely rich.

Our local post office had a letter carrier who was just a simple peasant. One day a strange letter carrier appeared. He had a long mustache, his jacket had gilded buttons, and he wore insignia on his cap. He brought a letter for which the recipient had to sign. For whom do you think it was? For Henne. She could no more sign her name than I can dance a quadrille. She daubed three marks on the receipt and somebody was a witness. To make it short, it was a letter containing money. Lippe, the teacher, came to read it and half the town listened.

"My dear mother, your worries are over. My husband has become rich. New York is a large city where white bread is eaten in the middle of the week. Everybody speaks English, the Jews too. At night it is as bright as day. Trains travel on tracks high up near the roofs. Make peace with Father and I will send you both passage to America."

The townspeople didn't know whether to laugh or cry. Henne listened but didn't say a word. She neither cursed nor blessed.

A month later another letter arrived, and two months after that, another. An American dollar was worth two rubles. There was an agent in town, and when he heard that Henne was getting money from America, he proposed all kinds of deals to her. Would she like to buy a house, or become a partner in a store? There was a man in our town called Leizer the messenger, although nobody ever sent him anywhere. He came to Henne and offered to go in search of her husband. If he was alive, Leizer was sure he would find him and either bring him home or make him send her a bill of divorcement. Henne's reply was: "If you bring him back, bring him back dead, and you should walk on crutches!"

Henne remained Henne, but the neighbors began to make a fuss over her. That is how people are. When they smell a groschen, they get excited. Now they were quick to greet her, called her Hennely, and waited on her. Henne just glowered at them, muttering curses. She went straight to Zrule's tavern, bought a big bottle of vodka, and took it home. To make a long story short, Henne began to drink. That a woman should drink is rare, even among the Gentiles, but that a Jewish woman should drink was unheard of. Henne lay in bed and gulped down the liquor. She sang, cried, and made crazy faces. She strolled over to the marketplace in her undergarments, followed by cat-calling urchins. It is sacrilegious to behave as Henne did, but what could the townspeople do? Nobody went to prison for drinking. The officials themselves were often dead drunk. The neighbors said that Henne got up in the morning and drank a cup of vodka. This was her breakfast. Then she went to sleep and when she awoke she began to drink in earnest. Once in a while, when the whim seized her, she would open the window and throw out some coins. The little ones almost killed themselves trying to pick them up. As they groped on the ground for the money, she would empty the slops over them. The rabbi sent for her but he might just as well have saved his breath. Everyone was sure that she would drink herself to death. Something entirely different happened.

As a rule, Henne would come out of her house in the morning. Sometimes she would go to the well for a pail of water. There were stray dogs in Butcher Alley and occasionally she would throw them a bone. There were no outhouses and the villagers attended to their needs in the open. A few days passed and nobody saw Henne. The neighbors tried to peer into her window, but the curtains were drawn. They knocked on her door and no one opened it. Finally they broke it open and what they saw should never be seen again. Some time before, Henne had bought an upholstered chair from a widow. It was an old piece of furniture. She used to sit in it drinking and babbling to herself. When they got the door open, sitting in the chair was a skeleton as black as coal.

My dear people, Henne had been burned to a crisp. But how? The chair itself was almost intact, only the material at the back was singed. For a person to be so totally consumed, you'd need a fire bigger than the one in the bathhouse on Fridays. Even to roast a goose, a lot of wood is needed. But the chair was untouched. Nor had the linen on the bed caught fire. She had bought a chest of drawers, a table, a wardrobe, and everything was undamaged. Yet Henne was one piece of coal. There was no body to be laid out, to be cleansed, or dressed in a shroud. The officials hurried to Henne's house and they could not believe their own eyes. Nobody had seen a fire, nobody had smelled smoke. Where could such a hell fire have come from? No ashes were to be found in the stove or under the tripod. Henne seldom cooked. The town's doctor, Chapinski, arrived. His eyes popped out of his head and there he stood like a figure of clay.

"How is it possible?" the chief of police asked.

"It's impossible," the doctor replied. "If someone were to tell me such a thing, I would call him a filthy liar."

"But it has happened," the chief of police interrupted.

Chapinski shrugged his shoulders and murmured, "I just don't understand."

Someone suggested that it might have been lightning. But there had been no lightning and thunder for weeks.

The neighboring squires heard of the event and arrived on the scene. Butcher Alley filled with carriages, britskas, and phaetons. The crowd stood and gaped. Everyone tried to find an explanation. It was beyond reason. The upholstery of the chair was filled with flax, dry as pepper.

A rumor spread that the vodka had ignited in Henne's stomach. But who ever heard of a fire in the guts? The doctor shook his head. "It's a riddle."

There was no point in preparing Henne for burial. They put her bones in a sack, carried it to the cemetery, and buried her. The gravedigger recited the Kaddish. Later her daughters came from Lublin, but what could they learn? Fires ran after Henne and a fire had finished her. In her curses she had often used the word "fire": fire in the head, fire in the belly. She would say, "You should burn like a candle." "You should burn in fever." "You should burn like kindling wood." Words have power. The proverb says: "A blow passes, but a word remains."

My dear people, Henne continued to cause trouble even after her death. Kopel the coachman bought her house from her daughters and turned it into a stable. But the horses sweated in the night and caught cold. When a horse catches cold that way, it's the end. Several times the straw caught fire. A neighbor who had quarreled with Henne about the washing swore that Henne's ghost tore the sheets from the line and threw them into the mud. The ghost also overturned a washtub. I wasn't there, but of a person such as Henne anything can be believed. I see her to this day, black, lean, with a flat chest like a man and the wild eyes of a hunted beast. Something was smouldering within her. She must have suffered. I remember my grandmother saying, "A good life never made anyone knock his head against the wall." However, no matter what misfortunes strike I say, "Burst, but keep a good face on things."

Thank God, not everyone can afford constantly to bewail his lot. A rabbi in our town once said: "If people did not have to work for their bread, everyone would spend his time mourning his own death and life would be one big funeral."

Translated by the author and Dorothea Straus

Getzel the Monkey

My dear friends, we all know what a mimic is. Once we
had such a man living in our town, and he was given a
fitting name. In that day they gave nicknames to
everybody but the rich people. Still, Getzel was even
richer than the one he tried to imitate, Todrus Broder.
Todrus himself lived up to his fancy name. He was tall,
broad-shouldered like a giant, with a black beard as
straight as a squire's and a pair of dark eyes that
burned through you when they looked at you. Now, I
know what I'm talking about. I was still a girl then,
and a good-looking one, too. When he stared at me with
those fiery eyes, the marrow in my bones trembled. If
an envious man were to have a look like that, he could,
God preserve us, easily give you the evil eye. Todrus
had no cause for envy, though. He was as healthy as an
ox, and he had a beautiful wife and two graceful
daughters, real princesses. He lived like a nobleman.
He had a carriage with a coachman, and a hansom as
well. He went driving to the villages and played around
with the peasant women. When he threw coins to
them, they cheered. Sometimes he would go horseback
riding through the town, and he sat up in the saddle as
straight as a Cossack.

His surname was Broder, but Todrus came from
Great Poland, not from Brody. He was a great friend of
all the nobles. Count Zamoysky used to come to his
table on Friday nights to taste his gefilte fish. On

Purim the count sent him a gift, and what do you imagine the gift turned out to be? Two peacocks, a male and a female!

Todrus spoke Polish like a Pole and Russian like a Russian. He knew German, too, and French as well. What didn't he know? He could even play the piano. He went hunting with Zamoysky and he shot a wolf. When the Tsar visited Zamosc and the finest people went to greet him, who do you think spoke to him? Todrus Broder. No sooner were the first three words out of his mouth than the Tsar burst out laughing. They say that later the two of them played a game of chess and Todrus won. I wasn't there, but it probably happened. Later Todrus received a gold medal from Petersburg.

His father-in-law, Falk Posner, was rich, and Falk's daughter Fogel was a real beauty. She had a dowry of twenty thousand rubles, and after her father's death she inherited his entire fortune. But don't think that Todrus married her for her money. It is said that she was traveling with her mother to the spas when suddenly Todrus entered the train. He was still a bachelor then, or perhaps a widower. He took one look at Fogel and then he told her mother that he wanted her daughter to be his wife. Imagine, this happened some fifty years ago. . . . Everyone said that it was love at first sight for Todrus, but later it turned out that love didn't mean a thing to him. I should have as many blessed years as the nights Fogel didn't sleep because of him! They joked, saying that if you were to dress a shovel in a woman's skirts, he would chase after it. In those days, Jewish daughters didn't know about love affairs, so he had to run after Gentile girls and women.

Not far from Zamosc, Todrus had an estate where the greatest nobles came to admire his horses. But he was a terrible spendthrift, and over the years his debts grew. He devoured his father-in-law's fortune, and that is the plain truth.

Now, Getzel the Monkey, whose name was really Getzel Bailes, decided to imitate everything about Todrus Broder. He was a rich man, and stingy to boot.

His father had also been known as a miser. It was said that he had built up his fortune by starving himself. The son had a mill that poured out not flour but gold. Getzel had an old miller who was as devoted as a dog to him. In the fall, when there was a lot of grain to mill, this miller stayed awake nights. He didn't even have a room for himself; he slept with the mice in the hayloft. Getzel grew rich because of him. In those times people were used to serving. If they didn't serve God, they served the boss.

Getzel was a moneylender, too. Half the town's houses were mortgaged to him. He had one precious little daughter, Dishke, and a wife, Risha Leah, who was as sick as she was ugly. Getzel could as soon become Todrus as I the rabbi of Turisk. But a rumor spread through the town that Getzel was trying to become another Todrus. At the beginning it was only the talk of the peddlers and the seamstresses, and who pays attention to such gossip? But then Getzel went to Selig the tailor and he ordered a coat just like Todrus's, with a broad fox collar and a row of tails. Later he had the shoemaker fit him with a pair of boots exactly the same as Todrus's, with low uppers and shiny toes. Zamosc isn't Warsaw. Sooner or later everyone knows what everyone else is doing. So why mimic anyone? Still, when the rumors reached Todrus's ears he merely said, "I don't care. It shows that he has a high opinion of my taste." Todrus never spoke a bad word about anyone. If he was going down Lublin Street and a girl of twelve walked by, he would lift his hat to her just as though she were a lady. Had a fool done this, they would have made fun of him. But a clever person can afford to be foolish sometimes. At weddings Todrus got drunk and cracked such jokes that they thought he, not Berish Venngrover, was the jester. When he danced a kozotsky, the floor trembled.

Well, Getzel Bailes was determined to become a second Todrus. He was small and thick as a barrel, and a stammerer to boot. To hear him try to get a word out was enough to make you faint. The town had something to mock. He bought himself a carriage, but it was a tiny carriage and the horses were two old nags. Getzel rode from the marketplace to the mill and from the mill to the marketplace. He wanted to be gallant, and he tried to take his hat off to the druggist's wife. Before he could raise his hand, she had already disappeared. People were barely able to keep from laughing in his face, and the town rascals immediately gave him his nickname.

Getzel's wife, Risha Leah, was a shrew, but she had sense enough to see what was happening. They began to quarrel. There was no lack in Zamosc of curious people who listened at the cracks in the shutters and looked through the keyhole. Risha Leah said to him, "You can as much become Todrus as I can become a man! You are making a fool of yourself. Todrus is Todrus; you stay Getzel."

But who knows what goes on in another person's head? It seemed to be an obsession. Getzel began to pronounce his words like a person from Great Poland and to use German expressions: *mädchen, schmädchen, grädchen.* He found out what Todrus ate, what he drank, and, forgive me for the expression, what drawers he wore. He began to chase women, too. And, my dear friends, just as Todrus had succeeded in everything, so Getzel failed. He would crack a joke and get a box on the ear in return. Once, in the middle of a wedding celebration, he tried to seduce a woman, and her husband poured chicken soup down the front of his gaberdine. Dishke cried and implored him, "Daddy, they are making fun of you!" But it is written somewhere that any fancy can become a madness.

Getzel met Todrus in the street and said, "I want to see your furniture."

"With the greatest pleasure," said Todrus and took him into his living room. What harm would it do Todrus, after all, if Getzel copied him?

So Getzel kept on mimicking. He tried to imitate Todrus's voice. He tried to make friends with the squires and their wives. He had studied everything in detail. Getzel had never smoked, but suddenly he came out with cigars and the cigars were bigger than he was. He also started a subscription to a newspaper in Petersburg. Todrus's daughters went to a Gentile boarding school, and Getzel wanted to send Dishke there, even though she was already too old for that. Risha Leah raised an uproar and she was barely able to prevent him from doing it. If he had been a pauper, Getzel would have been excommunicated. But he was loaded with money. For a long time Todrus didn't pay any attention to all of this, but at last in the marketplace he walked over to Getzel and asked: "Do you want to see how I make water?" He used plain language, and the town had something to laugh about.

2.

Now, listen to this. One day Risha Leah died. Of what did she die? Really, I couldn't say. Nowadays people run to the doctor; in those times a person got sick and it was soon finished. Perhaps it was Getzel's carryings on that killed her. Anyway, she died and they buried her. Getzel didn't waste any tears over it. He sat on the stool during the seven days of mourning and cracked jokes like Todrus. His daughter Dishke was already engaged. After the thirty days of bereavement the matchmakers showered him with offers, but he wasn't in a hurry.

Two months hadn't passed when there was bedlam in the town. Todrus Broder had gone bankrupt. He had borrowed money from widows and orphans. Brides had invested their dowries with him, and he owed money to nobles. One of the squires came over and tried to shoot him. Todrus's wife wept and fainted, and the girls hid in the attic. It came out that Todrus owed Getzel a large sum of money. A mortgage, or God knows what. Getzel came to Todrus. He was carrying a cane with a silver tip and an amber handle, just like Todrus's, and he pounded on the floor with it. Todrus tried to laugh off the whole business, but you could tell that he didn't

feel very good about it. They wanted to auction off all
his possessions, tear him to pieces. The women called
him a murderer, a robber, and a swindler. The brides
howled: "What did you do with our dowries?" and
wailed as if it were Yom Kippur. Todrus had a dog as
big as a lion, and Getzel had gotten one the image of
it. He brought the dog with him, and both animals
tried to devour each other. Finally Getzel whispered
something to Todrus; they locked themselves in a room
and stayed there for three hours. During that time the
creditors almost tore the house down. When Todrus
came out, he was as pale as death; Getzel was perspir-
ing. He called out to the men: "Don't make such a
racket! I'll pay all the debts. I have taken over the
business from Todrus." They didn't believe their own
ears. Who puts a healthy head into a sickbed? But
Getzel took out his purse, long and deep, just like
Todrus's. However, Todrus's was empty, and this one
was full of bank notes. Getzel began to pay on the
spot. To some he paid off the whole debt and to others
an advance, but they all knew that he was solvent.
Todrus looked on silently. Fogel, his wife, came to
herself and smiled. The girls came out of their hiding
places. Even the dogs made peace; they began to sniff
each other and wag their tails. Where had Getzel put
together so much cash? As a rule, a merchant has all
his money in his business. But Getzel kept on paying.
He had stopped stammering and he spoke now as if he
really were Todrus. Todrus had a bookkeeper whom
they called the secretary, and he brought out the
ledgers. Meanwhile, Todrus had become his old self
again. He told jokes, drank brandy, and offered a drink
to Getzel. They toasted *l'chayim*.

To make a long story short, Getzel took over everything. Todrus Broder left for Lublin with his wife and
daughters, and it seemed that he had moved out altogether. Even the maids went with him. But then why
hadn't he taken his feather beds with him? By law, no
creditor is allowed to take these. For three months
there was no word of them. Getzel had already become

the boss. He went here, he went there, he rode in
Todrus's carriage with Todrus's coachman. After three
months Fogel came back with her daughters. It was
hard to recognize her. They asked her about her husband and she answered simply, "I have no more husband." "Some misfortune, God forbid?" they asked, and
she answered no, that they had been divorced.

There is a saying that the truth will come out like oil
on water. And so it happened here. In the three hours
that Getzel and Todrus had been locked up in the
office, Todrus had transferred everything to Getzel—his
house, his estate, all his possessions, and on top of it
all, his wife. Yes, Fogel married Getzel. Getzel gave
her a marriage contract for ten thousand rubles and
wrote up a house—it was actually Todrus's—an estate.
For the daughters he put away large dowries.

The turmoil in the town was something awful. If you
weren't in Zamosc then, you have no idea how excited a
town can become. A book could be written about it. Not
one book, ten books! Even the Gentiles don't do such
things. But that was Todrus. As long as he could, he
acted like a king. He gambled, he lost, and then it was
all over; he disappeared. It seems he had been about to
go to jail. The squires might have murdered him. And
in such a situation, what won't a man do to save his
life? Some people thought that Getzel had known everything in advance and that he had plotted it all. He
had managed a big loan for Todrus and had lured him
into his snare. No one would have thought that Getzel
was so clever. But how does the saying go? If God wills,
a broom will shoot.

Todrus's girls soon got married. Dishke went to live
with her in-laws in Lemberg. Fogel almost never showed
her face outside. Todrus's grounds had a garden with a
pavilion, and she sat there all summer. In the winter
she hid inside the house. Todrus Broder had vanished
like a stone in the water. Some held that he was in
Krakow; others, that he had gone to Warsaw. Still
others said that he had converted and had married a
rich squiress. Who can understand such a man? If a

Jew is capable of selling his wife in such a way, he is no longer a Jew. Fogel had loved him with a great love, and it was clear that she had consented to everything just to save him. In the years that followed, nobody could say a word against Todrus to her. On Rosh Hashanah and Yom Kippur she stood in her pew in the women's section at the grating and she didn't utter a single word to anybody. She remained proud.

Getzel took over Todrus's language and his manners. He even became taller, or perhaps he put lifts in his boots. He became a bosom friend of the squires. It was rumored that he drank forbidden wine with them. After he had stopped stammering, he had begun to speak Polish like one of them.

Dishke never wrote a word to her father. About Todrus's daughters I heard that they didn't have a good end. One died in childbirth. Another was supposed to have hanged herself. But Getzel became Todrus and I saw it happen with my own eyes, from beginning to end. Yes, mimicking is forbidden. If you imitate a person, his fate is passed on to you. Even with a shadow one is not allowed to play tricks. In Zamosc there was a young man who used to play with his shadow. He would put his hands together so that the shadow on the wall would look like a buck with horns, eating and butting. One night the shadow jumped from the wall and gored the young man as if with real horns. He got such a butt that he had two holes in his forehead afterwards. And so it happened here.

Getzel did not need other people's money. He had enough. But suddenly he began to borrow from widows and orphans. Anywhere he could find credit he did, and he paid high interest. He didn't have to renovate his mill either. The flour was as white as snow. But he built a new mill and put in new millstones. His old and devoted miller had died, and Getzel hired a new miller who had long mustaches, a former bailiff. This one swindled him right and left. Getzel also bought an estate from a nobleman even though he already had an estate with a stable and horses. Before this he had kept to his Jewishness, but now he began to dress like a fop. He stopped coming to the synagogue except on High Holy Days. As if this wasn't enough, Getzel started a brewery and he sowed hops for beer. He didn't need any of this. Above all, it cost him a fortune. He imported machines, God knows from where, and they made such a noise at night that the neighbors couldn't sleep. Every few weeks he made a trip to Warsaw. Who can guess what really happened to him? Ten enemies don't do as much harm to a man as he does to himself. One day the news spread that Getzel was bankrupt. My dear friends, he didn't have to go bankrupt; it was all an imitation of Todrus. He had taken over the other's bad luck. People streamed from every street and broke up his windowpanes. Getzel had no imitator. No one wanted his wife; Fogel was older than Getzel by a good many years. He assured everyone that he wouldn't take anything away from them. But they beat him up. A squire came and put his pistol to Getzel's forehead in just the same way as the other had to Todrus.

To make a long story short, Getzel ran away in the middle of the night. When he left, the creditors took over and it turned out that there was more than enough for everybody. Getzel's fortune was worth God knows how much. So why had he run away? And where had he gone? Some said that the whole bankruptcy was nothing but a sham. There was supposed to have been a woman involved, but what does an old man want with a woman? It was all to be like Todrus. Had Todrus buried himself alive, Getzel would have dug his own grave. The whole thing was the work of demons. What are demons if not imitators? And what does a mirror do? This is why they cover a mirror when there is a corpse in the house. It is dangerous to see the reflection of the body.

Every piece of property Getzel had owned was taken away. The creditors didn't leave as much as a scrap of bread for Fogel. She went to live in the poorhouse. When this happened I was no longer in Zamosc. But may my enemies have such an old age as they say

Fogel had. She lay down on a straw mattress and she never got up again. It was said that before her death she asked to be inscribed on the tombstone not as the wife of Getzel but as the wife of Todrus. Nobody even bothered to put up a stone. Over the years the grave became overgrown and was finally lost.

What happened to Getzel? And what happened to Todrus? No one knew. Somebody thought they might have met somewhere, but for what purposes? Todrus must have died. Dishke tried to get a part of her father's estate, but nothing was left. A man should stay what he is. The troubles of the world come from mimicking. Today they call it fashion. A charlatan in Paris invents a dress with a train in front and everybody wears it. They are all apes, the whole lot of them.

I could also tell you a story about twins, but I wouldn't dare to talk about it at night. They had no choice. They were two bodies with one soul. Both sisters died within a single day, one in Zamosc and the other in Kovle. Who knows? Perhaps one sister was real and the other was her shadow?

I am afraid of a shadow. A shadow is an enemy. When it has the chance, it takes revenge.

Translated by the author and Ellen Kantarov

Yanda

The Peacock's Tail stood on a side street not far from the ruins of a Greek Orthodox church and cemetery. It was a two-story brick building with a weather vane on its crooked roof and a battered sign over its entrance depicting a peacock with a faded gold tail. The front of the inn housed a windowless tavern, dark as dusk on the sunniest mornings. No peasants were served there even on market days. The owner, Shalom Pintchever, had no patience with the peasant rabble, their dances and wild songs. Neither he nor Shaindel, his wife, had the strength to wait on these ruffians, or later when they got drunk, to throw them into the gutter. The Peacock's Tail was a stopping place for squires, for military men who were on their way to the Russian-Austrian border, and for salesmen who came to town to sell farm implements and goods from Russia. There was never any lack of guests. Occasionally a group of strolling players stayed the night. Once in a while the inn was visited by a magician or a bear trainer. Sometimes a preacher stopped there, or one of those travelers of whom the Lord alone knows what brought them there. The town coachman understood what kind of customers to bring to The Peacock's Tail.

When Shalom Pintchever, a stranger, bought the hotel and with his wife came to live in the town, they brought with them a peasant woman called Yanda. Yanda would have been a beauty but for a face as pockmarked as a potato grater. She had black hair which she wore in a braid, white skin, a short nose, red cheeks, and eyes as black as cherries. Her bosom was high, her waist narrow, her hips rounded. She was a woman of great physical strength. She did all the work in the hotel: made the beds, washed the linen, cooked, dumped the chamber pots, and, in addition, visited the male guests when requested. The moment a visitor registered, Shalom Pintchever would ask slyly, winking an eye under his bushy brows: "With or without?" The traveler understood and almost always answered: "With." Shalom added the price to the bill.

There were guests who invited Yanda to drink with them or go for a walk, but she never accepted. Shalom Pintchever was not going to have them taking up her time or turning her into a drunkard. He had once and for all forbidden her to drink liquor, and she never touched a drop, not even a glass of beer on a hot summer day. Shalom had rescued her from a drunkard father and a stepmother. In return she served him without asking for pay. Every few months he would give her pocket money. Yanda would grab Shalom's hand, kiss it, and hide the money in her stocking without counting it. From time to time she would order a dress or a pair of high-buttoned shoes or buy herself a shawl, a kerchief, a comb. Sunday, when she went to church, she invariably threw a coin into the alms box. Sometimes she brought a present for the priest or a candle to be lit for her patron saint. The old women objected to her entering a holy place, but she stood inside the door anyway. There was gossip that the priest was carrying on with her, even though he had a pretty housekeeper.

The Jews accused Shalom Pintchever of keeping a bawdy house. When the women quarreled with Shaindel, they called her Yanda. But, without Yanda, Shalom would have been out of business. Three maids could not have done her work. Besides, most servants stole and had to be watched. Neither Shalom nor Shaindel could be bothered with that. Husband and wife were mourning an only daughter who had died in a fire in the town in which they had previously lived. Shaindel suffered from asthma; Shalom had sick kidneys. Yanda carried the burden of the hotel. Summertime she got up at daybreak; in the winter she left her bed two hours before sunrise. She scrubbed floors, patched quilts and sheets, carried water from the well, even chopped wood when a woodchopper was not available. Shaindel was convinced Yanda would collapse from overwork. Husband and wife also feared that she might contract a contagious disease. But some devil or other impure power watched over her. Years passed, and she did not get sick or even catch a cold. Her employers did not stint on her food, but she preferred to eat the leftovers: cold soups, scraps of meat, stale bread. Shalom and Shaindel both suffered from toothaches, but Yanda had a mouth full of strong white teeth like a dog. She could crack peach pits with them.

"She is not a human being," Shaindel would say. "She's a beast."

The women spat when Yanda passed by, cursing her vehemently. Boys called her names and threw stones and mud at her. Young girls giggled, dropped their eyes, and blushed when they met her on the street. More than once the police called her in for questioning. But years passed and Yanda remained in Shalom Pintchever's service. With time the clientele of the inn changed. As long as the town belonged to Russia, its guests were mainly Russians. Later, when the Austrians took over, they were Germans, Magyars, Czechs, and Bosnians. Then, when Poland gained independence, it served the Polish officials who arrived from Warsaw and Lublin. What didn't the town live through— epidemics of typhoid and dysentery; the Austrian soldiers brought cholera with them and six hundred townspeople perished. For a short time, under Bolshevik rule, the inn was taken over by a Communist County Committee, and some commissar or other was put in charge. Yanda remained through it all. Somebody had to work, to wash, scour, serve the guests beer, vodka,

snacks. Whatever their titles, at night the men wanted
Yanda in their beds. There were some who kissed her
and some who beat her. There were those who cursed
her and called her names and those who wept before
her and confessed to her as if she were a priest. One
officer placed a glass of cognac on her head and shot at
it with his revolver. Another bit into her shoulder and
like a leech sucked her blood. Still, in the morning she
washed, combed her hair, and everything began anew.
There was no end to the dirty dishes. The floors were
full of holes and cracks, the walls were peeling. No
matter how often Yanda poured scalding water over
cockroaches and bedbugs, and used all kinds of poison,
the vermin continued to multiply! Each day the hotel
was in danger of falling apart. It was Yanda who kept
it together.

The owners themselves began to resemble the hotel.
Shaindel grew bent and her face became as white and
brittle as plaster. Her speech was unintelligible. She
no longer walked, but shuffled. She would find a
discarded caftan in a trunk and would try to patch it.
Shalom protested that he didn't need the rag, but half
blind as she was, she would sit for days, with her
glasses on the tip of her nose, trying to mend it. Again
and again she would ask Yanda to thread the needle,
muttering, "It isn't thread, it's cobweb. These needles
have no eyes."

Shalom Pintchever's face began to grow a kind of
mold. His brows became even shaggier. Under his eyes
there were bags and from them hung other bags. Between his wrinkles there was a black excrescence which
no water could remove. His head shook from side to
side. Nevertheless, when a guest arrived, Shalom would
reach for his hotel register with a trembling hand and
ask: "With or without?"

And the guest would almost invariably reply:
"With."

2.

It all happened quickly. First Shaindel lay down and breathed her last. It occurred on the first day of Rosh Hashanah. The following day, the oldest woman in the town gave up her own shroud, since it is forbidden to sew on the Holy Days. The women of the burial society treated themselves to cake and brandy at the cemetery. Shalom, confused by grief, forgot the text of the Kaddish and had to be prompted. Those who attended the funeral said that his legs were so shaky he almost fell into the grave. After Shaindel's death Shalom Pintchever became senile. He took money from the cashbox and didn't remember what he did with it. He became so deaf that even screaming into his ears did not help. The Feast of Tabernacles was followed by such a rain spell that even the oldest townspeople could not recall its like. The river overflowed. The wheel of the watermill had to be stopped. The roof of the inn sprang a leak. The guests who had rooms on the top floor came down in the middle of the night, complaining that water was pouring into their beds. Shalom lay helpless in his own bedroom. It was Yanda who apologized to the guests and made up beds for them downstairs. She even climbed a ladder up to the roof and tried to plug the leaks. But the shingles crumbled as soon as she touched them. In the morning the guests left without paying their bills. Early Saturday, as Shalom Pintchever picked up his prayer shawl and was about to leave for the synagogue, he began to sway and fell down. "Yanda, I am finished," he cried out. Yanda ran to get some brandy, but it was too late. Shalom lay stretched out on the floor, dead. There was an uproar in the town. Shalom had left no children. Irreverent people, for whom the sacredness of the Sabbath had little meaning, began to search for a will and tried to force his strongbox. Officials from the City Hall made a list of his belongings and sealed the drawer in which he kept his money. Yanda had begun to weep

the moment Shalom had fallen down and did not stop
until after the funeral. She had worked in the inn for
over twenty years but was left with barely sixty zlotys.
The authorities immediately ordered her to get out.
Yanda packed her belongings in a sack, put on a pair of
shoes, which she usually wore only to church, wrapped
herself in a shawl, and walked the long way to the
railroad station. There was nobody to say goodbye. At
the station she approached the ticket window and said,
"Kind sir, please give me a ticket to Skibica."

"There is no such station."

Yanda began to wail: "What am I to do, I am a
forsaken orphan!"

The peasants at the station jeered at her. The women
spat on her. A Jewish traveling salesman began to
question her about Skibica. Is it a village or a town? In
what county or district is it? At first Yanda remembered
nothing. But the Jew in his torn coat and sheepskin
hat persisted until Yanda finally remembered that the
village was somewhere near Kielce, between Chęczyn
and Sobkow. The salesman told Yanda to take out the
bank notes that she kept wrapped in a handkerchief
and helped her to count the money. He talked it over
with the ticket seller. There was no direct train to that
area. The best way to go was by horse and buggy to
Rozwadow, and from there on to Sandomierz, then to
Opola, where she could either get a ride in another cart
or go on foot to Skibica.

Just hearing the names of these familiar places
made Yanda weep. In Skibica she had once had a
father, a mother, a sister, relatives. Her mother had
died and her father, not long before he died, had
married another woman. Yanda had been about to
become engaged to Wojciech, a peasant boy, but the
blacksmith's daughter, a girl called Zocha, had taken
him away. During the years Yanda had worked for
Shalom Pintchever she had seldom thought of the past.
It all seemed so far away, at the end of the earth. But
now that her employer was dead there was nothing left
for her but to return home. Who knew, perhaps some of

her close ones were still alive. Perhaps somebody there still remembered her name.

Thank God, good people helped. No sooner had Yanda left the town where she had lived in shame than people stopped laughing at her, making grimaces, spitting. The coachmen did not overcharge her. Jews with beards and sidelocks seemed to know the whole of Poland as well as they knew the palms of their hands. They mentioned names of places which Yanda had already forgotten, and looked for shortcuts. In one tavern someone took out a map to find the shortest way home for her. Yanda marveled at the cleverness of men; how much knowledge they carried in their heads and how eager they were to help a homeless woman. But, despite all the good advice, Yanda walked more than she rode. Rains soaked her; there was snow and hail. She waded through ditches of water as deep as streams. She had grown accustomed to sleeping on pillows with clean pillowcases, between white sheets, under a warm eiderdown, but now she was forced to stretch out on the floors of granaries and barns. Her clothes were wet through. Somehow she managed to keep her paper money dry. As Yanda walked, she thought about her life. Once in a while Shalom Pintchever had given her money, but it had dwindled away. The Russians had counted in rubles and kopeks. When the Austrians came, the ruble lost its value and everything was exchanged for kronen and heller. The Bolsheviks used chervontsi; the Poles, złotys. How was someone like Yanda, uneducated as she was, to keep track of such changes? It was a miracle that she had anything left with which to get home.

God in heaven, men were still chasing her! Wherever she slept, peasants came to her and had their way with her. In a wagon, at night, somebody seized her silently. What do they see in me, Yanda asked herself. It's my bad luck. Yanda remembered that she had never been able to refuse anyone. Her father had beaten her for her submissiveness. Her stepmother had torn Yanda's hair. Even as a child, when she played with the other

children, they had smeared her face with mud, given
her a broom, and made her take the part of Baba Yaga.
With the guests in Shalom's hotel she had had such
savage and foolish experiences that she sometimes
hadn't known whether to laugh or cry. But to say no
was not in her nature. When she was young, while still
in her father's village, she had twice given birth to
babies, but they had both died. Several times heavy
work had caused her to miscarry. She could never
really forget Wojciech, the peasant boy to whom she
had almost been engaged but who at the last moment
had thrown her over. Yanda also had desired Shalom
Pintchever, perhaps because he had always sent her to
others and had never taken her himself. He would say,
"Yanda, go to number three. Yanda, knock at the door
of number seven." He himself had remained faithful to
his old wife, Shaindel. Perhaps he had been disgusted
by Yanda, but she had yearned for him. One kind word
from him pleased her more than all the wild games of
the others. Even when he scolded her, she waited for
more. As for the guests, there were so many of them
that Yanda had forgotten all but a few who stuck in her
memory. One Russian had demanded that Yanda spit
on him, tear at his beard, and call him names. Another,
a schoolboy with red cheeks, had kissed her and called
her mother. He had slept on her breast until dawn,
although guests in other rooms had been waiting for
her.

Now Yanda was old. But how old? She did not know
herself—certainly in her forties, or perhaps fifty? Other
women her age were grandmothers but she was
returning to her village alone, abandoned by God and
man. Yanda made a resolution: once home, she would
allow no man to approach her. In a village there was
always gossip and it usually ended in a quarrel. What
did she need it for? The truth was that all this whoring
had never given her any pleasure.

3.

The Jews who showed Yanda the way had not fooled
her. She reached Skibica in the morning, and even
though it had changed considerably, she recognized
her home. In a chapel at the outskirts of the village
God's mother still stood with a halo around her head
and the Christ child in her arms. The figure had
become dingy with the years and a piece of the Holy
Mother's shoulder was chipped off. A wreath of wilted
flowers hung around her neck. Yanda's eyes filled with
tears. She knelt in the snow and crossed herself. She
walked into the village, and a smell she had long
forgotten came to her nostrils: an odor of soggy potatoes, burned feathers, earth, and something else that
had no name but that her nose recognized. The huts
were half sunk into the ground, with tiny windows and
low doors. The thatched roofs were mossy and rotting.
Crows were cawing; smoke rose from the chimneys.
Yanda looked for the hut where her parents had lived
but it had disappeared and in its place was a smithy.
She put down the sack she was carrying on her back.
Dogs sniffed at her and barked. Women emerged from
the dwellings. The younger ones did not know her but
the old ones clapped their hands and pinched their
cheeks, calling, "Oh, Father, Mother, Jesu Maria."

"Yes, it's Yanda, as I love God."

Men, too, came to look at her, some from behind the
stoves where they had been sleeping, others from the
tavern. One peasant woman invited Yanda into her
hut. She gave her a piece of black bread and a cup of
milk. On the dirt floor stood bins filled with potatoes,
beets, black radishes, and cranberries. Chickens were
cackling in a coop. The oven had a built-in kettle for
hot water. At a spinning wheel sat an old woman with
a balding head from which hung tufts of hair as white
as flax. Someone screamed into her ear: "Grandma,
this is Yanda. Pawel Kuchma's daughter."

The old woman crossed herself. "Jesu Maria."

The peasant women all spoke together. Pawel Kuchma's home had burned down. Yanda's brother, Bolek, had gone to war and never returned. Her sister, Stasia, had married a man from Biczew and died there in childbirth. They also told Yanda what had happened to Wojciech, her former bridegroom-to-be. He had married Zocha and she had borne him fourteen children. Nine of them were still alive, but their mother had died of typhoid fever. As for Wojciech, he had been drinking all these years. Zocha had worked for others to support the family. After her death three years before, he had become a derelict. Everything went for drink and he was half crazy. His boys ran around wild. The girls washed clothes for the Jews of the town. His hut was practically in ruins. As the women spoke to Yanda, somebody opened the door and pushed a tall man inside. He was as lean as a stick, barefoot, with holes in his pants. He wore an open jacket without a shirt; his hair was long and disheveled—a living scarecrow. He did not walk, but staggered along as though on stilts. He had mad eyes, a dripping nose, and his crooked mouth showed one long tooth.

Somebody said, "Wojciech, do you recognize this woman?"

"Pockmarked Yanda."

There was laughter and clapping. For the first time in years Yanda blushed.

"See how you look."

"I heard you are a whore."

There was laughter again.

"Don't listen to him, Yanda. He's drunk."

"What am I drunk on? Nobody gives me a drop of vodka."

Yanda gaped at him. Could this be Wojciech? Some similarity remained. She wanted to cry. She remembered an expression of Shaindel's: "There are some in their graves who look better than he does." Yanda regretted that she had come back to Skibica.

A woman said, "Why don't you have a look at his children."

Yanda immediately lifted up her sack. She offered to pay for the bread and milk, but the peasant woman rebuked her, "This is not the city. Here you don't pay for a piece of bread."

Wojciech's hut was nearby. The roof almost touched the ground. Elflocks of straw hung from its edges. The windows had no panes. They were stuffed with rags or boarded up. One entered it as one would a cave. The floor had rotted away. The walls were as black as the inside of a chimney. In the semi-darkness Yanda saw boys, girls. The place stank of dirty linen, rot, and something rancid. Yanda clutched her nose. Two girls stood at the tub. Half-naked children smeared with mud crawled on the floor. One child was pulling the tail of a kitten. A boy with a blind eye was mending a trap. Yanda blinked. She was not accustomed to such squalor. At the inn the sheets had been changed each week. Every third day the guests got fresh towels. The leftover food had been enough to feed a whole family.

Well, dirt has to be removed. It won't disappear by itself.

Yanda rolled up her sleeves. She still had a few zlotys and she sent one of the girls to buy food. A Jew had a store in the village where one could get bagels, herring, chicory. God in heaven, how the children devoured those stale bagels! Yanda began to sweep and scrub. She went to the well for water. At first the girls ignored her. Then they told her not to meddle in their affairs. But Yanda said, "I will take nothing from you. Your mother, peace be with her, was my friend."

Yanda worked until evening. She heated water and washed the children. She sent an older child to buy soap, a fine comb, and kerosene, which kills lice. Every few minutes she poured out the slops. Neighbors came to look and shook their heads. They all said the same thing: Yanda's work was in vain. The vermin could not be removed from that hut. In the evening there was no lamp to light and Yanda bought a small kerosene lamp. The whole family slept on one wooden platform and there were few blankets. Yanda covered the children with her own clothes. Late in the evening the door opened and Wojciech intruded a leg. The girls began to giggle. Stefan, the boy with the blind eye, had already made friends with Yanda. He said, "Here he comes—the stinker."

"You must not talk like that about your father."

Stefan replied with a village proverb: "When your father is a dog, you say 'git' to him."

Yanda had saved a bagel and a piece of herring for Wojciech, but he was too drunk to eat. He fell down like a log, muttering and drooling. The girls stepped over him. Stefan mentioned that there was a straw mat in the shed behind the hut that Yanda could use to sleep on. He offered to show her where it was. As soon as she opened the door of the shed, the boy pushed her and she fell. He threw himself on her. She tried to tell him that it was a sin, but he stopped her mouth with his hand. She struggled but he beat her with a heavy fist. As she lay in the dark on wood shavings, garbage, and rotting rope, the boy satisfied himself. Yanda closed her eyes. Well, I'm lost anyhow, she thought. Aloud she muttered. "Woe is me, I might have been your mother."

Translated by the author and Dorothea Straus

The Needle

"My good people, nowadays all marriages are arranged by Mr. Love. Young folks fall in love and begin to date. They go out together until they start to quarrel and hate each other. In my time we relied on father and mother and the matchmaker. I, myself, did not see my Todie until the wedding ceremony, when he lifted the veil from my face. There he stood with his red beard and disheveled sidelocks. It was after Pentecost, but he wore a fur coat as if it were winter. That I didn't faint dead away was a miracle from heaven. I had fasted through the long summer day. Still, I wish my best friends no worse life than I had with my husband, he should intercede for me in the next world. Perhaps I shouldn't say this, but I can't wait until our souls are together again.

"Yes, love-shmuv. What does a young boy or girl know about what is good for them? Mothers used to know the signs. In Krasnostaw there lived a woman called Reitze Leah, and when she was looking for brides for her sons she made sure to drop in on her prospective in-laws early in the morning. If she found that the bed linens were dirty and the girl in question came to the door with uncombed hair, wearing a sloppy dressing gown, that was it. Before long everybody in the neighboring villages was onto her, and when she was seen in the marketplace early in the morning, all the young girls made sure their doors were bolted. She had six able sons. None of the matches she made for them was any good, but that is another story. A girl may be clean and neat before the wedding, but afterwards she becomes a slattern. Everything depends on luck.

"But let me tell you a story. In Hrubyeshow there lived a rich man, Reb Lemel Wagmeister. In those days we didn't use surnames, but Reb Lemel was so rich that he was always called Wagmeister. His wife's name was Esther Rosa, and she came from the other side of the Vistula. I see her with my own eyes: a beautiful woman, with a big-city air. She always wore a black-lace mantilla over her wig. Her face was as white and smooth as a girl's. Her eyes were dark. She spoke Russian, Polish, German, and maybe even French. She played the piano. Even when the streets were muddy, she wore high-heeled patent-leather shoes. One autumn I saw her hopping from stone to stone like a bird, lifting her skirt with both hands, a real lady. They had an only son, Ben Zion. He was as like his mother as two drops of water. We were distant relatives, not on her side but on her husband's. Ben Zion—Benze, he was called—had every virtue: he was handsome, clever, learned. He studied the Torah with the rabbi in the daytime and in the evening a teacher of secular subjects took over. Benze had black hair and a fair complexion, like his mother. When he took a walk in the summertime wearing his elegant gaberdine with a fashionable slit in the back, and his smart kid boots, all the girls mooned over him through the windows. Although it is the custom to give dowries only to daughters, Benze's father set aside for his son a sum of ten thousand rubles. What difference did it make to him? Benze was his only heir. They tried to match him with the richest girls in the province, but Esther Rosa was very choosy. She had nothing to do, what with three maids, a manservant, and a coachman in addition. So she spent her time looking for brides for Benze. She had already inspected the best-looking girls in half of Poland, but not one had she found without some defect.

One wasn't beautiful enough; another, not sufficiently clever. But what she was looking for most was nobility of character. 'Because,' she said, 'if a woman is coarse, it is the husband who suffers. I don't want any woman to vent her spleen on my Benze.' I was already married at the time. I married when I was fifteen. Esther Rosa had no real friend in Hrubyeshow and I became a frequent visitor to her house. She taught me how to knit and embroider and do needlepoint. She had golden hands. When the fancy took her, she could make herself a dress or even a cape. She once made me a dress, just for the fun of it. She had a good head for business as well. Her husband hardly took a step without consulting her. Whenever she told him to buy or sell a property, Reb Lemel Wagmeister immediately sent for Lippe the agent and said: 'My wife wants to buy or sell such-and-such.' She never made a mistake.

"Well, Benze was already nineteen, and not even engaged. In those days nineteen was considered an old bachelor. Reb Lemel Wagmeister complained that the boy was being disgraced by his mother's choosiness. Benze developed pimples on his forehead—because he needed a woman, it was said. We called them passion pimples.

"One day I came to see Esther Rosa to borrow a ball of yarn. And she said to me: 'Zeldele, would you like to ride to Zamosc with me?'

" 'What will I do in Zamosc?' I asked.

" 'What difference does it make,' she replied. 'You'll be my guest.'

"Esther Rosa had her own carriage, but this time she went along with someone else who was going to Zamosc. I guessed that the journey had something to do with looking over a bride, but Esther Rosa's nature was such that one didn't ask questions. If she were willing to talk, well and good. If not, you just waited. To make it short, I went to tell my mother about the trip. No need to ask my husband. He sat in the study house all day long. When he came home in the evening, my mother served him his supper. In those days a young

Talmud scholar barely knew he had a wife. I don't
believe that he would have recognized me if he met me
on the street. I packed a dress and a pair of bloomers—I
beg your pardon—and I was ready for the trip. We were
traveling in a nobleman's carriage and he did the
driving himself. Two horses like lions. The road was
dry and smooth as a table. When we arrived in Zamosc,
he let us off not at the marketplace but on a side street
where the Gentiles live. Esther Rosa thanked him and
he tipped his hat and waved his whip at us goodnaturedly. It all looked arranged.

"As a rule, when Esther Rosa traveled any place she
dressed as elegantly as a countess. This time she wore
a simple cotton dress, and a kerchief over her wig. It
was summer and the days were long. We walked to the
marketplace and she inquired for Berish Lubliner's
dry-goods store. A large store was pointed out to us.
Nowadays in a dry-goods store you can only buy yard
goods, but in those days they sold everything: thread,
wool for knitting, and odds and ends. What didn't they
sell? It was a store as big as a forest, filled with
merchandise to the ceiling. At a high desk stand a man
sat writing in a ledger, as they do in the big cities. I
don't know what he was, the cashier or a bookkeeper.
Behind a counter stood a girl with black eyes that
burned like fire. We happened to be the only customers
in the store, and we approached her. 'What can I do for
you?' she asked. 'You seem to be strangers.'

" 'Yes, we are strangers,' said Esther Rosa.

" 'What would you like to see?' the girl asked.

" 'A needle,' said Esther Rosa.

"The moment she heard the word 'needle,' the girl's
face changed. Her eyes became angry. 'Two women for
one needle,' she said.

"Merchants believe that a needle is unlucky. Nobody
ever dared to buy a needle at the beginning of the
week, because they knew it meant the whole week
would be unlucky. Even in the middle of the week the
storekeepers did not like to sell needles. One usually
bought a spool of thread, some buttons, and the needle

was thrown in without even being mentioned. A needle costs only half a groshen and it was a nuisance to make such small change.

" 'Yes,' said Esther Rosa. 'All I need is a needle.'

"The girl frowned but took out a box of needles. Esther Rosa searched through the box and said: 'Perhaps you have some other needles?'

" 'What's wrong with these?' the girl asked impatiently.

" 'Their eyes are too small,' Esther Rosa said. 'It will be difficult to thread them.'

" 'These are all I have,' the girl said angrily. 'If you can't see well, why don't you buy yourself a pair of eyeglasses.'

"Esther Rosa insisted. 'Are you sure you have no others? I must have a needle with a larger eye.'

"The girl reluctantly pulled out another box and slammed it down on the counter. Esther Rosa examined several needles and said: 'These too have small eyes.'

"The girl snatched away the box and screamed: 'Why don't you go to Lublin and order yourself a special needle with a big eye.'

"The man at the stand began to laugh. 'Perhaps you need a sackcloth needle,' he suggested. 'Some nerve,' the girl chimed in, 'to bother people over a half-groshen sale.'

"Esther Rosa replied: 'I have no use for sackcloth or for girls who are as coarse as sackcloth.' Then she turned to me and said: 'Come, Zeldele, they are not our kind.'

"The girl turned red in the face and said loudly, 'What yokels! Good riddance!'

"We went out. The whole business had left a bad taste in my mouth. A woman passed by and Esther Rosa asked her the way to Reb Zelig Izbitzer's dry-goods store. 'Right across the street,' she said, pointing. We crossed the marketplace and entered a store that was only a third of the size of the first one. Here too there was a young saleswoman. This one wasn't dark; she had red hair. She was not ugly but she had freckles.

Her eyes were as green as gooseberries. Esther Rosa asked if she sold needles. And the girl replied, 'Why not? We sell everything.'

" 'I'm looking for a needle with a large eye, because I have trouble threading needles,' Esther Rosa said.

" 'I'll show you every size we have and you can pick the one that suits you best,' the girl replied.

"I had already guessed what was going on and my heart began to beat like a thief's. The girl brought out about ten boxes of needles. 'Why should you stand?' she said. 'Here is a stool. Please be seated.' She also brought a stool for me. It was perfectly clear to me that Esther Rosa was going to test her too.

" 'Why are the needles all mixed together?' Esther Rosa complained. 'Each size should be in a different box.'

" 'When they come from the factory, they are all sorted out,' the girl said apologetically. 'But they get mixed up.' I saw Esther Rosa was doing her best to make the girl lose her temper. 'I don't see too well,' Esther Rosa said. 'It's dark here.'

" 'Just one moment and I'll move to stools to the door. There is more light there,' the girl replied.

" 'Does it pay you to make all this effort just to sell a half-penny needle?' Esther Rosa asked. And the girl answered: 'First of all, a needle costs only a quarter of a penny, and then as the Talmud says, the same law applies to a penny as it does to a hundred guilders. Besides, today you buy a needle and tomorrow you may be buying satins for a trousseau.'

" 'Is that so? Then how come the store is empty?' Esther Rosa wanted to know. 'Across the street, Berish Lubliner's store is so full of customers you can't find room for a pin between them. I bought my materials there but I decided to come here for the needle.'

"The girl became serious. I was afraid that Esther Rosa had overdone it. Even an angel can lose patience. But the girl said, 'Everything according to God's will.' Esther Rosa made a move to carry her stool to the door, but the girl stopped her. 'Please don't trouble yourself.

I'll do it.' Esther Rosa interrupted. 'Just a moment. I want to tell you something.'

" 'What do you want to tell me?' the girl said, setting down the stool.

" 'My daughter, Mazel Tov!' Esther Rosa called out.

"The girl turned as white as chalk. 'I don't understand,' she said.

" 'You will be my daughter-in-law,' Esther Rosa announced. 'I am the wife of Reb Lemel Wagmeister of Hrubyeshow. I have come here to look for a bride for my son. Not to buy a needle. Reb Berish's daughter is like a straw mat and you are like silk. You will be my Benze's wife. God willing.'

"That the girl didn't faint dead away was a miracle from heaven. Everybody in Zamosc had heard of Reb Lemel Wagmeister. Zamosc is not Lublin. Customers came in and saw what was happening. Esther Rosa took a string of amber beads out of her basket. 'Here is your engagement gift. Bend your head.' The girl lowered her head submissively and Esther Rosa placed the beads around her neck. Her father and mother came running into the store. There was kissing, embracing, crying. Someone immediately rushed to tell the story to Reb Berish's daughter. When she heard what had happened, she burst into tears. Her name was Itte. She had a large dowry and was known as a shrewd saleswoman. Zelig Izbitzer barely made a living.

"My good people, it was a match. Esther Rosa wore the pants in the family. Whatever she said went. And as I said, in those days young people were never asked. An engagement party was held and the wedding soon after. Zelig Izbitzer could not afford a big wedding. He barely could give his daughter a dowry, for he also had two other daughters and two sons who were studying in the yeshiva. But, as you know, Reb Lemel Wagmeister had little need for her dowry. I went to the engagement party and I danced at the wedding. Esther Rosa dressed the girl like a princess. She became really beautiful. When good luck shines, it shows on the face. Whoever did not see that couple standing under the wedding canopy and later dancing the virtue dance will never know what it means to have joy in children. Afterwards they lived like doves. Exactly to the year, she bore a son.

"From the day Itte discovered that Esther Rosa had come to test her, she began to ail. She spoke about the visit constantly. She stopped attending customers. Day and night she cried. The matchmakers showered her with offers, but first she wouldn't have anyone else and second what had happened had given her a bad name. You know how people exaggerate. All kinds of lies were invented about her. She had insulted Esther Rosa in the worst way, had spat in her face, had even beaten her up. Itte's father was stuffed with money and in a small town everybody is envious of his neighbor's crust of bread. Now his enemies had their revenge. Itte had been the real merchant and without her the store went to pieces. After a while she married a man from Lublin. He wasn't even a bachelor. He was divorced. He came to Zamosc and took his father-in-law's store. But he was as much a businessman as I am a musician.

"That is how things are. If luck is with you, it serves you well. And when it stops serving you, everything goes topsy-turvy. Itte's mother became so upset she developed gallstones, or maybe it was jaundice. Her face became as yellow as saffron. Itte no longer entered the store. She became a stay-at-home. It was hoped that when she became pregnant and had a child, she would forget. But twice she miscarried. She became half crazy, went on cursing Frieda Gittel—that is what Benze's wife was called—and insisted that the other had connived against her. Who knows what goes on in a madwoman's head? Itte also foretold that Frieda Gittel would die and that she, Itte, would take her place. When Itte became pregnant for the third time, her father took her to a miracle-worker. I've forgotten to mention that by this time her mother was already dead. The miracle-worker gave her potions and talismans, but she miscarried again. She began to run to doctors and to imagine all kinds of illnesses.

"Now listen to this. One evening Itte was sitting in her room sewing. She had finished her length of thread and wanted to rethread her needle. While getting the spool she placed the needle between her lips. Suddenly she felt a stab in her throat and the needle vanished. She searched all over for it, but—what is the saying,—'who can find a needle in a haystack?' My dear people, Itte began to imagine that she had swallowed the needle. She felt a pricking in her stomach, in her breast, her legs. There is a saying: 'A needle wanders.' She visited the leech, but what does a leech know? She went to doctors in Lublin and even in Warsaw. One doctor said one thing; another, something different. They poked her stomach but could find no needle. God preserve us. Itte lay in bed and screamed that the needle was pricking her. The town was in a turmoil. Some said that she had swallowed the needle on purpose to commit suicide. Others, that it was a punishment from God. But why should she have been punished? She had already suffered enough for her rudeness. Finally she went to Vienna to a great doctor. And he found the way out. He put her to sleep and made a cut in her belly. When she woke up he showed her the needle that he was supposed to have removed from her insides. I wasn't there. Perhaps he really found a needle, but that's not what people said. When she returned from Vienna, she was her former self again. The store had gone to ruin. Her father was already in the other world. Itte, however, opened a new store. In the new store she succeeded again, but she never had any children.

"I've forgotten to mention that after what happened between Esther Rosa and the two girls, the salesgirls of Zamosc became the souls of politeness, not only to strangers, but even to their own townspeople. For how could one know whether a customer had come to buy or to test? The book peddler did a fine trade in books on etiquette, and when a woman came to buy a ball of yarn, she was offered a chair.

"I can't tell you what happened later, because I

moved away from Zamosc. In the big cities one forgets about everything, even about God. Reb Lemel Wagmeister and Esther Rosa have long since passed away. I haven't heard from Benze or his wife for a long time. Yes, a needle. Because of a rooster and a chicken a whole town was destroyed in the Holy Land, and because of a needle a match was spoiled. The truth is that everything is fated from heaven. You can love someone until you burst, but if it's not destined, it will come to naught. A boy and a girl can be keeping company for seven years, and a stranger comes along and breaks everything up. I could tell you a story of a boy who married his girl's best friend out of spite, and she, to spite him kept to her bed for twenty years. Tell it? It's too late. If I were to tell you all the stories I know, we'd be sitting here for seven days and seven nights."

Translated by the author and Elizabeth Shub

Two Corpses Go Dancing

It has always tickled my fancy to amuse myself not only with the living but with the dead as well. That I do not have the power of resurrection is a well-known fact. This is something only the Almighty can accomplish. Nevertheless, I, the Evil One, can for a short time infuse a corpse with the breath of life, with animal spirits as the philosophers choose to call it, and send it to roam among the living. Woe unto such a one! one who is neither alive nor dead, but who exists somewhere on the borderline. What a delight it is for me to look in on a corpse as, wholly unaware of its status, it eats, worries about making a living, marries, sins—deceiving itself and others. When the game becomes boring, I end it. "Back to your sepulcher, Mr. Corpse," I order, "enough of your tricks." And the corpse crumbles like dust, for while it has been carousing, it has kept on rotting all the same.

This time I chose a young man named Itche-Godl. He had been dead more than a year and his widow, Tryna-Rytza, had remarried. Since he had lived in such a large city as Warsaw, had left behind no parents, no children, and certainly no estate, he had been completely forgotten. The truth of the matter is that he had been a corpse even when alive. You know the old saying: "A poor man is like a dead man." Well, Itche-Godl had been a pauper of the first magnitude. His wife had been the breadwinner, selling in the marketplace,

and the couple had made their home in a cellar that
was dark even during daylight hours. Itche-Godl, in
tatters, had moped about the study houses or dozed on
a bench behind the oven. A puny man, stooped, sleepy-
eyed, with a beard like the wattle of a chicken, he wore
trousers that drooped constantly, a ragged gaberdine
girdled with a rope, an old cap lining on his head, and
on his feet cracked shoes. So he had existed until his
thirty-sixth year, when he fell prey to some mysterious
illness. For several weeks he lay under a covering of
rags in the rotting straw of his bench bed, with his face
turning always yellower and more haggard. Until finally one morning while Tryna-Rytza was preparing
her wicker basket to take to the marketplace, she
realized her provider, her lord and master whose footstool she would one day become in paradise, was no
longer alive. Taking a pillow feather, she held it to his
nostrils and waited to see if it would flutter. But it did
not. Somehow or other, she managed to scrape together
a few gulden for the funeral, and Itche-Godl was
dispatched to the True World. Since the burial took
place on a Friday, the neighbors were too busy to walk
behind the hearse, and the body was hurriedly disposed of. Not even a marker was placed over the grave.

Usually after a man dies the Angel Dumah confronts
him, demands his name, and then proceeds to weigh up
his good against his evil deeds. But Itche-Godl lay
rotting for months without anyone coming to question
him, forgotten not only by the angels but by the devils
as well. It was only by accident that I learned of this
forsaken cadaver, and then it occurred to me why not
have some fun with it.

"Listen here, Itche-Godl," I shouted at him. "What's
the use of rotting underground? Why not get up and go
into the city? There are plenty of corpses roaming
around Warsaw. There might as well be another."

Itche-Godl rose, and since it was very late and the
sexton was fast asleep, I sent him to the mortuary,
where he stole the night watchman's trousers, boots, hat,
and gaberdine. Then he set off walking toward the city.

Although he was dressed like any other pauper, there was something about him that was frightening. Dogs howled. The night watch shuddered and clutched their sticks when they saw him silently approaching. A drunk, staggering across his path, sobered instantly and dropped back. Since Itche-Godl did not know that he was dead and that he had not been home in over a year, he was now on his way to his cellar. Coming into the narrow street where he lived, he felt his way sightlessly down the cellar steps, hanging on to the narrow wooden rail.

"How late it is! My, my! Why did I stay so long at the study house?" he mumbled. "Tryna-Rytza will surely make mincemeat out of me."

He pushed at the door but to his astonishment found it fastened by a lock and chain. She must be in a rage, he thought. He rapped once, then again. Suddenly he heard what sounded like a man's sigh from the other side. What's going on here, he asked himself. Is it possible Tryna-Rytza has fallen upon sinful ways? But that's foolish. I must have imagined it. . . . At that moment the door was flung open and in the darkness Itche-Godl made out the figure of a man. It occurred to him that perhaps he had made a mistake and knocked on the wrong door. "Does Tryna-Rytza live here?" he blurted out.

"Who are you?" rasped a coarse male voice. "What do you want?"

"But I am her husband," said Itche-Godl, confused.

"Her husband?" the other bellowed, backing away.

"Who is it?" Tryna-Rytza called, getting up from her bed. Presently she too was at the door. Itche-Godl recognized her familiar shape, her stride, the sweet-sour odor of her body.

"It's me, Itche-Godl," he said.

Instead of replying, Tryna-Rytza began to scream. The man slammed the door. Itche-Godl was shut outside. He trembled. Tryna-Rytza let out shriek after shriek. Then came a sudden silence, as if she had fallen into a swoon. A little later he heard whispers, mur-

murs, and then Tryna-Rytza and the man began to intone "Hear, O Israel."

"What goes on here?" Itche-Godl inquired of himself. Rooted there in the darkness, he pondered, scratched his beard, furrowed his brow, but the longer he thought about it, the more astounding the entire incident appeared.

"No doubt about it, the woman has committed adultery," he told himself.

Though it grieved him sorely to leave his woman and his pallet and to seek shelter for the night in the poorhouse, what choice had he? It was not his way to argue and he had never even learned how to raise his voice properly. He decided to withdraw.

"What can I do?" he thought. "It has been destined so."

And on shaky legs he climbed back up the stairs and out into the city.

2.

At daybreak, as Itche-Godl lay huddled on the floor in a corner of the poorhouse, believing himself asleep, I appeared before him in black, with the feet of a goose. "Why dream, Itche-Godl?" I said. "Man does not live forever. If you don't get your portion in this world, in the next it will be too late. If your wife is an adulteress, you must become a lecher!"

"But that is forbidden," Itche-Godl answered. "One is punished for that in hell."

"There is no such place as hell," I informed him. "A corpse knows nothing and feels nothing. There is no Judge and no Judgment."

"But how could I, ragged and scabby as I am, become a libertine?" asked Itche-Godl.

"The rich have plenty of money," I said. "Go to the market and steal some. I'll help you."

"And suppose they catch me and throw me into prison?"

"Don't worry. They won't be able to do a thing to you."

Early that same morning, Itche-Godl went to the marketplace and walked into a store as if to make a purchase. But although there were no other customers, the proprietress did not approach him, nor, when he ambled over to a sack of beans and dipped his hand in, did she berate him for handling her merchandise. Presently, when the woman went into the back room, leaving the store unattended, Itche-Godl sidled over to the counter, opened the cash drawer, took out a handful of money, and stuffed it into his pocket. Then he slipped outside and lost himself in the crowd.

Barely a minute later he heard the hue and cry. The shopwoman wailed that she had been robbed, and a great commotion ensued. Everyone was suspicious of everyone else. A beggar was stopped, searched, and, although nothing was found on him, severely beaten. But no one suspected Itche-Godl.

"What do I do now?" he asked.

"Aren't you at all hungry?"

"Yes and no."

"Well, never mind. Go to a soup kitchen and order a plate of tripe with calves' feet, egg noodles, a bowl of carrots and fried potatoes, and a glass of brandy to wash it all down. As you leave, take a decent fur coat and a sable hat from a hook. After that, we'll see."

Since Itche-Godl was not listed in the Book of Life, the angels were unaware of his existence and it was easy for me to bend him to my will. He followed my instructions and an hour later emerged on the street again, a well-dressed man. His face, to be sure, was pale and sunken and his eyes looked congealed in bony sockets, but the fur collar concealed nearly his whole visage. Since he appeared prosperous, the beggars pestered him for alms, but he, like any man of property, pretended not to see them.

"What shall I do now?" Itche-Godl asked me again.

"Would you care for a little sport with that harlot, your wife?" I asked him.

"Yes, why not?"

"Come along then, and do as I tell you. I'll see to it that all goes well."

I steered Itche-Godl to the marketplace, where Tryna-Rytza was standing over a basket of half-rotten apples. In contrast to Itche-Godl, she was a healthy wench with red cheeks and broad hips. As Itche-Godl was convinced that it was only yesterday she had deserted him, he could not fathom the changes he saw in her. Her face appeared more youthful, her voice lustier as she conversed with the other marketwomen, at the same time eating with gusto some fried groats from an earthen pot.

"Apparently sin agrees with her," thought Itche-Godl. It was I, of course, who caused him to think this, his mind being completely under my domination.

He went nearer. "Excuse me, woman, how much are the apples?"

Tryna-Rytza looked up and, bewildered at seeing such a distinguished man in a fur coat and sable hat, blurted out: "A penny a pound. Three pounds for two."

"Too cheap!" said Itche-Godl. "In Danzig, where I come from, such produce would bring at least three pennies a pound."

"Huh . . . what? That is a price!" Tyrna-Rytza exclaimed, staring in amazement at the stranger. "Here everything is dirt cheap."

"Why do you work in the market?" he asked. "Don't you have a husband to support you?"

"I have a husband, may he live to a hundred and twenty," she replied. "But I have to help out."

"What does he do?" Itche-Godl asked, laughing to himself. He was certain that she was speaking of him, Itche-Godl.

"You might say he's a jack of all trades—porter, secondhand clothes dealer, sometimes a barrelmaker, sometimes a cobbler. But you know the saying: 'Trades aplenty, pockets empty!' "

"Do you have children?" he asked. She said she did not. "And why not?" he asked slyly.

"I'm with my second husband," Tryna-Rytza explained. "My first, may he rest in peace, was, begging your pardon, a weakling and a simpleton. He died a year ago. My second, may God spare him, has only been with me a few weeks."

Itche-Godl strained to keep from laughter. How could the woman lie so shamelessly?

"Tell me the truth. Which one do you love best: the second or the first, blessed be his memory?"

"Why do you ask me such questions?" she demanded. "People from Danzig must be terribly curious."

"In Danzig, when one is asked a question it's the custom to answer it," he said, marveling at his daring. It seemed, he decided, that with money one acquired a goodly measure of impudence. Tryna-Rytza also seemed lost in thought as she swallowed the last spoonful of groats.

"Well, what's the use of lying to you?" she replied after some hesitation. "May God forgive me, but this one is a man. The other, may his rest be easy, was, alas, a schlemiel."

Suddenly she looked closely at the man in front of her. Her blood grew cold, her face paled, and the earthen pot fell from her hands and shattered into bits.

"Who are you? What do you want?" she screamed in a voice unlike her own. Before Itche-Godl could manage an answer, she had fainted. The tradeswomen cried out and scurried about. Itche-Godl edged away into the crowd.

3.

At the marketplace of the Old City stood a large dry-goods store belonging to a widow named Finkle. Widely known for her wisdom and education, she spoke both Polish and German and her witticisms and bons mots were repeated and relished among the merchants. The widow Finkle was olive-skinned and slim, with sharp eyes and an aquiline nose. She wore a curled wig topped by a silver comb, wore shoes with high heels and, even on weekdays, silk dresses and jewelry. She had her clothes custom-made for her by a tailor who sewed for the nobility.

She had been a widow for over twenty years but had never remarried. The reason? That was her secret. No one dared to ask. Her late husband, Reb Joseph Rappaport, had been heir to a fortune, a Talmud scholar, and learned in worldly matters as well. Obviously she could not forget him. It was rumored, too, that she had come to her husband on his deathbed and of her own volition made a vow never to remarry.

This widow, Finkle Rappaport, fell ill one winter with an internal ailment, and the most prominent Warsaw doctors were unable to help her. In Vienna at that time lived a doctor said to have performed miracles, literally bringing the dead to life again. So the widow Finkle traveled to Vienna, leaving the store in the care of her three clerks, a young man and two girls, all relatives upon whose trustworthiness she could rely.

When months passed without word from her, rumors began to circulate that she was no longer alive. Before her departure she had drawn up a will, leaving part of her estate to her relatives, the remainder to charity. Her costly gowns and silk undergarments were, in case of her death, to be distributed among indigent brides. And a sum of money was set aside to engage ten pious men to say Kaddish and to study the Mishnah for a full year after her demise. She had also provided that an eternal light in her memory be maintained in the prayer house. In short, the woman had attended to it that she should not arrive empty-handed at the Celestial Council of Justice.

But in the meantime no one knew what had happened to her and the Warsaw rabbis forbade that her estate be touched until there was definite proof of her death. Nine months passed. That the widow Finkle was no longer alive was clear to everyone, since in all that time nothing had been heard from her. Her near relatives had already mourned for her, and when her name came up, the usual eulogies were intoned. Several women had dreamed that she appeared before them in shrouds, pleading that her remains be returned to Warsaw so that she might be buried next to her ancestors and complaining that her soul could find no place in the impious cemetery of Vienna.

Suddenly the news spread that Finkle had returned. One evening, as her employees were about to light the oil lamp, Finkle entered. She was swathed all in black and her form appeared taller and more angular than it had been. The clerks were so frightened they were unable to speak.

"Apparently you decided you were already rid of me," Finkle said.

"God forbid," replied the male clerk, recovering himself.

"Why didn't Aunt write?" asked the older of the girls, bursting into tears.

"If I didn't write, obviously I was unable to write!" Finkle snapped in her severe manner.

She related tersely that she had been confined in a Vienna hospital, had been extremely ill, but was now recovered. It was clear that she was not disposed to discuss her absence. She seemed a changed person, her face drawn and spotted, her nose more crooked, her eyes sharper yet somehow more distant. In the days that followed, she sat behind the counter gazing into a volume of *The Lamp of Light*, although, as the younger of the girls observed, she never turned the page and the book remained open always at the same place. Women kept coming in to see her, to question her, but she received them coldly and unresponsively. She answered everyone in the same way, saying only that she had been very sick. And when the young matrons interrogated her about Vienna, how the women dressed, what the latest fashions were, and whether the city was truly as magnificent as some descriptions would have it, she simply reiterated: "I hardly saw the city. My mind was on other things."

Finkle was sitting in the store one day staring into

The Lamp of Light, the yardstick on one side of her, the shears on the other, when Itche-Godl came in to purchase material for an overcoat, as I had ordered him. Getting into a conversation with Finkle, he told her that he was a merchant from Danzig, a widower.

"Is it long since your wife passed away?" Finkle asked. And Itche-Godl told her how long it had been.

"What are you doing in Warsaw?" she asked. And he explained his plans to erect a building on the marketplace four stories high and with three courtyards.

"Why such a large building?" Finkle asked.

"One does not build for oneself alone but for posterity as well," he replied.

"You have children, then?" asked Finkle.

"My first wife, may she rest in peace, was barren," he answered. "But I am thinking of marrying again."

Finkle asked him how many yards of cloth he required.

"What's the difference?" he answered. "So long as it covers the body." And he looked at her with lackluster eyes, and she looked back, the depths of her eyes blank.

The next morning I bade Itche-Godl send a matchmaker to Finkle. "But how can I?" he protested. "I have a wife already." "Do as I tell you," I ordered. "You have nothing." So the marriage broker spoke to Finkle, and she consented. When the clerks and neighbors heard that Finkle was contemplating marriage, they were greatly surprised. They came to offer congratulations but were thanked curtly. When they inquired: "Who is the groom? Where is he from? What does he do?" she said sharply: "Who knows? He's erecting a building or something in the marketplace."

"But there isn't an empty lot there," they pointed out.

"For my part, he can build on the wind," Finkle answered. But although her mouth smiled, her eyes remained stark. Moreover, the women noticed when they were near her a weird odor that seemed to emanate from her person. Mostly they stayed at a distance, however, for Finkle always reapplied herself quickly to her volume with its yellowed pages. The women, leaving the store, whispered among themselves. "Somehow it's not the old Finkle," they said and departed with heavy hearts.

The clerks in the store assumed that Finkle's wedding trousseau would be a costly one, but she ordered no new garments sewn. At home, too, her maid observed that she was behaving strangely. She barely touched the food placed before her, never attended to personal needs or washed herself or changed her clothing. In the morning her bed appeared unslept in, never disarranged, as smooth and cold as the day before. When she walked through the house, her footsteps made no sound, and often when the maid spoke to her there was no reply. The wedding date was set, yet Finkle made no preparations. One time the maid asked her: "Where will the master sleep?"

"What master?" Finkle answered.

"I mean . . . after the wedding," stammered the maid.

Finkle shrugged. "He'll sleep in the same place as the first."

On the evening of the wedding Finkle appeared at the ritual bath and the women, who had not counted on her coming, were greatly astonished. She looked, in her black clothes, unusually fleshless and elongated, nor did her figure cast any shadow on the wall. The bath attendant came to help her undress, but Finkle pushed past her and sitting down on the edge of the bench began to remove her clothes herself. Her torn stockings and spotted undergarments surprised everyone. When she was naked, she descended the steps promptly and silently lowered herself into the water. Her body was wasted, one could count every rib. Though she remained underwater for a long time, not even one bubble rose to the surface. Finally she poked her skull out, a skull that was neither trimmed nor shaved as is customary among pious women, but was overgrown with clumps of disheveled hair.

The next night was the night of the wedding, and the bride, having dressed herself in a black silk dress with a train, stationed herself at a window to wait for the groom. Her girls had filled the candelabra and chandeliers with lighted wax candles. Itche-Godl hastened in, accompanied by an assistant rabbi and by some street loungers who were to make up the quorum. The ceremony went off in the usual way. The marriage contract was filled in by the assistant rabbi with a goose quill. Itche-Godl slipped the ring from his bosom pocket and placed it on Finkle's index finger. When the canopy had been dismantled and the poles stacked behind the oven, the maid served cakes and brandy to the guests while they tendered their congratulations to the bride and groom. When the assistant rabbi said to Finkle: "May we soon celebrate a circumcision!" she snickered, revealing a row of blackish teeth, while Itche-Godl, lowering his head, giggled.

"A good night! A lucky night!" chorused the guests as they left.

The servant girl, who had been given the night off, had gone to sleep at her mother's, and the clerks had retired to their quarters in the basement. Finkle and Itche-Godl were left to themselves.

"Shall I put out the lights?" asked Finkle.

"As you wish," said Itche-Godl.

"You're mournful. Why?" asked Finkle.

"You're imagining it," answered Itche-Godl.

"Would you prefer to eat or sleep?" whispered Finkle.

"Sleep," said Itche-Godl.

"I, too." Finkle sighed.

She began to walk toward the bedroom, and Itche-Godl trailed behind, his legs shaky. The corridor was dark.

"How's your house coming?" Finkle asked.

"The lot—it's already there," replied Itche-Godl in an undertone.

"The lots are always there," said Finkle sternly. Itche-Godl suddenly felt as if she were moving far away from him. "Where are you going?" he called. "Come on. Don't be afraid," she replied.

The bedroom was not only unaccountably wide and

dark, but it didn't seem to have any walls and a wind seemed to be blowing as if they were outdoors. "Get undressed," Finkle ordered.

"I'm cold," complained Itche-Godl. He was stumbling around in the dark looking for a chair where he could sit down and take off his shoes.

"What are you doing? Where are you?" called Finkle.

"Are you in bed already?" asked Itche-Godl, and Finkle murmured, "I think so."

"I can't find a chair . . ." said Itche-Godl.

"Truly, you are helpless," sighed Finkle.

Having no other choice, Itche-Godl laid his coat and hat on the floor. With trembling knees, he started for the bed. Suddenly it seemed to him that he was looking down into a pit.

"What's the matter? Why don't you come?" Finkle grumbled.

"I think I see a pit," whispered Itche-Godl.

"What kind of pit?" Finkle cried out.

"A pit . . . it looks like a pit . . . what else could it be?" At these words he fell in and there was the sound of rattling bones.

"What's happened?" Finkle demanded.

"I've fallen in! Save me!" moaned Itche-Godl, whose tongue was becoming numb. Finkle tried to get up but was unable to move.

"I don't understand. Where could you have fallen? There aren't any pits here!" she screamed. For a long time both were silent. Then Finkle spoke: "Woe is me . . . We have made fools of ourselves."

"What's the matter? Are you sick or something, God forbid?" asked Itche-Godl in a muffled voice.

And Finkle answered, her voice funereal: "I am worse than sick!"

"Good heavens! Hear, O Israel: the Lord our God, the Lord is One," gasped Itche-Godl, and those were his last words. The God-fearing widow Finkle answered: "Blessed be His Name, Whose glorious kingdom is forever and ever. . . ."

The following morning the news spread throughout

Warsaw that Finkle and her bridegroom had vanished on their wedding night. At first it was thought that the couple must have fled to Danzig, but why they should flee or from whom no one could conceive. Sometime afterward a letter came from Vienna which stated that Finkle had died three months earlier and been buried in a local cemetery. Only then did the people realize that the Finkle who had returned had been nothing but a phantom and the entire series of events an illusion. They discovered, too, that over a year ago a pauper named Itche-Godl had died in Warsaw. This man had returned twice to haunt his wife, who had remarried. In every household in the neighborhood the mezuzahs were examined. Ten Jews went to Itche-Godl's grave to beg his forgiveness, to pledge him to remain in eternal rest and to torment the living no more. To appease the corpse, the community erected a tombstone over his grave. Thus Itche-Godl, who went unmourned from the world, became famous after death. And when Tryna-Rytza, his former wife, was, with luck, delivered of a son, she named him after her first husband: Itche-Godl.

So much for two of the corpses I sent dancing. But Itche-Godl and Finkle are not the only ones. I play such tricks often. The world is full of dead ones in sable capes and fur coats who carouse among the living. Maybe your neighbor, maybe your wife, maybe you yourself. . . . Unbutton your shirt. It's possible that underneath your clothes your body is wrapped in a shroud.

Translated by Joseph Singer and Elizabeth Pollet

The Parrot

Outside, the moon was shining, but in the prison cell it was almost dark. Although the single window was barred and screened, enough light filtered into disclose parts of faces. New snow had fallen and gave a violet glow to the speck of sky which came through the window as through a sieve. By midnight it had become as cold as in the street and the prisoners had covered themselves with all the rags they had: cotton vests, jackets, overcoats. They slept in their caps, with rags stuffed in their shoes. In summer the chamber pot had given off a stench, but now the winter wind came in and blew away the odor. It had begun to get dark at half past three in the afternoon, and by six Stach the watchman put out the kerosene lamp. The prisoners went on talking for a little while until they fell asleep. Their snoring kept up till about one o'clock, when they began to wake.

The first one to awake was Leibele the thief, a married man, a father of daughters. He yawned like a bell. Mottele Roiskes woke up with a belch; then Berele Zakelkover sat up and went to urinate. The three had been there for months and had told one another all their stories. But this morning there was a new prisoner, a giant of a man with a snub nose, a straight neck, thick mustaches the color of beer, dressed in a new jacket, tight high boots, and a cap lined with fur. He had brought a padded blanket and an additional pair of new boots which hung over his shoulders. He seemed like a big shot who had influence with the police. In the beginning they thought him a Gentile. They even spoke about him in thieves' jargon. But he proved to be a Jew, a silent man, a recluse. When they spoke to him, he scarcely answered. He stretched out on the bench and lay there for hours without a word. Stach brought him a bowl of kasha and a piece of black bread, but he was in no hurry to eat. Leibele asked him, "A word from you is like a gold coin, eh?"

To which he answered, "Two coins."

They couldn't get any more out of him.

"Well, he'll soften up, the snob," Mottele Roiskes said.

If this new inmate had been a weaker fellow, the others would have known what to do with him, but he had the shoulders and hands of a fighter. Such a man might have a hidden knife. As long as there was light, Leibele, Mottele Roiskes, and Berele Zakelkover played Sixty-six with a pack of marked cards. Then they went to sleep with heavy hearts. In prison it's not good when a man thinks too highly of himself. But sooner or later he has to break down.

Presently all three of them were silent and listened to the stranger. Since he didn't snore, it was hard to know if he was asleep or awake. The few words which he had spoken he pronounced with hard *r*'s, a sign that he was not from around Lublin. He must have come from Great Poland, on the other side of the Vistula. Then what was he doing in the prison at Yanev? They seldom sent anyone from so far away. Mottele Roiskes was the first to talk. "What time can it be?" Nobody answered. "What happened to the rooster?" he continued. "He stopped crowing."

"Maybe it's too cold for him to crow," Berele Zakelkover answered.

"Too cold? They get warm from crowing. There was a teacher in our town, Reb Itchele, who said that when a rooster crows he burns behind his wings. That's the reason he flaps his wings—to cool off."

"What nonsense," Leibele growled.

"It's probably written in a holy book."

"A holy book can also say silly things."

"It's probably from the Gemara."

"How does the Gemara know what's happening behind a rooster's wings? They sit in the study house and they invent things."

"They know some things. A preacher came to us and he said that all the philosophers wanted to know how long a snake is pregnant and nobody knew. But they asked a tanna and he said seven years."

"So long?"

They became quiet; conversation petered out. Berele Zakelkover began to scratch his foot. He suffered from eczema. He scratched and hissed softly at the same time. Suddenly the stranger said in a deep voice, "A snake is not pregnant seven years, perhaps not even seven months."

All became tense. All became cheerful.

"How do you know how long a snake is pregnant?" Leibele asked. "Do you breed snakes?"

"No creature is pregnant seven years. How long does a snake live?"

"There are all kinds of snakes."

"How can the Gemara know? To know you have to keep two snakes in the house, a he and a she, and let them mate."

"Perhaps God told him."

"Yes."

They became quiet again. The stranger was now sitting up. One could barely see his silhouette but his eyes reflected the gold of the moon. After a little while he said, "God says nothing. God is silent."

"He spoke to Moses."

"I wasn't there."

"An unbeliever, eh?"

"How can you know what God said to Moses?" the stranger argued. "It's written in the Pentateuch, but who wrote the Pentateuch? With a pen you can write anything. I come from Kalisch, where there are two rabbis. When one pronounced a thing kosher, the other said unkosher. Before Passover the miller asked one of them to make the mill kosher. So the other one got angry that he hadn't received ten rubles and he said the Passover flour was unkosher. Does all this come from God?"

Mottele Roiskes was about to answer, but Leibele interrupted. "If you are from Kalisch, what are you doing here?"

"That's a different matter."

"What do you mean?"

The stranger gave no reply. The stillness became heavy and tense.

"Do you have a smoke?" the stranger asked.

"We're all out."

"I can do without food, but I have to have a smoke. Can you get it from the watchman?"

"We have no money."

"I have some."

"With money you can buy anything. Even in the clink," Leibele answered. "But not now. Wait until morning."

"The winter nights are rough," Berele Zakelkover began to say. "You go to sleep with the chickens, and by twelve o'clock you're already slept out. You lie in the dark and all kinds of thoughts come into your mind. Here you've got to talk or you'll go crazy."

"What is there to talk about?" the stranger asked. "There's a proverb: man spouts, God flouts. I'm not an unbeliever, but God sits in the seventh heaven and snaps his fingers at everything."

"Why did they put you in this cage?" Leibele asked.

"For singing psalms."

"No, I'm serious."

The stranger was silent.

"A big pile, eh?"

"No pile at all. I'm not a thief and I don't like anyone to steal from me. If somebody tries it, I break him in pieces. That's the reason I'm here now."

"In what yeshiva did they keep you before?"

"First in Kielc and then in Lublin."

"Did you polish off someone?"

"Yes, that's exactly what I did."

2.

The stranger stretched out on the bench again. Berele Zakelkover went to scratching his foot. Mottele Roiskes asked, "Are you going to stay here?"

"They'll probably send me to Siberia."

Leibele walked over to the window. "A blizzard."

"It's a sin to let out a dog in weather like this," Mottele Roiskes said.

"I'd like to be the dog," Berele joked.

The stranger sat up again. He leaned his back against the wall and supported his chin on his knees. Broken moon rays reflected on his shiny boot tops. He said, "So what if they let you out? In half a year you'd be sitting here again."

"A half a year isn't anything to sneeze at."

"This is the last time for me," Leibele said, both to himself and to the stranger. "I've eaten enough half-baked bread. I have a wife and children."

"That's the usual song they all sing," remarked the stranger. "Where do you all come from? From Piask?"

"You're a thief yourself."

"I'm not a thief, and till now I wasn't a murderer. I could always swap blows, but for many years I've never touched anyone, not even a fly."

"So what happened all of a sudden?" Leibele asked.

The stranger hesitated. "It was fated."

"Who did you finish off? A merchant?"

"A woman."

"Your own wife?"

"No. She wasn't my wife."

"Did you catch her red-handed?"

The stranger gave no answer. He seemed to doze off while sitting there. Suddenly he said, "It all happened because of a bird."

"A bird? No kidding."

"It's the truth."

"What kind of a bird?"

"A parrot."

"Tell us about it. If you hold it in, you'll lose your mind."

"That wouldn't be so bad, but you can't choose when to lose your mind. I'm a horse dealer, or, rather, that's what I was. They knew me in Kalisch as Simon the horse trader. My father also dealt in horses; my grandfather too. When the horse thieves in Kalisch tried to sell me bargains, I sent them packing. I didn't need stolen goods. Sometimes I used to buy a half-dead nag, but under my care it recovered. I love animals, all animals. We're a family of horse traders. My wife died two years after our marriage and for thirteen years I was alone. I loved her and I couldn't forget her. We had no child. I had a house, stables; I kept a Gentile maid—not a young shiksa, an older woman. And not for what you think either. I lived, as they say, respectably. The matchmakers proposed all kinds of women, but I didn't like any of them. I'm one of those men who must love, and if I don't love a woman I can't live with her. It's as simple as that."

"Aha."

"I like animals. For me a horse is not just a horse. When I sold a horse, I wanted to know to whom I was selling it. There was a coachman in our town who used to whip the horses, and I refused to sell to him. For sixteen years I traded in horses and I never lifted a whip to one. You can get anything out of an animal with good treatment. It's the same with a horse, a dog, or a cat. Animals understand what you say to them; they even guess your thoughts. Animals see in the dark and have a better memory than men. Many times I've lost my way and my horses have led me to the right spot. The snow might be knee-deep, but my horses would take me to the peasant's hut and stop in front of it. Sometimes my horse would even turn his head, as though to say, 'Here it is, boss.'

"If you're alone, you have time to observe these creatures. Besides horses, I had dogs, cats, rabbits, a cow, a goat. I lived in the suburbs because in the city you can't keep a big stable, and can't take a horse to pasture. Oats and hay are good in winter, but in summer a horse needs fresh grass, green grass with flowers, and all the rest. The peasants hobble their horses and leave them all night in the pasture, but a hobbled animal is like a hobbled human being. Is it good to be in prison? I made a fence around my pasture, and the peasants laughed at me. It doesn't pay to build a fence around six acres of land, they told me, but I didn't want to hobble my horses, or let them stray into strange fields and get beaten. That's how I used to be before I became a murderer.

"What about the bird?"

"Wait. I'm coming to that. I kept fowl, and birds too. In the beginning, they weren't in my house but under the roof and in the granary. Storks used to come after Passover from the warm countries and build nests on my roof. They didn't have to build new ones, they just mended last year's nests after the rain and snow. Under the eaves, starlings had built theirs. People believe that crows bring bad luck, but actually crows are clever birds. I also had pigeon cotes. Some people eat squabs but I never tasted one. How much meat is there in a squab?"

"You seem to be a regular saint."

"I'm not a saint, but when you live in the suburbs you see all sorts of things. A bird flies in with a broken wing. A dog comes in limping. I'm not softhearted, but when you see a bird tottering on the ground and not able to lift itself up, you want to help it. I once took such a bird into my house and kept it until its wing was healed. I bandaged it like a doctor. Of course, the Jews laughed at me, but what do Jews know about animals? Some Gentiles understood. In summer my windows are wide open. As long as a bird wants to, it can stay and get its seed. When it's healthy again, it flies away. Once a bird returned to me, not alone, but with a wife. I

was sitting on a stool fixing a saddle and suddenly two
birds flew in. I recognized the male immediately
because he had a scar on his leg. They stood on
a shelf and sang me a good morning. It was like a
dream.

"Matchmakers used to come to me and propose all
kinds of arrangements, but when I looked over the
merchandise she never pleased me. One was ugly, the
other fat, the third one talked too much—I can't stand
chatterboxes. Animals are silent; that's why I love
them."

"A parrot talks."

"Yes."

"Well, what else?"

"Nothing. The years go by. One day it's my wife's
first anniversary, then the second, then the eighth.
Other horse dealers became rich, but I just made a
living. I didn't fool the customer. I decided how much
profit I wanted and that was all. I got used to being
alone."

"What did you do when you needed a female?"

"What do you do?"

"In a prison you have no choice."

"If you don't like anyone, it's like being in a prison.
There were whores in Kalisch, but when I looked at
them I felt like vomiting. You could get a peasant girl
or even a woman, but they were all lousy. Mine was a
clean one. Each night she combed her hair. In the
summer we bathed in a pond. She died from a lump in
her breast. They cut it out but it grew again. Such
suffering I don't wish my worst enemy."

"Was she beautiful?"

"A princess."

3.

"Well, what about the parrot?"

"Wait. Where can I begin? I'm not a grandmother
and I don't tell grandmothers' tales. Gypsies used to
come to me to sell horses, but I never bought them.

First of all, they're thieves. Second, their horses are
seldom healthy and, if you're not an expert, you find
the defect later. But I see everything the first minute.
The gypsies knew that they couldn't put anything over
on me.

"Once I was sitting and eating breakfast, millet with
milk. I used to eat the same thing every morning. I
always had a sack full of it for myself and for the birds.
As I sat there, I saw a gypsy woman, a fat black one
with large earrings and many strings of beads around
her neck. She came in and said, 'Master, show me your
hand.' I had never been to a fortune-teller; I didn't
believe in it. Besides, what is the good of knowing
things in advance? What must happen will happen.
But, for some reason, I gave her my hand and she
looked at my right palm and clucked in dismay. Then
she asked for my left hand. 'Why do you need my left
hand?' I asked. She said, 'The right one shows your
fortune and the left one the fortune of your wife.' 'But I
have no wife,' I said. 'My wife died.' And she said,
'There will be a second one.' 'When will she come?' I
asked. 'She will fly into your window like a bird.' 'Will
she have wings?' I asked. She smiled and showed her
white teeth. I gave her a few groschen and a slice of
bread, and she left. I paid no attention to her talk. Who
cares about the babble of gypsies? But somehow the
words were stored in my head and I remembered them
and thought about them. Sometimes an idea ticks in
your mind and you can't get rid of it.

"Now listen to what happened. They had just called
me into a village to buy horses and I stayed overnight.
The next day I came riding home with four horses, one
my own mare and three which I had bought from a
peasant. I walked into my house and there was a
parrot. I didn't believe my own eyes. Local birds flew in
and out, but where did a parrot come from? Parrots are
not of this country. He stood on my wardrobe and
looked at me as though he had been expecting me. He
was as green as an unripe lemon but on his wings he
had dark spots and his neck was yellow. He was not a

large parrot; in fact, he seemed a young one. I gave him
some millet and he ate it. I held out a saucer of water
and he drank. I stretched out a finger to him and he
perched on it like an old friend. I forgot all my business. I loved him immediately like my own child. In the
beginning I wanted to close the window, because he
could fly out as easily as he flew in. But it was summer,
and besides, I thought, if he's destined to stay here,
he'll stay.

"He didn't fly away. I bought him a cage, put in a
saucer of millet, a dish of water, vegetables, a little
mirror, and whatever else a bird needs. I named him
Metzotze and the name stuck. In the beginning he
didn't talk; he just clucked and cawed. Then suddenly
he began to speak in a strange language. It must have
been gypsy talk because it wasn't Polish or Russian or
Yiddish. He must have escaped from the gypsies.

"The moment he came I knew that what the gypsy
foretold would come true. Somehow I felt that this
would happen. The summer was over and winter was
coming on. I closed the windows to keep the house
warm. He began to talk Yiddish and call me Simon,
and when the Gentiles spoke in Polish he imitated
them. The moment I entered the room he would fly up
to my shoulder. When I went to the stable he stayed
sitting there. He put his beak to my ear and played
with my earlobe, telling me secrets in bird language.
In the beginning I didn't know if he was a he or a she,
but a magician passed by and told me it was a he. I
began to look for a wife for him and at the same time I
knew I would find my intended."

"A strange story," Mottele Roiskes interrupted.

"Just wait. Once I had to go to an estate to deliver
horses, but since I loved my Metzotze so much, it was
hard for me to leave him. But—how do they say it?—
making a living is like waging a war. I took my horses
and went to the estate. I told my maid—Tekla was her
name—that she should watch the parrot like the eyes
in her head. I didn't have to tell her—she was attached
to the bird herself, as was my stable man. In a word, he

was not among strangers. I sold my horses for a good price and everything went as smoothly as on greased wheels. I wanted to go home, but new business came up. The bird had brought me luck. I had to spend the night at an inn and the moment I entered I saw a woman: small, dark, with black eyes, a short nose. She looked at me and smiled familiarly as though I were an old friend. Outside, there was a blizzard, much as today, and we were the only guests. The landlady heated a samovar for us, but I said, 'Perhaps you have some vodka?' I'm not a drunkard but in business you sometimes have to drink. When the deal is finished, the buyer and the seller strike their palms together and have a drink. The landlady brought us a bottle and a bowl of pretzels. I asked the woman, 'Perhaps you want to taste some?' and she answered, 'Why not? I'm still able to enjoy life.' I poured a full glass for her and she tossed it off as if it were nothing at all. She didn't even take a pretzel afterwards. I saw that she could pour it down. When the landlady went to see a peasant about a cow, we were left alone. I took a glass, she took a glass. I don't get drunk quickly—I can pour down a large bottle and still stay sober. I was afraid she would get fuddled but she sat there and smiled, and we just became more cheerful and familiar. We talked like old cronies. She told me her name was Esther and she came from somewhere in Volhynia. 'What is a young woman doing alone in an inn?' I asked her.

" 'I'm waiting for a smuggler.'

" 'What do you need a smuggler for?' I asked, and she told me she was going to America. 'What's wrong with this country?'

"She told me she had had an affair and the man left her. She learned that he had a wife. He was a traveling salesman, one of those skirt chasers who think tricking a woman is something to boast about. 'Well,' she said, 'I played and lost. I couldn't show my face at home any more.' It came out that she had had a husband and had divorced him. Her father was a pious man and it was below his dignity. In short, she had to leave. Some smuggler was going to lead her to the German border.

" 'What will you do in faraway America?' I said. And she answered, 'Sew blouses. If you do something silly, you have to pay for it.' I poured her a fourth glass, a fifth glass. She said, 'Why didn't I meet you before? A man like you would make a good husband for me.' 'It's never too late,' I said. Why should I drag it out? By the time the landlady came back from the peasant, everything was settled between us. I was drawn to her as to a magnet and she felt the same way. We held hands, kissed, and her kissing drove you crazy. She wasn't a female, she was a piece of fire. I didn't want the landlady to know what was going on and I went to sleep in my room, but I lay there in a fever. She slept right next door and I heard through the thin wall how she tossed on her bed. At dawn I fell asleep and in the morning I had to leave. We had already decided that she was going with me. The whole business of America was out. She didn't need a smuggler any more.

"I came out of my room and found my woman already packed and ready. She smiled at me and her eyes shone. When the landlady heard that she was going with me, she understood what had happened, but what did I care? My heart was with Esther. I took her in my sleigh and she sat near me on the driver's seat. She was afraid of falling and she held on to me and excited me all over again. Riding along, we decided to get married. We didn't need any special ceremonies. I was a widower and she was a divorcée. We would go to Getzel, the assistant rabbi, and he would lead us under a canopy. I told her about the bird and she said, 'I will be a mother to him.' We spoke about him as though he would be our child."

"Did you really marry her?" Leibele asked.

"No."

"Why not?"

"Because she was divorced and I was a Cohen. I had forgotten the law."

"Who reminded you? The assistant rabbi?"

"Who else?"

"What a story!"

4.

"When Rabbi Getzel told me that we couldn't marry, I wanted to tear him to pieces, but was it his fault? I never went to pray except at Rosh Hashanah and Yom Kippur. Suddenly I was a Cohen, descended from a priestly line! I took Esther and went home with her. 'Let's pretend that I'm a Catholic priest and you're my housekeeper.' I lived far from the city and nobody would look through the keyhole. At first she was disappointed. What should she write to her family? But we were both so much in love that we could barely wait till night. Metzotze immediately became pals with her. The moment she entered, he perched on her shoulder and she kissed him on the back and he kissed back. I said to her, 'He's our matchmaker,' and I told her the story of the gypsy and the rest of it.

"In the beginning everything went well. We lived like two doves. They gossiped about us in the city, but who cared? So what if Simon the horse dealer isn't pious? So they won't call me up to the reading of the scroll. Well, but Esther wanted a baby and that was bad. It would mean that the baby would be a bastard. Some student from the study house told me that such a baby is not exactly a bastard but is called by some other name. But it's bad just the same. Esther had written to her parents that she got married and they wanted to visit us. Now the complications began. I was satisfied to be alone with her. Esther and Metzotze were enough for me. But she only wanted to go to town. She asked me if I had friends, wanted to invite guests to show off her cooking and baking. Her cooking was fit for a king. She could bake a cake which you couldn't match in the best bakeries. She dressed nicely too, but for whom? In the fields she wore a corset. She tried to persuade me to go with her to America. I wish I had listened to her, but I had no desire to travel thousands of miles. I had a house, stables, grounds. If you have to sell all this, you get almost nothing in return. What could I do in America? Press pants? Besides, I was so attached to the bird that I couldn't leave him. And it's not so easy to drag a parrot over borders and oceans. I was attached to my mare too. And where could I leave her? She wasn't young any more and if she fell into the hands of a coachman he would whip her to pieces. I said to Esther, 'We love each other, let's live quietly. Who cares what people babble about?' But she was only drawn to people. She went to the city, made acquaintances, entangled herself with low characters and the devil knows what. I let her persuade me to invite a few horse dealers to a party, but in the years when I was a widower I had kept away from everybody and no one wanted to come to the suburbs. Those who came did us a great favor. After they left, Esther burst into tears and cried until daybreak.

"Why drag it out? We began to quarrel. I mean, she quarreled. She scolded, she cursed, she cried and screamed that I had trapped her. Why didn't I tell her I was a Cohen? I didn't remember that I was a Cohen any more than you remember what you ate in your mother's belly. She lay beside me at night and kept talking as though possessed by a dybbuk. One moment she laughed; the next moment she cried. She was putting on an act, but for whom? She talked to herself and did such strange things that you wouldn't believe it was the same Esther. She called me names that you don't hear in my part of the country. Suddenly she began to be hostile to the bird. He screamed too much, he dirtied the house, he didn't let her sleep at night. She was jealous too, complaining that I loved him more than I did her.

"When this began I knew that it would have a bad ending. Was it Metzotze's fault? He was as good as an angel. At night he was quiet, but in the morning a bird doesn't lie under a quilt and snore. A bird begins to sing at daybreak. Esther, however, went to sleep at two o'clock in the morning, and at eleven at night she might begin to wash her hair or bake a cake. I saw I was in a mess, but what could I do? One minute she was sane, the next minute crazy. There's a teahouse in Kalisch where all the scum gather together. She kept on dragging me there. I sat and drank tea while she made friends with all the roughnecks. She met some strange nobody and told him all our secrets. I must have been stronger than iron not to bury myself from shame. She could be clever, but when she wanted she could act like the worst fool. It was all from spite, but what did I do to deserve it? Another man in my place would take her by the hair and throw her out, but I get used to a person. Also, I have pity.

"I can tell you, it became worse from day to day. I never knew what Gehenna was, but I had Gehenna in my own house. She picked quarrels with the maid, the Gentile, and made her leave. I had never touched her, but Esther suspected the worst. She was only looking for excuses to make trouble. She also began to pick fights with the stable boy. For years both had worked for me with devotion. Now they had to run away, and in my business you need help. You can't do everything by yourself. Horses have to be scrubbed and groomed. There are imps that come into the stables at night. Don't laugh at me. I didn't believe it either until I saw it with my own eyes. I would buy a horse and put him in the stable. I'd come in the morning and he was bathed in sweat as though he had been driven all night long over hills and ditches. He was foaming at the mouth. I would look at the mane and it would be in pigtails. Who would come at night to braid pigtails on a horse? It happened not once but ten times. These imps can torture a horse to death. I had to go down at night and keep watch. But when the groom left, I had to do his work too. In short, it was bad. When I talked she flared up; when I was silent she complained that I ignored her. She was only looking for something to pick on. I couldn't write, and she tried to teach me. She gave me one lesson and that was it. We played cards just to kill time, but she cheated. Why did she have to cheat? I gave her enough money."

"For such a piece of merchandise there is only one remedy," said Leibele. "A good swat in the kisser."

"Just what I wanted to say," Mottele Roiskes chimed in.

"I tried that too. But I have a heavy hand and when I give a blow I can cripple someone. If I touched her I had to pay the doctor. She also threatened to denounce me. But what was there to denounce? I didn't make counterfeit money. She was far from religious, but if she felt like it she could become pious. To make a fire on the Sabbath was all right, but to pour out the slops was forbidden. She changed the rules whenever it suited her. The women in the city knew of my misfortune and laughed in my face.

"It happened two years ago in the winter. I don't know how it was here, but around Kalisch there were terrible frosts. Old men couldn't remember such cold, and heating the stoves didn't help. The wind blew and broke the trees. On my place, the wind tore off a piece of the fence. Usually it's warm in the stable, but I was afraid for my horses, for when a horse catches cold it's the end. To this day I don't remember what we quarreled about that evening, but then, when didn't we quarrel? It was one long war. Sometimes at night we made peace for a few minutes, but later we didn't even do this. She slept in the bed and I on a bench. When I had to get up, she went to sleep. I'm a light sleeper—it's easy to disturb me. She crept around, boiled tea, moved chairs; she began to say the Shema and suddenly she burst out laughing like mad. She wasn't mad—she did it to spite me. She knew that I loved the parrot and she had it in for him. A parrot comes from a warm climate and if he catches a draft he's finished. But she opened the doors and let the wind blow in. He could have flown away, because he was an animal, not a man with understanding. I told her clearly, 'If anything happens to Metzotze, it's all over with you.' And she screamed, 'Go and marry him. A Cohen is allowed to marry a parrot.' I know now that it was all predestined. It's written on a man's palm or on his forehead: he will live this long; he will do this and that. But what did she have against me? I didn't stop her from going to America. I was even ready to pay her expenses.

"Where am I? Oh. Yes, I warned her, 'You can do with me whatever you want, but don't take it out on Metzotze.' Nonetheless, she screamed at him and scolded him as though he were a man. 'He's scabby, lousy, a demon's in him,' and so on. You know, a bird needs to have darkness at night. When a lamp is lit, he thinks it's day. She kept on lighting the candles, and the bird couldn't stand light at night and tucked his head under his wing. What does a bird need? A few grains of seed and a little sleep. How can a man torture a bird? One night I heard noises in the stable. I took my lantern and went to look at the horses. As I stepped over the threshold I somehow knew there would be misfortune."

For a while all was silent. Then Leibele asked, "What did she do? Chase out the parrot?"

The stranger began to murmur and to clear his throat. "Yes, in the middle of the night, in a burning frost."

"He wasn't found, huh?"

"He flew away."

"And you finished her, huh?"

The stranger paused.

"As I came back from the stable and I saw that the parrot wasn't there, I went over to her and said, 'Esther, it's your end.' I grabbed her by the hair, took her outside, and threw her into the well."

"She didn't fight back?"

"No, she went quietly."

"Still, one has to be a murderer to do something like that," Mottele Roiskes remarked.

"I am a murderer."

"What else?"

"Nothing. I went to the police and said, 'This is what I did. Take me.'"

"In the middle of the night?"

"It was already beginning to get light."

"Did they let you go to the funeral?"

"No funeral."

"They say that a Cohen is an angry man," Berele Zakelkover threw in.

"It looks that way."

"How much did they give you?"

"Eight years."

"Well, you got off easy."

"I'll never get out," the stranger said.

For a long while all were quiet. Then the stranger said, "Metzotze is still around."

"What do you mean?"

"You'll think I'm crazy, but what do I care?"

"What do you mean, around?"

"He comes to me. He perches on my shoulder."

"Are you dreaming?"

"No, it's the truth."

"You imagine it."

"He speaks. I hear his voice."

"In that case you're a little touched."

"He sleeps on my forehead."

"Well, you're out of your mind."

"A parrot has a soul."

"Nonsense," Leibele said. "If a parrot has a soul, so has a chicken. If all the chickens, geese, and ducks had souls, the world would be full of souls."

"All I know is that Metzotze visits me."

"It's because you miss him so much."

"He comes, he kisses me on the mouth. He flutters his tail against my ear."

"Will he come here too?"

"Perhaps."

"And how will he know that they sent you to Yanev?"

"He knows everything."

"Nonsense. Tell it to the doctor. They'll send you to the nuthouse. It's easy to run away from there. What about Esther? Does she visit you too?"

"No, she doesn't."

"Fantasies. The dead are dead. Men as well as animals."

The stranger stretched out on the bench again. "I know the truth."

Translated by Ruth Whitman

The Brooch

When Wolf Ber returned from the road, he always
bought gifts for Celia and the girls. This time Wolf Ber
had been in luck. He had broken into a safe and stolen
740 rubles. In addition, traveling on the railroad
second-class, he had met a wealthy Russian and had
won 150 rubles from him in a card game. Wolf Ber had
long ago reached the conclusion that everything
depended on fate: sometimes everything goes wrong;
sometimes it doesn't. This particular trip had started
right immediately. Just for fun he had tried to pick a
pocket (a safecracker is not a pickpocket) and pulled
out a purse full of bank notes. Then he had gone to a
Turkish bath, and there he found a gold watch! After
such "business" he always gave thanks to God and
dropped a coin in the poor box. Wolf Ber did not belong
to a gang and he conducted himself respectably. He
knew that thieving was a sin. But were the merchants
any better? Didn't they buy cheap and sell dear? Didn't
they bleed the poor dry? Didn't they, every few years,
go bankrupt and settle for a fraction? Wolf Ber had
once worked as a tanner in Lublin. But he had been
unable to stand the dust, the heat, the stench. The
foreman had yelled at the tanners and was forever trying
to get more work out of them. The earnings had
amounted to no more than water for groats. It was
better to rot in prison.

Wolf Ber had long since gotten used to earning his

living as a thief. He had been caught a few times but had been let off easily. He knew how to speak to the *natchalniks*: Sir .... I have a wife and children! He never talked back and did not try to play tough. In jail, far from fighting with the other prisoners, he shared his money and cigarettes with them and wrote letters for them. Wolf Ber came from a respectable home. His father, a pious man, had been a house painter. His mother had peddled tripe and calves' legs. He, Wolf Ber, was the only member of the family to become a thief. Already near forty, Wolf Ber was of medium height, with broad shoulders, brown eyes, and a beer-yellow mustache twisted in the Polish way. He wore riding pants, and boots with tight uppers that made him look like a Gentile; the Poles believed a Jew could not get his feet into such boots, because Jewish feet grew always wider and never longer. Wolf Ber's cap had a leather visor. Over his vest a watch chain dangled, with a little spoon to clean out ear wax attached to it. Other thieves carried guns or spring-knives, but Wolf Ber never had any weapons on his person. A gun will sooner or later shoot; a knife will sooner or later stab. And why shed blood? Why take upon oneself a severe punishment? Wolf Ber was a self-controlled and careful man; he was inclined to think about things and liked to read storybooks and even newspapers. Women were always trying to entice him with their charms. But Wolf Ber had one God and one wife. What could he find in others that Celia did not have? Loose females disgusted him. He never stepped over the threshold of a brothel and he detested liquor. He had a faithful wife and two well-brought-up children. He had a house and garden in Kozlow. His girls went to school. On Purim, Wolf Ber sent the rabbi a gift. Before Passover the community elders came to him to collect for the poor.

Coming home this time, Wolf Ber had bought a pair of gold earrings for Celia from a jeweler in Lublin, and for his daughters, Masha and Anka, two medallions. Until Reivitz, the last station, he had traveled by train;

then he had taken a carriage wagon, sitting up front with the driver and helping him drive. Wolf Ber had no patience with the sort of jokes and puns that the businessmen riding inside exchanged with the women. They always tried to make Wolf Ber join in the conversation but he preferred to look in silence at the trees and sky and to listen to the twittering birds. The snow was melting in the fields; the winter grain was sprouting; the sun hung low, yellow and golden, as if painted on a canvas. Now and again he saw cows nibbling fresh grass in their pastures. Warm breezes drifted over from the woods as if a summer land were hidden in the thickets. Once in a while a hare or a deer peeked out at the edge of the forest; or a turtle moved slowly across the road like a living stone.

As a rule, Wolf Ber set out from home four times a year. When things went smoothly, he never stayed away longer than six weeks. He went to the same towns, the same fairs. In Kozlow they knew what Wolf Ber did for a living—but he never stole from anyone there; and in his absence Celia could always get credit at the stores. All such debts were entered in a book, and when Wolf Ber returned he paid them to the last grosz. Once Wolf Ber had been imprisoned for several months in the Yanow jail, but the Kozlow merchants did not let Celia down. They advanced her goods for hundreds of rubles. Many times Celia complained to Wolf Ber that the shopkeepers had given her false weight or short measure or had padded the bill, but he refused to argue. That was how the world was.

As always, Wolf Ber came back to Kozlow longing for Celia and the girls, looking forward to Celia's dishes, which he could not get on the road, and to the soft bed, better than at any inn. Celia's pillowcases and sheets, luxuriously clean, were as smooth as silk and smelled of lavender. Celia always came to him in the bedroom freshly washed and combed, with her hair braided, her feet in slippers with pompoms, and dressed in a fancy nightgown. She kissed him like a bride and murmured sweet secrets into his ear. The girls were growing up:

one was ten; the other, eleven. Yet, like small children, they fell all over him, covered him with kisses, showed him their schoolbooks, their compositions, their marks, their drawings. His children were dressed like those of the gentry, in starched and pleated dresses, with alpaca aprons, hair ribbons, and shiny shoes. They spoke not only Yiddish but Russian and Polish too. They talked about foreign countries and cities of which Wolf Ber had never heard; they were versed in the histories of kings and wars and could recite by heart poems and rhymes. Wolf Ber never stopped wondering how so much knowledge could enter into such small heads. Their father's occupation was never mentioned. He was supposed to be a traveling salesman. His house stood on Church Street near the toll bridge. The Gentile neighbors did not know what he did, or perhaps only professed not to. On Christmas and Easter he would send them gifts.

The carriage wagon bringing Wolf Ber home stopped in the marketplace. Although it was not long after Purim, the sun already had a touch of Passover warmth. Golden rivulets trickled in the mud. Birds picked grain from horse dung. Peasant women, wading barefoot through the puddles, were selling horseradish, parsley, beets, and onions. Wolf Ber paid the coachman and, in the big-city manner, added twenty groszy "for beer." Lifting up his leather valise with its copper locks and sidepockets, he began to walk toward Church Street. The storekeepers followed him with their eyes. Girls parted their window curtains, wiping the mist off the glass. From somewhere Chazkele the fool emerged and Wolf Ber handed him some coins. Even the dogs around the butcher shop wagged their tails.

Thank God! Wolf Ber was going to be home for Passover. Celia would prepare a Seder; he would drain the four goblets, eat matzo pancakes, matzo balls, and gefilte fish. Since he had brought home a large sum of money, he would dress up the whole family. With such a trade as his, it was best to spend the money at once. Wolf Ber was suddenly aware of a familiar smell. He was passing a matzo bakery and stopped to look in the window. Women with flushed faces, wearing white aprons and kerchiefs on their heads, were rolling out the matzos, stopping frequently to scrape their rolling pins with pieces of glass. One woman was pouring water; another was kneading the dough; a third perforated the matzos with a pointed stick. At the oven a man was shoveling out those already baked. Near him another man with sidelocks and a skullcap gesticulated and grimaced—the overseer. Wolf Ber suddenly remembered his parents. Where were they now? Most probably in paradise. True, their son had not chosen the righteous way, but he had put up a headstone over their graves. Every year he lit a memorial candle, recited the Kaddish, and hired a man to study the Mishnah in their memory. God was merciful to sinners. If not, He would have sent down a second deluge long ago.

2.

When Wolf Ber entered Church Street, where he lived, a sudden fear came over him. A power that knows more than man seemed to be warning him against too much exuberance. Inside him, a voice seemed to say: It's not yet Passover; you are not yet at the Seder. Wolf Ber halted. Was Celia ill? Had something happened to the children? Was he, Wolf Ber, destined to end up in prison? But how? He never left any traces. Trying to dispel the premonition, he began to walk briskly between the two rows of houses, built low as for midgets and closed in with spiked fences. Through the half-melted snow pocked with holes like a sieve, the stems of last year's sunflowers stuck out. On Marchinsky's roof the storks had already returned and were mending last year's nest. Wolf Ber soon approached his own house, which had a roof shaped like a mushroom. White smoke was curling from the chimney. One pane in the front window reflected the midday sun. Well, everything is all right, Wolf Ber comforted himself. He opened the door and there was the whole family. Celia was standing at the kitchen stove in a short under-skirt, her blond hair brushed up with a knot on top, her face white and girlish, her waist cinched in; she was wearing a pair of red slippers, and her legs, broad at the calf, were narrow at the ankle. She had never looked so fresh and charming to him. The girls were sitting on stools, playing some game with bonesticks.

There was an outcry as they all ran toward him. Celia almost tipped over the pot on the stove. The girls hung on him, covering him with kisses. In the next room the parrot, apparently recognizing his master's voice, began to shriek. The moment Wolf Ber touched Celia's lips, he was full of desire. He kissed her again and again. Masha and Anka fought over him. After a while he opened his valise to take out the gifts, and that set off another outcry. When Wolf Ber went to greet the parrot, the bird, which was perched on one foot on the top of its cage, flapped its wings and landed on his shoulder. Wolf Ber kissed the bird's beak and let it taste a pretzel which he had bought for it in Lublin. The parrot had lost its winter feathers and had sprouted brightly colored new ones.

The parrot spoke. "Papa, Papa, Papa."

"Do you love Papa?"

"Love, love, love."

Well, there was no reason for fear. Wolf Ber examined the house with an expert eye. Everything gleamed: the floor, the copper pans above the oven, the brass samovar. It was the custom to whitewash the walls each year before Passover, but he could see no blemishes. "There is no better wife anywhere in the world," Wolf Ber said aloud. Earlier in the day, sitting on the wagon, he had felt tired and barely able to keep his eyes open, but now he was wide awake and gay. Celia brought him a Sabbath cookie and a glass of Vishniak.

When they had been alone in the room for a while, Celia questioned him with a glint in her eye. "How was business?"

"As long as I have you, everything goes well," Wolf Ber answered, ashamed of his profession. As a rule, Celia asked nothing about what he had done while away and he seldom told her anything. But now it seemed she had made peace with his way of making a living. Presently Wolf Ber started to talk about new clothes for her and the girls. Celia doubted that any tailor would accept new orders so near Passover. Nevertheless, they decided that she would walk over to the dry-goods stores and select materials. Celia loved to shop. Wolf Ber handed her a wad of bills and she left, taking the children with her. While shopping, she would also pay up her accounts. Wolf Ber lay down on the sofa to get some sleep. He knew Celia would prepare a rich supper and he wanted to be rested. He dozed off immediately and dreamed that he was in Lublin. He stood in an alcove somewhere, half undressed, washing himself from a trough; his body gave off a bad smell. He was again a tanner. A door opened and a women in a disheveled wig, with a dirty face, looked in and spoke angrily to him: "How long are you going to wash yourself? It's time for the Seder." Wolf Ber woke with a start. What kind of a dream was that? There was a bitter taste in his mouth. The dream had been unusually vivid. In his nostrils he could still feel the stench of rawhide. Wolf Ber reached into his breast pocket to take out the Havana cigar which had been presented to him by the Russian from whom he had won 150 rubles. Wolf Ber never smoked cigars; he rolled his own cigarettes. But he was curious now to taste a cigar that cost half a ruble. He remembered that he had once had an amber cigar holder trimmed with gold. If he was going to smoke a Havana, he might as well do it in style.

Wolf Ber got up to hunt for the cigar holder but couldn't find it. He hated to lose things. He opened all the drawers, rummaged in nooks and crannies, and searched through the oaken chest. In a drawer in the linen closet there was a tin box where Wolf Ber kept the birth certificates, the marriage contract, the mortgage papers, and other valuable documents which were seldom looked at. It was improbable that the cigar holder would be there, but Wolf Ber opened the tin box just the same. The cigar holder was not there, but on the marriage contract lay a brooch with big diamonds. Wolf Ber was stunned. What was this? He knew jewelry. These were real diamonds, not imitations. The brooch looked like an antique. The longer Wolf Ber examined it, the more his amazement grew. How did this brooch come to be here? It was neither his nor Celia's. Could Celia have saved up a nest egg and bought herself a brooch for hundreds of rubles? But such a piece could not be bought in Kozlow! Wolf Ber examined the brooch carefully and found on the reverse side two engraved letters: an aleph and a gimel. After a time he put the brooch in his inner pocket. He became depressed. He returned to the sofa and closed his eyes, trying to solve the riddle, but no matter how he racked his brain, he could find no answer. Finally he dozed off again and once more he was washing himself in that alcove in Lublin. Once more it smelled of rawhide and of chemicals used in tanneries. The disheveled woman with the wrinkled face warned him again that he would be late for the Seder. Wolf Ber woke up. What explanation could there be? Did Celia have a lover who had given her the brooch as a present? Wolf Ber felt a bitterness on his palate. He hiccuped and an unsavory taste came up from his stomach. He spat into his handkerchief. Well, there must be some answer. And what did the letters aleph and gimel mean? Was there a Jew in Kozlow who would have an affair with a married woman? And was Celia likely to do anything like that? The longer Wolf Ber pondered, the stranger the whole thing seemed to him. He paced the room. He spoke to the parrot: "You know the truth. Speak up!"

"Papa, Papa, Papa! Love, love, love!"

Dusk fell. The windowpanes turned green. Purple reflections from the sunset trembled on the wall. The parrot entered its cage, ready for the night. Wolf Ber lit the Havana cigar and sat in the dark, inhaling deeply.

The outlandish aroma made him drunk. Again and again he put his hand into his inner pocket and touched the brooch. Whenever he heard a noise outside, he listened intently. Where was his wife? Why was she taking so long? He decided not to get into any argument so long as the children were up. After a while he heard steps and voices. Celia was back. She and the girls, all three carrying packages, burst in gaily.

Celia spoke happily. "Wolf Ber, are you here? Why are you sitting in the dark? What's that you're smoking—a cigar?"

"A Russian gave it to me on the train."

"The smell makes me dizzy. We've bought out the store. Just a minute. I'll light the lamp."

"I had an amber cigar holder once. Where is it?"

"Where is it? I don't know."

The girls pranced about with the packages in their arms. Celia lit the table lamp first and then a hanging lamp that was suspended from the ceiling on bronze chains and had a gourd filled with lead pellets attached to keep it in balance. Celia had bought yards and yards of all kinds of materials, silks, woolens, velvet, and she had already had a talk with Leizer the tailor, who had promised to finish a few dresses before Passover. Now, with housewifely dispatch, she began to prepare supper. Usually the children went to bed early, but the day their father came home was a holiday. Celia had already promised them they would not have to go to school tomorrow.

3.

Wolf Ber sat at the table, praised Celia's dishes, and joked with the children, but he was not as jolly as he had been earlier. He hurried through his dinner, didn't eat much, and from time to time looked sharply at Celia. Immediately after the tea and jam and honeycake, he urged the girls to go to bed. They protested that they hadn't celebrated their father's homecoming enough. They wanted to show him their books, their maps, their drawings. But Wolf Ber insisted that all this could wait until tomorrow and that children should not sit up till all hours of the night.

After some haggling and delaying, the girls said good night. Celia had seemed to side with him, but at the same time she smiled knowingly. Apparently he was in a rush to be with her. You are eager, eh? her look seemed to ask. Wolf Ber went into the bedroom and undressed. His boots with the stiff uppers stood by the bed in soldierly fashion. He sat down on the freshly made bed. Celia was in the kitchen combing her hair and washing herself as she always did before coming to her husband. She donned a fresh nightgown, sprinkled herself with lotion, and brushed her teeth with paste the way they did in the big cities. Glancing at her image in the mirror, she thought: He will certainly not poison himself with me. . . . Celia expected Wolf Ber to extinguish the lamp immediately and make love to her, but he remained sitting up in his bed and looked at her sideways.

"Be so good as to close the door."

"Has something happened?"

"Close the door."

"It's closed."

Wolf Ber brought out the brooch from under his pillow. "Where did you get this?"

Celia lifted her eyes and her expression changed. She looked at the brooch, her face astonished, grave. "I've had it for a long time."

"How long?"

"A few years."

"Where did you get it?"

Celia did not answer immediately. Finally she raised her eyebrows. "I found it," she replied in the tone of one who does not expect to be believed.

"You found it? Where?"

"In the women's section of the synagogue."

"How often do you go to the synagogue?"

"It was Rosh Hashanah."

"And you didn't ask who'd lost it?"

"No."

"How is it you've never told me?" Wolf Ber asked after a pause.

Celia shook her head. "I don't have to tell you everything."

Man and wife spoke in low voices since the girls were not yet asleep. Wolf Ber thought it over. "Two letters are engraved on the back, an aleph and a gimel."

"Yes."

"Whose is it?"

Celia was silent. She turned to the door and made sure it was firmly shut. She moved as though she were trying to block the sounds of their conversation with her person, to keep them from reaching the children. For the first time Wolf Ber saw signs of insolence in her eyes.

"After all, you are not an investigating attorney!"

"Whose is it?" Wolf Ber raised his voice.

"Don't shout. Alte Gitel's."

In one second Wolf Ber knew everything. He remembered it all. "Alte Gitel lost her brooch at Hanukkah—not Rosh Hashanah. The whole town was in an uproar."

"Have it your way."

"How did you get it?"

"I found it."

"Where?"

"In the street."

"A minute ago you said you found it in the synagogue."

"What if I did?"

"Alte Gitel lost her brooch at Deborah Lea's wedding." Wolf Ber spoke half to Celia, half to himself. "You were there. . . . You even told me everyone was searched. . . . I remember your telling me. . . . Well, where did you hide it?"

Celia laughed shortly. "See how he interrogates me! One would think he was a saint!"

"You are a thief, aren't you?"

"If you are, why shouldn't I be?" Celia spoke rapidly

and in whispers. "Why all the fuss? The whole town knows what you do. Our children are taunted. The teachers make fun of them. If a girl loses something at school, it's our Masha and Anka who are suspected. I haven't told you all this because I didn't want to hurt you, but I'm disgraced ten times a day. So now why do you suddenly play the honest man? If I were a holy woman I would never have become your wife. That's plain enough."

"You did steal it, didn't you?"

"Yes, I stole it."

And Celia's eyes turned to him with a mixture of laughter and fear.

"How did you do it?"

"I took it off her cape—when the jester was reciting. I don't know myself why I did it. It's lain around here for years. Why were you going through my drawers?"

"I was hunting for my cigar holder."

"Your cigar holder I didn't take."

It became quiet. Wolf Ber sat up straight in his bed, his face stern, stiff. It was not that he was angry, but a sadness had come over him, as if he had heard belated news of a near relative's death. All these years he had thought Celia an honest woman and had reproached himself for bringing shame to the daughter of a good house. Occasionally she had complained about the bitter way of making a living he had chosen, telling him how the townspeople ignored her, reminding him how important it was for their children to grow up decent and with a good education. Then, when he had been arrested a few years ago in Yanow and had been in danger of a severe sentence, it was Celia who had come to Yanow and gotten him released. She had told him how she had thrown herself at the district attorney's feet, crying and pleading until he finally stopped her: "Get up, my beauty, I can't bear to see your tears any longer." It had never occurred to Wolf Ber before that perhaps this story was not the whole truth. Many times in the big cities women of dubious character had tried to entangle him, but he had always answered that he had a faithful wife in Kozlow, a fine woman who was a devoted mother of their children. He had risked his freedom so that she should want for nothing. He had even denied himself the more expensive restaurants and theaters. Now it was all for nothing. Something within him laughed: You are a fool, Wolf Ber, a damned fool! He felt nauseous and as though in these last few minutes old age had overtaken him.

He heard Celia's voice. "Shall I put out the lamp?"

"If you want to."

Celia blew out the night lamp and went to her bed. For a long time there was silence. Wolf Ber listened to himself. An icy coldness enveloped him, like a cold poultice around his chest.

"Did you sleep with the district attorney?"

"I don't know what you're talking about."

"You know very well!"

"You must have lost your mind."

Wolf Ber stretched out, closed his eyes, and lay silently on the cool sheet. In the other room the girls still whispered and giggled. An early spring breeze was blowing outside and it shook the shutters. Beams of moonlight sifted in through the cracks. From time to time Celia's bed creaked. Wolf Ber had come home full of lust for Celia, but now all desire had left him. Everything is finished, he said to himself. The seven good years are over. Something in him mourned. Who could tell—perhaps the children were not his own? There was no more point to dragging himself about on trains, sleeping in cheap hostelries, endangering his life at fairs. If she is a thief, I must become an honest man, he murmured. There is no place in the family for two thieves!

Wolf Ber was himself baffled at this queer idea. Nevertheless, he knew there was no other way. For some time he lay quietly and listened in the dark. Then he put his feet down on the floor.

"Where are you going?"

"To Lublin."

"In the middle of the night?"

"In the middle of the night."

"What are you going to do in Lublin?" Celia asked. And Wolf Ber answered: "Become a tanner."

Translated by Alma Singer and Elizabeth Pollet

The Letter Writer

Herman Gombiner opened an eye. This was the way he woke up each morning—gradually, first with one eye, then the other. His glance met a cracked ceiling and part of the building across the street. He had gone to bed in the early hours, at about three. It had taken him a long time to fall asleep. Now it was close to ten o'clock. Lately, Herman Gombiner had been suffering from a kind of amnesia. When he got up during the night, he couldn't remember where he was, who he was, or even his name. It took a few seconds to realize that he was no longer in Kalomin, or in Warsaw, but in New York, uptown on one of the streets between Columbus Avenue and Central Park West.

It was winter. Steam hissed in the radiator. The Second World War was long since over. Herman (or Hayim David, as he was called in Kalomin) had lost his family to the Nazis. He was now an editor, proofreader, and translator in a Hebrew publishing house called Zion. It was situated on Canal Street. He was a bachelor, almost fifty years old, and a sick man.

"What time is it?" he mumbled. His tongue was coated, his lips cracked. His knees ached; his head pounded; there was a bitter taste in his mouth. With an effort he got up, setting his feet down on the worn carpet that covered the floor. "What's this? Snow?" he muttered. "Well, it's winter."

He stood at the window awhile and looked out. The

broken-down cars parked on the street jutted from the snow like relics of a long-lost civilization. Usually the street was filled with rubbish, noise, and children—Negro and Puerto Rican. But now the cold kept everyone indoors. The stillness, the whiteness made him think of his old home, of Kalomin. Herman stumbled toward the bathroom.

The bedroom was an alcove, with space only for a bed. The living room was full of books. On one wall there were cabinets from floor to ceiling, and along the other stood two bookcases. Books, newspapers, and magazines lay everywhere, piled in stacks. According to the lease, the landlord was obliged to paint the apartment every three years, but Herman Gombiner had bribed the superintendent to leave him alone. Many of his old books would fall apart if they were moved. Why is new paint better than old? The dust had gathered in layers. A single mouse had found its way into the apartment, and every night Herman set out for her a piece of bread, a small slice of cheese, and a saucer of water to keep her from eating the books. Thank goodnes she didn't give birth. Occasionally, she would venture out of her hole even when the light was on. Herman had even given her a Hebrew name: Huldah. Her little bubble eyes stared at him with curiosity. She stopped being afraid of him.

The building in which Herman lived had many faults, but it did not lack heat. The radiators sizzled from early morning till late at night. The owner, himself a Puerto Rican, would never allow his tenants' children to suffer from the cold.

There was no shower in the bathroom, and Herman bathed daily in the tub. A mirror that was cracked down the middle hung inside the door, and Herman caught a glimpse of himself—a short man, in oversize pajamas, emaciated to skin and bone, with a scrawny neck and a large head, on either side of which grew two tufts of gray hair. His forehead was wide and deep, his nose crooked, his cheekbones high. Only in his dark eyes, with long lashes like a girl's, had there remained any trace of youthfulness. At times, they even seemed to twinkle shrewdly. Many years of reading and poring over tiny letters hadn't blurred his vision or made him nearsighted. The remaining strength in Herman Gombiner's body—a body worn out by illnesses and undernourishment—seemed to be concentrated in his gaze.

He shaved slowly and carefully. His hand, with its long fingers, trembled, and he could easily have cut himself. Meanwhile, the tub filled with warm water. He undressed, and was amazed at his thinness—his chest was narrow, his arms and legs bony; there were deep hollows between his neck and shoulders. Getting into the bathtub was a strain, but then lying in the warm water was a relief. Herman always lost the soap. It would slip out of his hands playfully, like a live thing, and he would search for it in the water. "Where are you running?" he would say to it. "You rascal!" He believed there was life in everything, that the so-called inanimate objects had their own whims and caprices.

Herman Gombiner considered himself to be among the select few privileged to see beyond the façade of phenomena. He had seen a blotter raise itself from the desk, slowly and unsteadily float toward the door, and, once there, float gently down, as if suspended by an invisible string held by some unseen hand. The whole thing had been thoroughly senseless. No matter how much Herman thought about it, he was unable to figure out any reason for what had taken place. It had been one of those extraordinary happenings that cannot be explained by science, or religion, or folklore. Later, Herman had bent down and picked up the blotter, and placed it back on the desk, where it remained to this day, covered with papers, dusty, and dried out—an inanimate object that for one moment had somehow freed itself from physical laws. Herman Gombiner knew that it had been neither a hallucination nor a dream. It had taken place in a well-lit room at eight in the evening. He hadn't been ill or even upset that day. He never drank liquor, and he had been wide awake. He had been standing next to the chest, about to take a handkerchief out of a drawer. Suddenly his gaze had been attracted to the desk and he had seen the blotter rise and float. Nor was this the only such incident. Such things had been happening to him since childhood.

Everything took a long time—his bath, drying himself, putting on his clothes. Hurrying was not for him. His competence was the result of deliberateness. The proofreaders at Zion worked so quickly they missed errors. The translators hardly took the time to check meanings they were unsure of in the dictionary. The majority of American and even Israeli Hebraists knew little of vowel points and the subtleties of grammar. Herman Gombiner had found the time to study all these things. It was true that he worked very slowly, but the old man, Morris Korver, who owned Zion, and even his sons, the half Gentiles, had always appreciated the fact that it was Herman Gombiner who had earned the house its reputation. Morris Korver, however, had become old and senile, and Zion was in danger of closing. It was rumored that his sons could hardly wait for the old man to die so they could liquidate the business.

Even if Herman wanted to, it was impossible for him to do anything in a hurry. He took small steps when he walked. It took him half an hour to eat a bowl of soup. Searching for the right word in a dictionary or checking something in an encyclopedia could involve hours of work. The few times that he had tried to hurry had ended in disaster; he had broken his foot, sprained his hand, fallen down the stairs, even been run over. Every trifle had become a trial to him—shaving, dressing, taking the wash to the Chinese laundry, eating a meal in a restaurant. Crossing the street, too, was a problem, because no sooner would the light turn green than it turned red again. Those behind the wheels of cars possessed the speed and morals of automatons. If a person couldn't run fast enough, they were capable of driving right over him. Recently, he had begun to suffer from tremors of the hands and feet. He had once had a meticulous handwriting, but he could no longer write. He used a typewriter, typing with his right index finger. Old Korver insisted that all Gombiner's troubles came from the fact that he was a vegetarian; without a piece of meat, one loses strength. Herman couldn't take a bite of meat if his life depended on it.

Herman put one sock on and rested. He put on the second sock, and rested again. His pulse rate was slow—fifty or so beats a minute. The least strain and he felt dizzy. His soul barely survived in his body. It had happened on occasion, as he lay in bed or sat on a chair, that his disembodied spirit had wandered around the house, or had even gone out the window. He had seen his own body in a faint, apparently dead. Who could enumerate all the apparitions, telepathic incidents, clairvoyant visions, and prophetic dreams he experienced! And who would believe him? As it was, his co-workers derided him. The elder Korver needed only a glass of brandy and he would call Herman a superstitious greenhorn. They treated him like some outlandish character.

Herman Gombiner had long ago arrived at the conclusion that modern man was as fanatic in his nonbelief as ancient man had been in his faith. The rationalism of the present generation was in itself an example of preconceived ideas. Communism, psychoanalysis, Fascism, and radicalism were the shibboleths of the twentieth century. Oh, well! What could he, Herman Gombiner, do in the face of all this? He had no choice but to observe and be silent.

"Well, it's winter, winter!" Herman Gombiner said to himself in a voice half chanting, half groaning. "When will it be Hanukkah? Winter has started early this year." Herman was in the habit of talking to himself. He had always done so. The uncle who raised him had been deaf. His grandmother, rest her soul, would wake up in the middle of the night to recite penitential prayers and lamentations found only in outdated prayer books. His father had died before Herman—Hayim David—was born. His mother had remarried in a far-

away city and had had children by her second husband.
Hayim David had always kept to himself, even when
he attended heder or studied at the yeshiva. Now, since
Hitler had killed all of his family, he had no relatives
to write letters to. He wrote letters to total strangers.

"What time is it?" Herman asked himself again. He
dressed in a dark suit, a white shirt, and a black tie,
and went out to the kitchenette. An icebox without ice
and a stove that he never used stood there. Twice a
week the milkman left a bottle of milk at the door.
Herman had a few cans of vegetables, which he ate on
days when he didn't leave the house. He had discovered
that a human being requires very little. A half cup of
milk and a pretzel could suffice for a whole day. One
pair of shoes served Herman for five years. His suit,
coat, and hat never wore out. Only his laundry showed
some wear, and not from use but from the chemicals
used by the Chinese laundryman. The furniture certainly never wore out. Were it not for his expenditures
on cabs and gifts, he could have saved a good deal of
money.

He drank a glass of milk and ate a biscuit. Then he
carefully put on his black coat, a woolen scarf, rubbers,
and a felt hat with a broad brim. He packed his
briefcase with books and manuscripts. It became heav-
ier from day to day, not because there was more in it
but because his strength diminished. He slipped on a
pair of dark glasses to protect his eyes from the glare of
the snow. Before he left the apartment, he bade farewell to the bed, the desk piled high with papers (under
which the blotter lay), the books, and the mouse in the
hole. He had poured out yesterday's stale water, refilled
the saucer, and set out a cracker and a small piece of
cheese. "Well, Huldah, be well!"

Radios blared in the hallway. Dark-skinned women
with uncombed hair and angry eyes spoke in an
unusually thick Spanish. Children ran around half
naked. The men were apparently all unemployed. They
paced idly about in their overcrowded quarters, ate
standing up, or strummed mandolins. The odors from

the apartments made Herman feel faint. All kinds of
meat and fish were fried there. The halls reeked of
garlic, onion, smoke, and something pungent and nau-
seating. At night his neighbors danced and laughed
wantonly. Sometimes there was fighting and women
screamed for help. Once a woman had come pounding
on Herman's door in the middle of the night, seeking
protection from a man who was trying to stab her.

2.

Herman stopped downstairs at the mailboxes. The
other residents seldom received any mail, but Herman
Gombiner's box was packed tight every morning. He
took his key out, fingers trembling, inserted it in the
keyhole, and pulled out the mail. He was able to
recognize who had sent the letters by their envelopes.
Alice Grayson, of Salt Lake City, used a rose-colored
envelope. Mrs. Roberta Hoff, of Pasadena, California,
sent all her mail in the business envelopes of the
undertaking establishment for which she worked. Miss
Bertha Gordon, of Fairbanks, Alaska, apparently had
many leftover Christmas-card envelopes. Today Herman
found a letter from a new correspondent, a Mrs. Rose
Beechman, of Louisville, Kentucky. Her name and
address were hand-printed, with flourishes, across the
back of the envelope. Besides the letters, there were
several magazines on occultism to which Herman
Gombiner subscribed—from America, England, and
even Australia. There wasn't room in his briefcase for
all these letters and periodicals, so Herman stuffed
them into his coat pocket. He went outside and waited
for a taxi.

It was rare for a taxi, particularly an empty one, to
drive down this street, but it was too much of an effort
for him to walk the half block to Central Park West or
Columbus Avenue. Herman Gombiner fought his weakness with prayer and autosuggestion. Standing in the
snow, he muttered a prayer for a taxi. He repeatedly
put his hand into his pocket and fingered the letters in

their envelopes. These letters and magazines had become the essence of his life. Through them he had established contact with souls. He had acquired the friendship and even the love of women. The accounts he received from them strengthened his belief in psychic powers and in the world beyond. He sent gifts to his unknown correspondents and received gifts from them. They called him by his first name, revealed their thoughts, dreams, hopes, and the messages they received through the Ouija board, automatic writing, table turning, and other supernatural sources.

Herman Gombiner had established correspondences with these women through the periodicals he subscribed to, where not only accounts of readers' experiences were published but their contributors' names and addresses as well. The articles were mainly written by women. Herman Gombiner always selected those who lived far away. He wished to avoid meetings. He could sense from the way an experience was related, from a name or an address, whether the woman would be capable of carrying on a correspondence. He was almost never wrong. A small note from him would call forth a long letter in reply. Sometimes he received entire manuscripts. His correspondence had grown so large that postage cost him several dollars a week. Many of his letters were sent out special delivery or registered.

Miracles were a daily occurrence. No sooner had he finished his prayer than a taxi appeared. The driver pulled up to the house as if he had received a telepathic command. Getting into the taxi exhausted Herman, and he sat a long while resting his head against the window with his eyes shut, praising whatever Power had heard his supplication. One had to be blind not to acknowledge the hand of Providence, or whatever you wanted to call it. Someone was concerned with man's most trivial requirements.

His disembodied spirit apparently roamed to the most distant places. All his correspondents had seen him. In one night he had been in Los Angeles and in

Mexico City, in Oregon and in Scotland. It would come to him that one of his faraway friends was ill. Before long, he would receive a letter saying that she had indeed been ill and hospitalized. Over the years, several had died, and he had had a premonition each time.

For the past few weeks, Herman had had a strong feeling that Zion was going to close down. True, this had been predicted for years, but Herman had always known that it was only a rumor. And just recently the employees had become optimistic; business had improved. The old man talked of a deficit, but everybody knew he was lying in order to avoid raising salaries. The house had published a prayer book that was a best-seller. The new Hebrew-English dictionary that Herman Gombiner was completing had every chance of selling tens of thousands of copies. Nevertheless, Herman sensed a calamity just as surely as his rheumatic knees foretold a change in the weather.

The taxi drove down Columbus Avenue. Herman glanced out the window and closed his eyes again. What is there to see on a wintry day in New York? He remained wrapped up in his gloom. No matter how many sweaters he put on, he was always cold. Besides, one is less aware of the spirits, the psychic contacts, during the cold weather. Herman raised his collar higher and put his hands in his pockets. A violent kind of civilization developed in cold countries. He should never have settled in New York. If he were living in southern California, he wouldn't be enslaved by the weather in this way. Oh, well . . . And was there a Jewish publishing house to be found in southern California?

3.

The taxi stopped on Canal Street. Herman paid his fare and added a fifty-cent tip. He was frugal with himself, but when it came to cabdrivers, waiters, and elevator men, he was generous. At Christmastime he even bought gifts for his Puerto Rican neighbors. Today

Sam, the elevator man, was apparently having a cup of coffee in the cafeteria across the street, and Herman had to wait. Sam did as he pleased. He came from the same city as Morris Korver. He was the only elevator man, so that when he didn't feel like coming in the tenants had to climb the stairs. He was a Communist besides.

Herman waited ten minutes before Sam arrived—a short man, broad-backed, with a face that looked as if it had been put together out of assorted pieces: a short forehead, thick brows, bulging eyes with big bags beneath them, and a bulbous nose covered with cherry-red moles. His walk was unsteady. Herman greeted him, but he grumbled in answer. The Yiddish leftist paper stuck out of his back pocket. He didn't shut the elevator door at once. First he coughed several times, then lit a cigar. Suddenly he spat and called out, "You've heard the news?"

"What's happened?"

"They've sold the building."

"Aha, so that's it!" Herman said to himself. "Sold? How come?" he asked.

"How come? Because the old wise guy is senile and his sonny boys don't give a damn. A garage is what's going up here. They'll knock down the building and throw the books on the garbage dump. Nobody will get a red cent out of these Fascist bastards!"

"When did it happen?"

"It happened, that's all."

Well, I *am* clairvoyant, Herman thought. He remained silent. For years, the editorial staff had talked about joining a union and working out a pension plan, but talk was as far as they had got. The elder Korver had seen to that. Wages were low, but he would slip some of his cronies an occasional five- or ten-dollar bonus. He gave out money at Hanukkah, sent Purim gifts, and in general acted like an old-style European boss. Those who opposed him were fired. The bookkeepers and other workers could perhaps get jobs elsewhere, but the writers and editors would have nowhere to go.

Judaica was becoming a vanishing specialty in America. When Jews died, their religious and Hebrew books were donated to libraries or were simply thrown out. Hitlerism and the war had caused a temporary upsurge, but not enough to make publishing religious works in Hebrew profitable.

"Well, the seven fat years are over," Herman muttered to himself. The elevator went up to the third floor. It opened directly into the editorial room—a large room with a low ceiling, furnished with old desks and outmoded typewriters. Even the telephones were old-fashioned. The room smelled of dust, wax, and something stuffy and stale.

Raphael Robbins, Korver's editor-in-chief, sat on a cushioned chair and read a manuscript, his eyeglasses pushed down to the tip of his nose. He suffered from hemorrhoids and had prostate trouble. A man of medium height, he was broad-shouldered, with a round head and a protruding belly. Loose folds of skin hung under his eyes. His face expressed a grandfatherly kindliness and an old woman's shrewdness. For years his chief task had consisted of eating lunch with old Korver. Robbins was known to be a boaster, a liar, and a flatterer. He owned a library of pornographic books—a holdover from his youth. Like Sam, he came from the same city as Morris Korver. Raphael Robbins's son, a physicist, had worked on the atomic bomb. His daughter had married a rich Wall Street broker. Raphael Robbins himself had accumulated some capital and was old enough to receive his Social Security pension. As Robbins read the manuscript, he scratched his bald pate and shook his head. He seldom returned a manuscript, and many of them were lying about gathering dust on the table, in his two bookcases, and on cabinets in the kitchenette where the workers brewed tea.

The man who had made Morris Korver rich and on whose shoulders the publishing house had rested for years was Professor Yohanan Abarbanel, a compiler of dictionaries. No one knew where his title came from. He had never received a degree or even attended a university. It was said that old Korver had made him a professor. In addition to compiling several dictionaries, Abarbanel had edited a collection of sermons with quotations for rabbis, written study books for bar-mitzvah boys, and put together other handbooks, which had run into many editions. A bachelor in his seventies, Yohanan Abarbanel had had a heart attack and had undergone surgery for a hernia. He worked for a pittance, lived in a cheap hotel, and each year worried that he might be laid off. He had several poor relatives whom he supported. He was a small man, with white hair, a white beard, and a small face, red as a frozen apple; his little eyes were hidden by white bushy eyebrows. He sat at a table and wheezed and coughed, and all the while wrote in a tiny handwriting with a steel pen. The last few years, he couldn't be trusted to complete any work by himself. Each word was read over by Herman Gombiner, and whole manuscripts had to be rewritten.

For some reason, no one in the office ever greeted anyone else with a "hello" or a "good morning" on arrival, or said anything at closing time. During the day, they did occasionally exchange a few friendly words. It might even happen that, not having addressed a word to one another for months, one of them might go over to a colleague and pour out his heart, or actually invite him to supper. But then the next morning they would again behave as if they had quarreled. Over the years they had become bored with one another. Complaints and grudges had accumulated and were never quite forgotten.

Miss Lipshitz, the secretary, who had started working at Zion when she was just out of college, was now entirely gray. She sat at her typewriter—small, plump, and pouting, with a short neck and an ample bosom. She had a pug nose and eyes that seemed never to look at the manuscript she was typing but stared far off, past the walls. Days would pass without her voice being heard. She muttered into the telephone. When she ate lunch in the restaurant across the street, she would sit alone at a table, eating, smoking, and reading a newspaper simultaneously. There was a time when everyone in the office—old Mr. Korver included—had either openly or secretly been in love with this clever girl who knew English, Yiddish, Hebrew, stenography, and much more. They used to ask her to the theater and the movies and quarreled over who should take her to lunch, For years now, Miss Lipshitz had isolated herself. Old man Korver said that she had shut herself up behind an invisible wall.

Herman nodded to her, but she didn't respond. He walked past Ben Melnick's office. Melnick was the business manager—tall, swarthy, with a young face, black bulging eyes, and a head of milky-white hair. He suffered from asthma and played the horses. All sorts of shifty characters came to see him—bookies. He was separated from his wife and was carrying on a love affair with Miss Potter, the chief bookkeeper, another relative of Morris Korver's.

Herman Gombiner went into his own office. Walking through the editorial room, and not being greeted, was a strain for him. Korver employed a man to keep the place clean—Zeinvel Gitzis—but Zeinvel neglected his work; the walls were filthy, the windows unwashed. Packs of dusty manuscripts and newspapers had been lying around for years.

Herman carefully removed his coat and laid it on a stack of books. He sat down on a chair that had horsehair sticking through its upholstery. Work? What was the sense of working when the firm was closing down? He sat shaking his head—half out of weakness, half from regret. "Well, everything has to have an end," he muttered. "It is predestined that no human institution will last forever." He reached over and pulled the mail out of his coat pocket. He inspected the envelopes, without opening any of them. He came back to Rose Beechman's letter from Louisville, Kentucky. In a magazine called the *Message*, Mrs. Beechman had reported her contacts over the last fifteen years with her dead grandmother, Mrs. Eleanor Brush. The grandmother usually materialized during the night, though sometimes she would also appear in the daylight, dressed in her funeral clothes. She was full of advice for her granddaughter, and once she even gave her a recipe for fried chicken. Herman had written to Rose Beechman, but seven weeks had passed without a reply. He had almost given up hope, although he had continued sending her telepathic messages. She had been ill—Herman was certain of it.

Now her letter lay before him in a light-blue envelope. Opening it wasn't easy for him. He had to resort to using his teeth. He finally removed six folded sheets of light-blue stationery and read:

Dear Mr. Gombiner:

I am writing this letter to you a day after my return from the hospital where I spent almost two months. I was operated on for the removal of a spinal tumor. There was danger of paralysis or worse. But fate, it seems, still wants me here. . . . Apparently, my little story in the *Message* caused quite a furor. During my illness, I received dozens of letters from all parts of the country and from England.

It so happened that my daughter put your letter at the bottom of the pile, and had I read them in order, it might have taken several weeks more before I came to yours. But a premonition—what else can I call it?—made me open the very last letter first. It was then that I realized, from the postmark, yours had been among the first, if not the very first, to arrive. It seems I always do things not as I intend to but according to a command from someone or something that I am unaware of. All I can say is: this "something" has been with me as long as I can remember, perhaps even since before I was capable of thinking.

Your letter is so logical, so noble and fascinating, that I may say it has brightened my homecoming. My daughter has a job in an office and has neither the time nor the patience to look after the house. When I returned, I found things in a sorry state. I am by nature a meticulous housekeeper who cannot abide disorder, and so you can imagine my feelings. But your profound and truly remarkable thoughts, as well as the friendliness and humanity implicit in them, helped me to forget my troubles. I read your letter three times and thanked God that people with your understanding and faith exist.

You ask for details. My dear Mr. Gombiner, if I were to relate all the facts, no letter would suffice. I could fill a whole book. Don't forget that these experiences have been going on for fifteen years. My saintly grandmother visited me every day in the hospital. She literally took over the work of the nurses, who are not, as you may know, overly devoted to their patients—nor do they have the time to be. Yes, to describe it all "exactly," as you request, would take weeks, months. I can only repeat that everything I wrote in the *Message* was the honest truth. Some of my correspondents call me "crackpot," "crazy," "charlatan." They accuse me of lying and publicity-seeking. Why should I tell lies and why do I need publicity? It was, therefore, especially pleasing to read your wonderful sentiments. I see from the letterhead that you are a Jew and connected with a Hebrew publishing house. I wish to assure you that I have always had the highest regard for Jews, God's chosen people. There are not very many Jews here in Louisville, and my personal contact has been only with Jews who have little interest in their religion. I have always wanted to become acquainted with a real Jew, who reveres the tradition of the Holy Fathers.

Now I come to the main point of my letter, and I beg you to forgive my rambling. The night before I left the hospital, my beloved grandmother, Mrs. Brush, visited with me till dawn. We chatted about various matters, and just before her departure she said to me, "This winter you will go to New York, where you will meet a man who will change the direction of your life." These were her parting words. I must add here that although for the past fifteen years I have been fully convinced that my grandmother never spoke idly and that whatever she said had meaning, at that moment for the first time I felt some doubt. What business did I, a widow living on a small pension, have in a far-off New York? And what man in New York could possibly alter my existence?

It is true I am not yet old—just above forty—and considered an attractive woman. (I beg you not to think me vain. I simply wish to clarify the situation.) But when my husband

died eight years ago, I decided that was that. I was left with a
twelve-year-old daughter and wished to devote all my ener-
gies to her upbringing, and I did. She is today good-looking,
has gone through business school and has an excellent position with a real-estate firm, and she is engaged to marry an
extremely interesting and well-educated man (a government
official). I feel she will be very happy.

I have since my husband's death received proposals from
men, but I have always rejected them. My grandmother, it
seems, must have agreed with me, because I never heard
anything to the contrary from her. I mention this because my
grandmother's talk of a trip to New York and the man I
would meet there seemed so unlikely that I believed she had
said it just to cheer me up after my illness. Later, her words
actually slipped my mind.

Imagine my surprise when today, on my return from the
hospital, I received a registered letter from a Mr. Ginsburg, a
New York lawyer, notifying me of the death of my great-aunt
Catherine Pennell and telling me that she had left me a sum
of almost five thousand dollars. Aunt Catherine was a
spinster and had severed her ties with our family over fifty
years ago, before I was born. As far as we knew, she had lived
on a farm in Pennsylvania. My father had sometimes talked
about her and her eccentricities, but I had never met her nor
did I know whether she was alive or dead. How she wound up
in New York is a mystery to me, as is the reason for her
choosing to leave me money. These are the facts, and I must
come to New York concerning the bequest. Documents have
to be signed and so forth.

When I read the lawyer's letter and then your highly
interesting and dear one, I suddenly realized how foolish I
had been to doubt my grandmother's words. She has never
made a prediction that didn't later prove true, and I will
never doubt her again.

This letter is already too long and my fingers are tired from
holding the pen. I simply wish to inform you that I will be in
New York for several days in January, or at the latest in
early February, and I would consider it a privilege and an
honor to meet you personally.

I cannot know what the Powers that be have in store for

me, but I know that meeting you will be an important event in my life, as I hope meeting me will be for you. I have extraordinary things to tell you. In the meantime, accept my deepest gratitude and my fondest regards.

I am, very truly yours,
Rose Beechman

4.

Everything happened quickly. One day they talked about closing down the publishing house, and the next day it was done. Morris Korver and his sons called a meeting of the staff. Korver himself spoke in Yiddish, pounded his fist on a bookstand, and shouted with the loud voice of a young man. He warned the workers that if they didn't accept the settlement he and his sons had worked out, none of them would get a penny. One son, Seymour, a lawyer, had a few words to say, in English. In contrast with his father's shouting, Seymour spoke quietly. The older employees who were hard of hearing moved their chairs closer and turned up their hearing aids. Seymour displayed a list of figures. The publishing house, he said, had in the last few years lost several hundred thousand dollars. How much can a business lose? There it all was, written down in black and white.

After the bosses left, the writers and office workers voted whether or not to agree to the proposed terms. The majority voted to accept. It was argued that Korver had secretly bribed some employees to be on his side, but what was the difference? Every worker was to receive his final check the following day. The manuscripts were left lying on the tables. Sam had already brought up men from the demolition company.

Raphael Robbins carefully put into his satchel the little cushion on which he sat, a magnifying glass, and a drawerful of medicine. He took leave of everyone with the shrewd smile of a man who knew everything in advance and therefore was never surprised. Yohanan Abarbanel took a single dictionary home with him. Miss Lipshitz, the secretary, walked around with red,

weepy eyes all morning. Ben Melnick brought a huge
trunk and packed his private archives, consisting of
horse-racing forms.

Herman Gombiner was too feeble to pack the letters
and books that had accumulated in his bookcase. He
opened a drawer, looked at the dust-covered papers,
and immediately started coughing. He said goodbye to
Miss Lipshitz, handed Sam a last five-dollar tip, went
to the bank to cash the check, and then waited for a
taxi.

For many years, Herman Gombiner had lived in fear
of the day when he would be without a job. But when
he got into the taxi to go home at one o'clock in the
afternoon, he felt the calm of resignation. He never
turned his head to look back at the place in which he
had wasted almost thirty years. A wet snow was falling. The sky was gray. Sitting in the taxi, leaning his
head back against the seat, with eyes closed, Herman
Gombiner compared himself to a corpse returning from
its own funeral. This is probably the way the soul
leaves the body and starts its spiritual existence, he
thought.

He had figured everything out. With the almost two
thousand dollars he had saved in the bank, the money
he had received from Morris Korver, and unemploy-
ment insurance, he would be able to manage for two
years—perhaps even a few months longer. Then he
would have to go on relief. There was no sense in even
trying to get another job. Herman had from childhood
begged God not to make him dependent on charity, but
it had evidently been decided differently. Unless, of
course, death redeemed him first.

Thank God it was warm in the house. Herman looked
at the mouse's hole. In what way was he, Herman,
better than she? Huldah also had to depend on someone. He took out a notebook and pencil and started to
calculate. He would no longer need to pay for two taxis
daily, or have to eat lunch in a restaurant, or leave a
tip for the waiter. There would be no more contribu-
tions for all kinds of collections—for Palestine, for

employees' children or grandchildren who were getting married, for retirement gifts. He certainly wouldn't be paying any more taxes. Herman examined his clothes closet. He had enough shirts and shoes to last him another ten years. He needed money only for rent, bread, milk, magazines, and stamps. There had been a time when he considered getting a telephone in his apartment. Thank God he had not done it. With these six dollars he could manage for a week. Without realizing it would come to this, Herman had for years practiced the art of reducing his expenditures to a minimum, lowering the wick of life, so to speak.

Never before had Herman Gombiner enjoyed his apartment as he did on that winter day when he returned home after the closing of the publishing house. People had often complained to him about their loneliness, but as long as there were books and stationery and as long as he could sit on a chair next to the radiator and meditate, he was never alone. From the neighboring apartments he could hear the laughter of children, women talking, and the loud voices of men. Radios were turned on full blast. In the street, boys and girls were playing noisily.

The short day grew darker and darker, and the house filled with shadows. Outside, the snow took on an unusual blue coloring. Twilight descended. "So, a day has passed," Herman said to himself. This particular day, this very date would never return again, unless Nietzsche was right in his theory about the eternal return. Even if one did believe that time was imaginary, this day was finished, like the flipped page of a book. It had passed into the archives of eternity. But what had he, Herman Gombiner, accomplished? Whom had he helped? Not even the mouse. She had not come out of her hole, not a peep out of her all day. Was she sick? She was no longer young; old age crept up on everyone. . . .

As Herman sat in the wintry twilight, he seemed to be waiting for a sign from the Powers on high. Sometimes he received messages from them, but at other

The Letter Writer **239**

times they remained hidden and silent. He found himself thinking about his parents, grandparents, his sisters, brother, aunts, uncles, and cousins. Where were they all? Where were they resting, blessed souls, martyred by the Nazis. Did they ever think of him? Or had they risen into spheres where they were no longer concerned with the lower worlds? He started to pray to them, inviting them to visit him on this winter evening.

The steam in the radiator hissed, singing its one note. The steam seemed to speak in the pipes, consoling Herman: "You are not alone, you are an element of the universe, a child of God, an integral part of Creation. Your suffering is God's suffering, your yearning His yearning. Everything is right. Let the Truth be revealed to you, and you will be filled with joy."

Suddenly Herman heard a squeak. In the dimness, the mouse had crawled out and looked cautiously around, as if afraid that a cat lurked nearby. Herman held his breath. Holy creature, have no fear. No harm will come to you. He watched her as she approached the saucer of water, took one sip, then a second and a third. Slowly she started gnawing the piece of cheese.

Can there be any greater wonder, Herman thought. Here stands a mouse, a daughter of a mouse, a granddaughter of mice, a product of millions, billions of mice who once lived, suffered, reproduced, and are now gone forever, but have left an heir, apparently the last of her line. Here she stands, nourishing herself with food. What does she think about all day in her hole? She must think about something. She does have a mind, a nervous system. She is just as much a part of God's creation as the planets, the stars, the distant galaxies.

The mouse suddenly raised her head and stared at Herman with a human look of love and gratitude. Herman imagined that she was saying thank you.

5.

Since Herman Gombiner had stopped working, he realized what an effort it had been for him to wake up in

the morning, to wait outside for a cab, to waste his time
with dictionaries, writing, editing, and traveling home
again each evening. He had apparently been working
with the last of his strength. It seemed to him that the
publishing house had closed on the very day that he
had expended his last bit of remaining energy. This
fact in itself was an excellent example of the presence
of Godly compassion and the hand of Providence. But
thank heaven he still had the will to read and write
letters.

Snow had fallen. Herman couldn't recall another
New York winter with as much snow as this. Huge
drifts had piled up. It was impossible for cars to drive
through his street. Herman would have had to plow his
way to Columbus Avenue or Central Park West to get
a taxi. He would surely have collapsed. Luckily, the
delivery boy from the grocery store didn't forget him.
Every other day he brought up rolls, sometimes eggs,
cheese, and whatever else Herman had ordered. His
neighbors would knock on his door and ask him whether
he needed anything—coffee, tea, fruit. He thanked
them profusely. Poor as he was, he always gave a
mother a nickel to buy some chocolate for her child. The
women never left at once; they lingered awhile and
spoke to him in their broken English, looking at him as
if they regretted having to go. Once, a woman stroked
Herman's head gently. Women had always been
attracted to him.

There had been times when women had fallen
desperately in love with him, but marriage and a
family were not for Herman. The thought of raising
children seemed absurd to him. Why prolong the human
tragedy? Besides, he had always sent every last cent to
Kalomin.

His thoughts kept returning to the past. He was back
in Kalomin. He was going to heder, studying at a
yeshiva, secretly teaching himself modern Hebrew,
Polish, German, taking lessons, instructing others. He
experienced his first love affair, the meetings with
girls, strolls in the woods, to the watermill, to the

cemetery. He had been drawn to cemeteries even as a youngster, and would spend hours there, meditating among the tombstones and listening to their stony silence. The dead spoke to him from their graves. In the Kalomin cemetery there grew tall, white-barked birch trees. Their silvery leaves trembled in the slightest breeze, chattering their leafy dialect all day. The boughs leaned over each other, whispering secrets.

Later came the trip to America and wandering around New York without a job. Then he went to work for Zion and began studying English. He had been fairly healthy at that time and had had affairs with women. It was difficult to believe the many triumphs he had had. On lonely nights, details of old episodes and never-forgotten words came to him. Memory itself demonstrates that there is no oblivion. Words a woman had uttered to him thirty years before and that he hadn't really understood at the time would suddenly become clear. Thank God he had enough memories to last him a hundred years.

For the first time since he had come to America, his windows froze over. Frost trees like those in Kalomin formed on the windowpanes—upside-down palms, exotic shrubs, and strange flowers. The frost painted like an artist, but its patterns were eternal. Crystals? What were crystals? Who had taught the atoms and molecules to arrange themselves in this or that way? What was the connection between the molecules in New York and the molecules in Kalomin?

The greatest wonders began when Herman dozed off. As soon as he closed his eyes, his dreams came like locusts. He saw everything with clarity and precision. These were not dreams but visions. He flew over Oriental cities, hovered over cupolas, mosques, and castles, lingered in strange gardens, mysterious forests. He came upon undiscovered tribes, spoke foreign languages. Sometimes he was frightened by monsters.

Herman had often thought that one's true life was lived during sleep. Waking was no more than a marginal time assigned for doing things.

Now that he was free, his entire schedule was turned around. It seemed to happen of itself. He stayed awake at night and slept during the day. He ate lunch in the evening and skipped supper altogether. The alarm clock had stopped, but Herman hadn't rewound it. What difference did it make what time it was? Sometimes he was too lazy to turn the lights on in the evening. Instead of reading, he sat on a chair next to the radiator and dozed. He was overcome by a fatigue that never left him. Am I getting sick, he wondered. No matter how little the grocery boy delivered, Herman had too much.

His real sustenance was the letters he received. Herman still made his way down the few flights of stairs to his letter box in the lobby. He had provided himself with a supply of stamps and stationery. There was a mailbox a few feet from the entrance of the house. If he was unable to get through the snow, he would ask a neighbor to mail his letters. Recently, a woman who lived on his floor offered to get his mail every morning, and Herman gave her the key to his box. She was a stamp collector; the stamps were her payment. Herman now spared himself the trouble of climbing stairs. She mailed his letters and slipped the ones he received under the door, and so quietly that he never heard her footsteps.

He often sat all night writing, napping between letters. Occasionally he would take an old letter from the desk drawer and read it through a magnifying glass. Yes, the dead were still with us. They came to advise their relatives on business, debts, the healing of the sick; they comforted the discouraged, made suggestions concerning trips, jobs, love, marriage. Some left bouquets of flowers on bedspreads, and apported articles from distant places. Some revealed themselves only to intimate ones at the moment of death, others returned years after they had passed away. If this were all true, Herman thought, then his relatives, too, were surely living. He sat praying for them to appear to him.

The spirit cannot be burned, gassed, hanged, shot. Six million souls must exist somewhere.

One night, having written letters till dawn, Herman inserted them in envelopes, addressed and put stamps on them, then went to bed. When he opened his eyes, it was full daylight. His head was heavy. It lay like a stone on the pillow. He felt hot, yet chills ran across his back. He had dreamed that his dead family came to him, but they had not behaved appropriately for ghosts; they had quarreled, shouted, even come to blows over a straw basket.

Herman looked toward the door and saw the morning mail pushed under it by his neighbor, but he couldn't move. Am I paralyzed, he wondered. He fell asleep again, and the ghosts returned. His mother and sisters were arguing over a metal comb. "Well, this is too ridiculous," he said to himself. "Spirits don't need metal combs." The dream continued. He discovered a cabinet in the wall of his room. He opened it and letters started pouring out—hundreds of letters. What was this cabinet? The letters bore old datemarks; he had never opened them. In his sleep he felt troubled that so many people had written to him and he hadn't answered them. He decided that a postman must have hidden the letters in order to save himself the trouble of delivering them. But if the postman had already bothered to come to his house, what was the sense of hiding the letters in the cabinet?

Herman awoke, and it was evening. "How did the day pass so quickly?" he asked himself. He tried to get up to go to the bathroom, but his head spun and everything turned black. He fell to the floor. Well, it's the end, he thought. What will become of Huldah?

He lay powerless for a long time. Then slowly he pulled himself up, and by moving along the wall he reached the bathroom. His urine was brown and oily, and he felt a burning sensation.

It took him a long time to return to his bed. He lay down again, and the bed seemed to rise and fall. How strange—he no longer needed to tear open the envelopes of his letters. Clairvoyant powers enabled him to read their contents. He had received a reply from a woman in a small town in Colorado. She wrote of a now dead neighbor with whom she had always quarreled, and of how after the neighbor's death her ghost had broken her sewing machine. Her former enemy had poured water on her floors ripped open a pillow and spilled out all the feathers. The dead can be mischievous. They can also be full of vengeance. If this was so, he thought, then a war between the dead Jews and the dead Nazis was altogether possible.

That night, Herman dozed, twitched convulsively, and woke up again and again. Outside, the wind howled. It blew right through the house. Herman remembered Huldah; the mouse was without food or water. He wanted to get down to help her, but he couldn't move any part of his body. He prayed to God, "I don't need help any more, but don't let that poor creature die of hunger!" He pledged money to charity. Then he fell asleep.

Herman opened his eyes, and the day was just beginning—an overcast wintry day that he could barely make out through the frost-covered windowpanes. It was as cold indoors as out. Herman listened but could hear no tune from the radiator. He tried to cover himself, but his hands lacked the strength. From the hallway he heard sounds of shouting and running feet. Someone knocked on the door, but he couldn't answer. There was more knocking. A man spoke in Spanish, and Herman heard a woman's voice. Suddenly someone pushed the door open and a Puerto Rican man came in, followed by a small woman wearing a knitted coat and matching hat. She carried a huge muff such as Herman had never seen in America.

The woman came up to his bed and said, "Mr. Gombiner?" She pronounced his name so that he hardly recognized it—with the accent on the first syllable. The man left. In her hand the woman held the letters she had picked up from the floor. She had fair skin, dark eyes, and a small nose. She said, "I knew that you were sick. I am Mrs. Beechman—Rose Beechman." She held out a letter she had sent him that was among those she found at the door.

Herman understood, but was unable to speak. He heard her say, "My grandmother made me come to you. I was coming to New York two weeks from now. You are ill and the furnace in your house has exploded. Wait, I'll cover you. Where is your telephone?"

She pulled the blanket over him, but the bedding was like ice. She started to move about, stamping her boots and clapping her hands. "You don't have a telephone? How can I get a doctor?"

He wanted to tell her he didn't want a doctor, but he was too weak. Looking at her made him tired. He shut his eyes and immediately forgot that he had a visitor.

6.

"How can anyone sleep so much?" Herman asked himself. This sleepiness had transformed him into a helpless creature. He opened his eyes, saw the strange woman, knew who she was, and immediately fell asleep again. She had brought a doctor—a tall man, a giant—and this man uncovered him, listened to his heart with a stethoscope, squeezed his stomach, looked down his throat. Herman heard the word "pneumonia"; they told him he would have to go to the hospital, but he amassed enough strength to shake his head. He would rather die. The doctor reprimanded him goodnaturedly; the woman tried to persuade him. What's wrong with a hospital? They would make him well there. She would visit him every day, would take care of him.

But Herman was adamant. He broke through his sickness and spoke to the woman. "Every person has the right to determine his own fate." He showed her where he kept his money; he looked at her pleadingly, stretched out his hand to her, begging her to promise that he would not be moved.

One moment he spoke clearly as a healthy man, and

the next he returned to his torpor. He dreamed again—whether asleep or awake he himself didn't know. The woman gave him medicine. A girl came and administered an injection. Thank God there was heat again. The radiator sang all day and half the night. Now the sun shone in—the bit of sunlight that reached his window in the morning; now the ceiling light burned. Neighbors came to ask how he was, mostly women. They brought him bowls of grits, warm milk, cups of tea. The strange woman changed her clothes; sometimes she wore a black dress or a yellow dress, sometimes a white blouse or a rose-colored blouse. At times she appeared middle-aged and serious to him, at others girlishly young and playful. She inserted a thermometer in his mouth and brought his bedpan. She undressed him and gave him alcohol rubs. He felt embarrassed because of his emaciated body, but she argued, "What is there to be ashamed of? We are all the way God made us." Sick as he was, he was still aware of the smoothness of her palms. Was she human? Or an angel? He was a child again, whose mother was worrying about him. He knew very well that he could die of this sleepiness, but he had ceased being afraid of death.

Herman was preoccupied with something—an event, a vision that repeated itself with countless variations but whose meaning he couldn't fathom. It seemed to him that his sleeping was like a long book which he read so eagerly he could not stop even for a minute. Drinking tea, taking medicine were merely annoying interruptions. His body, together with its agonies, had detached itself from him.

He awoke. The day was growing pale. The woman had placed an ice pack on his head. She removed it and commented that his pajama top had blood on it. The blood had come from his nose.

"Am I dying? Is this death?" he asked himself. He felt only curiosity.

The woman gave him medicine from a teaspoon, and the fluid had the strength and the smell of cognac.

Herman shut his eyes, and when he opened them again he could see the snowy blue of the night. The woman was sitting at a table that had for years been cluttered with books, which she must have removed. She had placed her fingertips at the edge of the table. The table was moving, raising its front legs and then dropping them down with a bang.

For a while he was wide awake and as clearheaded as if he were well. Was the table really moving on its own accord? Or was the woman raising it? He stared in amazement. The woman was mumbling; she asked questions that he couldn't hear. Sometimes she grumbled; once she even laughed, showing a mouthful of small teeth. Suddenly she went over to the bed, leaned over him, and said, "You will live. You will recover."

His listened to her words with an indifference that surprised him.

He closed his eyes and found himself in Kalomin again. They were all living—his father, his mother, his grandfather, his grandmother, his sisters, his brother, all the uncles and aunts and cousins. How odd that Kalomin could be part of New York. One had only to reach a street that led to Canal Street. The street was on the side of a mountain, and it was necessary to climb up to it. It seemed that he had to go through a cellar or a tunnel, a place he remembered from other dreams. It grew darker and darker, the ground became steeper and full of ditches, the walls lower and lower and the air more stuffy. He had to open a door to a small chamber that was full of the bones of corpses, slimy with decay. He had come upon a subterranean cemetery, and there he met a beadle, or perhaps a warden or a gravedigger who was attending to the bones.

"How can anyone live here?" Herman asked himself. "Who would want such a livelihood?" Herman couldn't see this man now, but he recalled previous dreams in which he had seen him—bearded and shabby. He broke off limbs like so many rotten roots. He laughed with secret glee. Herman tried to escape from this labyrinth, crawling on his belly and slithering like a snake, overexerting himself so that his breathing stopped.

He awakened in a cold sweat. The lamp was not lit, but a faint glow shone from somewhere. Where is this light coming from, Herman wondered, and where is the woman? How miraculous—he felt well.

He sat up slowly and saw the woman asleep on a cot, covered with an unfamiliar blanket. The faint illumination came from a tiny light bulb plugged into a socket near the floor. Herman sat still and let the perspiration dry, feeling cooler as it dried.

"Well, it wasn't destined that I should die yet," he muttered. "But why am I needed here?" He could find no answer.

Herman leaned back on the pillow and lay still. He remembered everything: he had fallen ill, Rose Beechman had arrived, and had brought a doctor to see him. Herman had refused to go to the hospital.

He took stock of himself. He had apparently passed the crisis. He was weak, but no longer sick. All his pains were gone. He could breathe freely. His throat was no longer clogged with phlegm. This woman had saved his life.

Herman knew he should thank Providence, but something inside him felt sad and almost cheated. He had always hoped for a revelation. He had counted on his deep sleep to see things kept from the healthy eye. Even of death he had thought, Let's look at what is on the other side of the curtain. He had often read about people who were ill and whose astral bodies wandered over cities, oceans, and deserts. Others had come in contact with relatives, had had visions; heavenly lights had appeared to them. But in his long sleep Herman had experienced nothing but a lot of tangled dreams. He remembered the little table that had raised and lowered its front legs one night. Where was it? It stood not far from his bed, covered with a pile of letters and magazines, apparently received during his illness.

Herman observed Rose Beechman. Why had she come? When had she had the cot brought in? He saw her face distinctly now—the small nose, hollow cheeks, dark hair, the round forehead a bit too high for a woman. She slept calmly, the blanket over her breast. Her breathing couldn't be heard. It occurred to Herman that she might be dead. He stared at her intently; her nostrils moved slightly.

Herman dozed off again. Suddenly he heard a mumbling. He opened his eyes. The woman was talking in her sleep. He listened carefully but couldn't make out the words. He wasn't certain whether it was English or another language. What did it mean? All at once he knew: she was talking to her grandmother. He held his breath. His whole being became still. He made an effort to distinguish at least one word, but he couldn't catch a single syllable. The woman became silent and then started to whisper again. She didn't move her lips. Her voice seemed to be coming out of her nostrils. Who knows? Perhaps she wasn't speaking a known language, Herman Gombiner thought. He fancied that she was suggesting something to the unseen one and arguing with her. This intensive listening soon tired him. He closed his eyes and fell asleep.

He twitched and woke up. He didn't know how long he had been sleeping—a minute or an hour. Through the window he saw that it was still night. The woman on the cot was sleeping silently. Suddenly Herman remembered. What had become of Huldah? How awful that throughout his long illness he had entirely forgotten her. No one had fed her or given her anything to drink. "She is surely dead," he said to himself. "Dead of hunger and thirst!" He felt a great shame. He had recovered. The Powers that rule the world had sent a woman to him, a merciful sister, but this creature who was dependent on him for its necessities had perished. "I should not have forgotten her! I should not have! I've killed her!"

Despair took hold of Herman. He started to pray for the mouse's soul. "Well, you've had your life. You've served your time in this forsaken world, the worst of all worlds, this bottomless abyss, where Satan, Asmodeus,

Hitler, and Stalin prevail. You are no longer confined
to your hole—hungry, thirsty, and sick, but at one with
the God-filled cosmos, with God Himself. . . . Who knows
why you had to be a mouse?"

In his thoughts, Herman spoke a eulogy for the
mouse who had shared a portion of her life with him
and who, because of him, had left this earth. "What do
they know—all those scholars, all those philosophers,
all the leaders of the world—about such as you? They
have convinced themselves that man, the worst transgressor of all the species, is the crown of creation. All
other creatures were created merely to provide him
with food, pelts, to be tormented, exterminated. In
relation to them, all people are Nazis; for the animals
it is an eternal Treblinka. And yet man demands
compassion from heaven." Herman clapped his hand to
his mouth. "I mustn't live, I mustn't! I can no longer be
a part of it! God in heaven—take me away!"

For a while his mind was blank. Then he trembled.
Perhaps Huldah was still alive? Perhaps she had found
something to eat. Maybe she was lying unconscious in
her hole and could be revived? He tried to get off the
bed. He lifted the blanket and slowly put one foot
down. The bed creaked.

The woman opened her eyes as if she hadn't been
asleep at all but had been pretending. "Where are you
going?"

"There is something I must find out."

"What? Wait one second." She straightened her nightgown underneath the blanket, got out of bed, and went
over to him barefooted. Her feet were white, girlishly
small, with slender toes. "How are you feeling?"

"I beg you, listen to me!" And in a quiet voice he told
her about the mouse.

The woman listened. Her face, hidden in the shadows, expressed no surprise. She said, "Yes, I did hear
the mice scratching several times during the night.
They are probably eating your books."

"It's only one mouse. A wonderful creature."

"What shall I do?"

"The hole is right here. . . . I used to set out a dish of water for her and a piece of cheese."

"I don't have any cheese here."

"Perhaps you can pour some milk in a little dish. I'm not sure that she is alive, but maybe . . ."

"Yes, there is milk. First I'll take your temperature." She took a thermometer from somewhere, shook it down, and put it in his mouth with the authority of a nurse.

Herman watched her as she busied herself in the kitchenette. She poured milk from a bottle into a saucer. Several times she turned her head and gave him an inquiring look, as if she didn't quite believe what she had just heard.

How can this be, Herman wondered. She doesn't look like a woman with a grown daughter. She looks like a girl herself. Her loose hair reached her shoulders. He could make out her figure through her bathrobe: narrow in the waist, not too broad in the hips. Her face had a mildness, a softness that didn't match the earnest, almost severe letter she had written him. Oh, well, where is it written that everything must match? Every person is a new experiment in God's laboratory.

The woman took the dish and carefully set it down where he had indicated. On the way back to the cot, she put on her house slippers. She took the thermometer out of his mouth and went to the bathroom, where a light was burning. She soon returned. "You have no fever. Thank God."

"You have saved my life," Herman said.

"It was my grandmother who told me to come here. I hope you've read my letter."

"Yes, I read it."

"I see that you correspond with half the world."

"I'm interested in psychic research."

"This is your first day without fever."

For a while, both were silent. Then he asked, "How can I repay you?"

The woman frowned. "There's no need to repay me."

7.

Herman fell asleep and found himself in Kalomin. It
was a summer evening and he was strolling with a girl
across a bridge on the way to the mill and to the
Russian Orthodox Cemetery, where the gravestones
bear the photographs of those interred. A huge lumi-
nous sphere shimmered in the sky, larger than the
moon, larger than the sun, a new incomparable heavenly body. It cast a greenish glow over the water,
making it transparent, so that fish could be seen as
they swam. Not the usual carp and pike but whales
and sharks, fish with golden fins, red horns, with skin
similar to that on the wings of bats.

"What is all this?" Herman asked. "Has the cosmos
changed? Has the earth torn itself away from the sun,
from the whole Milky Way? Is it about to become a
comet?" He tried to talk to the girl he was with, but she
was one of the ladies buried in the graveyard. She
replied in Russian, although it was also Hebrew. Herman
asked, "Don't Kant's categories of pure reason any
longer apply in Kalomin?"

He woke up with a start. On the other side of the
window it was still night. The strange woman was
asleep on the cot. Herman examined her more carefully now. She no longer mumbled, but her lips trembled occasionally. Her brow wrinkled as she smiled in
her sleep. Her hair was spread out over the pillow. The
quilt had slid down, and he could see the bunched-up
folds of her nightgown and the top of her breast.
Herman stared at her, mute with amazement. A woman
had come to him from somewhere in the South—not a
Jewess, but as Ruth had come to Boaz, sent by some
Naomi who was no longer among the living.

Where had she found bedding, Herman wondered.
She had already brought order to his apartment—she
had hung a curtain over the window, cleaned the
newspapers and manuscripts from the large table.
How strange, she hadn't moved the blotter, as if she

had known that it was the implement of a miracle.

Herman stared, nodding his head in wonder. The books in the bookcases did not look so old and tattered. She had brought some kind of order to them, too. The air he breathed no longer smelled moldy and dusty but had a moist, cool quality. Herman was reminded of a Passover night in Kalomin. Only the matzos hanging in a sheet from the ceiling were lacking. He tried to remember his latest dream, but he could only recall the unearthly light that fell across the lake. "Well, dreams are all lost," Herman said to himself. "Each day begins with amnesia."

He heard a slight noise that sounded like a child sucking. Herman sat up and saw Huldah. She appeared thinner, weak, and her fur looked grayer, as if she had aged.

"God in heaven! Huldah is alive! There she stands, drinking milk from the dish!" A joy such as he had seldom experienced gripped Herman. He had not as yet thanked God for bringing him back to life. He had even felt some resentment. But for letting the mouse live he had to praise the Higher Powers. Herman was filled with love both for the mouse and for the woman, Rose Beechman, who had understood his feelings and without question had obeyed his request and given the mouse some milk. "I am not worthy, I am not worthy," he muttered. "It is all pure Grace."

Herman was not a man who wept. His eyes had remained dry even when he received the news that his family had perished in the destruction of Kalomin. But now his face became wet and hot. It wasn't fated that he bear the guilt of a murderer. Providence—aware of every molecule, every mite, every speck of dust—had seen to it that the mouse received its nourishment during his long sleep. Or was it perhaps possible that a mouse could fast for that length of time?

Herman watched intently. Even now, after going hungry for so long, the mouse didn't rush. She lapped the milk slowly, pausing occasionally, obviously confident that no one would take away what was rightfully hers. "Little mouse, hallowed creature, saint!" Herman cried to her in his thoughts. He blew her a kiss.

The mouse continued to drink. From time to time, she cocked her head and gave Herman a sidelong glance. He imagined he saw in her eyes an expression of surprise, as if she were silently asking, "Why did you let me go hungry so long? And who is this woman sleeping here?" Soon she went back to her hole.

Rose Beechman opened her eyes. "Oh! You are up? What time is it?"

"Huldah has had her milk," Herman said.

"What? Oh, yes."

"I beg you don't laugh at me."

"I'm not laughing at anyone."

"You've saved not one life but two."

"Well, we are all God's creatures. I'll make some tea."

Herman wanted to tell her that it wasn't necessary, but he was thirsty and his throat felt dry. He even felt a pang of hunger. He had come back to life, with all its needs.

The woman immediately busied herself in the kitchenette, and shortly she brought Herman a cup of tea and two biscuits. She had apparently bought new dishes for him. She sat down on the edge of a chair and said, "Well, drink your tea. I don't believe you realize how sick you were."

"I am grateful."

"If I had been just two days later, nothing would have helped."

"Perhaps it would have been better that way."

"No. People like you are needed."

"Today I heard you talking to your grandmother." Herman spoke, not sure if he should be saying this.

She listened and was thoughtfully silent awhile. "Yes, she was with me last night."

"What did she say?"

The woman looked at him oddly. He noticed for the first time that her eyes were light brown. "I hope you won't make fun of me."

"God in heaven, no!"

"She wants me to take care of you; you need me more than my daughter does—those were her words."

A chill ran down Herman's spine. "Yes, that may be true, but—"

"But what? I beg you, be honest with me."

"I have nothing. I am weak. I can only be a burden. . ."

"Burdens are made to be borne."

"Yes. Yes."

"If you want me to, I will stay with you. At least until you recover completely."

"Yes, I do."

"That is what I wanted to hear." She stood up quickly and turned away. She walked toward the bathroom, embarrassed as a young Kalomin bride. She remained standing in the doorway with her back toward him, her head bowed, revealing the small nape of her neck, her uncombed hair.

Through the window a gray light was beginning to appear. Snow was falling—a dawn snow. Patches of day and night blended together outside. Clouds appeared. Windows, roofs, and fire escapes emerged from the dark. Lights went out. The night had ended like a dream and was followed by an obscure reality, self-absorbed, sunk in the perpetual mystery of being. A pigeon was flying through the snowfall, intent on carrying out its mission. In the radiator, the steam was already whistling. From the neighboring apartments were heard the first cries of awakened children, radios playing, and harassed housewives yelling and cursing in Spanish. The globe called Earth had once again revolved on its axis. The windowpanes became rosy—a sign that in the east the sky was not entirely overcast. The books were momentarily bathed in a purplish light, illuminating the old bindings and the last remnants of gold-engraved and half-legible titles. It all had the quality of a revelation.

Translated by Alizah Shevrin and Elizabeth Shub

SHOSHA

By Isaac Bashevis Singer

An unusual love story about a young writer, Aaron Greidenger, who grows up in Warsaw between the two world wars.

When the Nazis threaten to invade Poland, Aaron is faced with the most important decision of his life. Should he go to New York with the only two people who could guarantee his safety and success? Or should he remain in Poland to face the Holocaust with his people and his childhood sweetheart, Shosha?

"Shosha is funny, tragic, human: it celebrates a place that once pulsed with rich, teeming life, and was erased from the earth by the Nazis."

—Pete Hamill, *New York Daily News*

SHOSHA   23997 $2.95